JMT

D0295711

OUTCASTS OF PICTURE ROCKS

OUTCASTS OF PICTURE ROCKS

CHERRY WILSON

Five Star
Unity, Maine

Five Star Western
Published in conjunction with
Golden West Literary Agency.

June 1999

First Edition, Second Printing

Five Star Standard Print Western Series.

The text of this edition is unabridged.

Set in 11 pt. Plantin by Al Chase.

Printed in the United States on permanent paper.

Library of Congress Cataloging in Publication Data

Wilson, Cherry.
   Outcasts of Picture Rocks : a western story / by Cherry
Wilson. — 1st ed.
     p.   cm.
   ISBN 0-7862-1902-5 (hc : alk. paper)
   I. Title.
PS3545.I62215O98 1999
  813'.52—dc21   99-14742

OUTCASTS OF PICTURE ROCKS

Foreword

Today, only the aficionado of Western fiction is familiar with the Western stories of Cherry Wilson. Yet, over the span of her writing career — approximately from 1924 to 1943 — her stories regularly appeared in *Western Story Magazine*, the highest paying of the Street & Smith publications, where her work was held to be equal in stature to the works of Max Brand by both editors and readers. She produced over two hundred short stories, short novels, and serials — five of the latter of which were brought out as hard cover books — and six motion pictures were based on her fiction. Despite her popularity, little is known about her, including her maiden name. What is known is that, when she was sixteen, her family moved to the Pacific Northwest from Pennsylvania. She married Bob Wilson, and the two led a nomadic life, during which Cherry gained some experience writing for newspapers. In 1924, when Bob fell ill, the couple stopped traveling, took up a homestead, and to earn money Wilson decided to write Western fiction. When her first story was accepted by *Western Story Magazine*, it began what would prove a long-standing professional relationship with Street & Smith magazine editors.

Thematically Wilson's fiction was similar to B. M. Bower's, but stylistically her stories are less episodic and, with growing experience, exhibit a greater maturity of sensibility. Her early work, especially, parallels Bower rather closely in that she developed a series of interconnected tales about the cowhands of the Triangle Z Ranch. There is also a similar emphasis on male bonding and comedic scenes — "All-in" in *Western Story Magazine* (11/8/24) explains how the cowpunchers acquire instruments to form the Triangle Z all-brass band and "Triangle Z's All-Brass Serenade" in *Western Story Magazine* (12/13/26) has this band serenading a Spanish *señorita* with an imperfect rendition of "Old Black Joe"! She varied the series by borrowing an idea from Peter B. Kyne's THE THREE GODFATHERS (1913), making her cowpunchers co-operative caretakers of an orphan in seven of the stories, beginning with "Hushaby's Partner" in *Western Story Magazine* (5/29/26). Perhaps the most unusual and interesting of the Triangle Z stories is "Shootin'-up Sheriff" in the June 15, 1929 issue of *Western Story Magazine* in which a town is taken over by women who occupy all the public offices and outlaw gambling, smoking, swearing, and for entertainment show educational films.

Wilson stressed human relationships in preference to gun play and action which generally occurs *en camera*. In fact, some of her best work can be found in those stories where the focus is on relationships between children and men, as in her novel, STORMY (Chelsea House, 1929), and short stories like "Ghost Town Trail" in *Western Story Magazine* (10/25/30) — a fascinating tale with an eerie setting and a storyline filled with mystery which can be found in THE MORROW ANTHOLOGY OF GREAT WESTERN SHORT STORIES (Morrow, 1997), edited by Jon Tuska and Vicki Piekarski — and "The Swing Man's Trail" in *Western Story Magazine* (12/13/30) in which a boy doggedly pursues a herd of rustled cattle that has swept up his family's only cow. She wrote poignantly about man's relationships with animals, and like Max Brand had an especial fondness for horses. Black Wing in the following story is a good example of this love.

OUTCASTS OF PICTURE ROCKS tells the story of two generations of the Jore family, feared and ostracized by all others, and both protected and imprisoned by their Arizona mountain stronghold. "Lovin' folks is strings on a man," Zion Jore says at one point, and it is the bonds of family and friendship that make this story such an emotionally powerful journey for the reader.

Vicki Piekarski
Portland, Oregon

Chapter One

THEY SAY

From the rambling, adobe hostelry, Trail's End, in Big Sandy, Arizona, one looks across vast sweeps of tawny range lands to the jagged summits of the Montezuma Mountains. And immediately the eye is drawn to a great, flat-topped dome, veiled in mists of palest violet, that towers a full thousand feet above the highest peak. It resembles nothing so much as a gigantic, exquisitely tinted cup, with fluted rim and one thin, time-seasoned crack splitting it from rim to base.

Wonderingly, seeing it for the first time and enjoying the sunset from the wide, shaded gallery, the latest guest asks just what that cup contains. The answer comes from old Dad Peppin, the genial, picturesque host of Trail's End who had lived long in the land: "Sure death for the curious!"

But this seeming a reproof, when, heaven knew, no one was more curious in this respect than himself, quickly the old man explained: "Why, that's the Picture Rocks Basin."

Picture Rocks? Every section of Arizona had its quota of them — the sign writing of a prehistoric people, which modernity could not decipher, a perpetual challenge to students of antiquity, and an unfailing source of interest to everyone. But — death to be curious about them? Some foolish legend!

"It's a crater, of course," mused the stranger, unimpressed. "The core of an old volcano. Burned out ages ago."

His host solemnly agreed. "It's a volcano, all right, but it ain't burnt out by a blamed sight. Every now and then it flares up and overflows." Meeting a smile of disbelief, he said, in simple explanation: "The Jores live there."

He felt a certain pride at the way the stranger whipped around in his chair. "Not the Jores! Not the outlaws who've kept this state in hot water for thirty years?"

"The same," replied old Dad Peppin, nodding his head. "That basin's been their refuge for two generations. What's in there, you're free to guess. But the Jores taboo all trespass and enforce it with fast rifles. You see that split, runnin' down from them two highest spires? Waal, that's Sentry Crags, the one known pass. Day and night, they guard it. Right this minute there's a sentinel on watch. They can see a rider comin' for miles. And if one gits too close . . . waal, the Jores don't miss."

Eagerly succumbing to the lure of the forbidden, the visitor said: "I'd like to see the Picture Rocks Basin."

"Nothin' original about that." Dad's sun wrinkles deepened. "Half the men in Arizony has the same itch. Especially Pat Dolan, our esteemed sheriff. But he's wise enough to take it out in wishin'."

"You don't seriously mean to say," protested the guest, "they'd shoot a man for goin' in?"

Mighty serious, Dad Peppin said: "They'd no more hesitate than you'd think twice about shootin' a man who was breakin' into your home with murder in his heart. They wouldn't dare hesitate! It's them against the world. They'd shoot . . . and I don't blame them. A man's home is his castle. And the Picture Rocks has been home to the Jores ever since ol' Jerico took refuge in that basin and defied a whole troop of U. S. cavalry to take him."

"Jerico Jore? I've heard of him. A leader in the old Los Lobos range war. A renegade of the worst kind!"

12

Queer, the smile that played upon Dad Peppin's lips. "Mebbe," he admitted slowly. "Mebbe he was. Reckon all us ole-timers was renegades, lookin' back at us. We're sure misfits now . . . caught betwixt two civilizations. But Jerico, he was a product of his time. And he sure did fit in then. Just the kind of man you wanted around when Apaches was on the warpath, or where there was other fightin' to be done. Life hung by the flame of a six-gun. It was as sweet then . . . sweeter, for you wa'n't sure of a tomorrow. No law but the six-gun. And a man what's had to make his own law and enforce it is kinda apt to forgit.

"But Jerico," the old man broke in firmly on his own rambling, "wa'n't cold-blooded. But warm, and loyal to the core. I never knowed a honester man. Oh, mebbe he had careless ideas about other men's cows, and corralled cash . . . like banks and payrolls . . . but he was as far above any low-down picayune thievin' as you or me. And when the law come to Los Lobos, the government offered him a pardon, if he'd put up his gun. But he'd made enemies what wouldn't let him. It was kill 'em, or be killed. He got some. And the state went out for his scalp. He holed up in the Picture Rocks, and, havin' a family to support, he often made forays where the biggest surplus was."

Affected by this way of putting it — "What happened to him?" — asked the guest.

"Leaded," was the terse answer. "A posse rounded him up over on the Verde, and buried him there years ago. It's his boys that's holdin' the Picture Rocks."

"Then it was his sons who made a foray on the surplus of the Whitestone Bank last . . . ?"

"And committed every crime from arson to mayhem in this state, to hear tell of it," interrupted Dad Peppin with considerable heat. "Give a dog a bad name. Oh, I ain't upholdin' 'em. Nor I ain't blamin' 'em. They was raised in that basin . . . was outlaws before they knowed what it was all about. They're dangerous and desperate. But they got to live. If you cage a wolf and don't feed it, you got no kick comin' if it busts out and helps itself."

Suppressing a smile at this novel defense, realizing it was the viewpoint of most Big Sandy old-timers, so at variance with the rest of Arizona, the stranger mused: "I judge from the howl that goes up, there's quite a pack of these wolves. How many sons did Jerico have?"

"Just three . . . Yance, Abel, and Joel. Joel ain't apt to cause any more trouble. He's servin' a life sentence in state prison. But Yance and Abel's up there. And Shang Haman . . . a devil, if ever there was one! Nobody knows how Shang got in with them. He's no kin, though it's rumored he's got ambitions in that direction. They say he's plumb loco about Joel's daughter, Eden."

His interest flaming, the man cried out: "A girl in that basin?"

"Aye," old Dad affirmed gently. "As Big Sandy folks can swear. We all seen her, when she come down to attend her father's trial. And no man who seen her will ever forget her. She stayed in this house. Stood by her father till they sent him up for life. Her mother didn't appear, nor the boy, Zion. A feather in Pat Dolan's cap, that was. His taste has run to feathers since. Swears he won't rest till Yance and Abel is keepin' company with Joel."

"But the girl?" demanded the stranger, his eyes on the ragged rims up there. "Did she go back?"

"Yes, poor lass. Right after the verdict. Wanted to. Why, nights after the trial was done, she'd set out here, right in that chair where you're a-settin', and look up at them ol' rims, longin' like a bird that's left its cage and hones to get back."

14

The stranger was silent then, his heart gripped by something in the picture drawn.

"She was just a slip of a girl then, sixteen," the old man rambled on. "That would make her . . . le's see, around eighteen now. And if she lives up to the promise she give then, she'll be a woman worth riskin' a heap to see. She's got Jore eyes . . . blue . . . waal, the purple blue that's on the rims now. But she takes after her mother other ways. And Revel Jore, they say, was the flower of the whole Southwest in her day. Come of a fine ol' family, and could have had her pick of men. But one luckless day she met the dashin' outlaw, Joel Jore, and give up everything to go with him."

The old man sighed. "They say," he continued in lowered tone, "the strain of sharin' a fugitive's life unsettled her reason. They say she rules the clan, since Joel went to prison, by some strange gift of prophecy.

"They say," he went on, and, taut with interest, the stranger bent to him, "the mother's unfortunate destiny has left its stamp on her young son, Zion. That he's wild as any mustang, kin to all wild things, and rides the basin like an avengin' demon. They say the spirit of ol' Jerico was born again in him." He broke off, seeming to feel that he had said too much. And, to extenuate it he added, as he smiled plaintively: "They say a lot about the Picture Rocks. You can't tell where fact leaves off and fancy begins. Just seein' that ol' crater, knowin' what it holds, whets the imagination. Sets you to wonderin' what's goin' to happen to them it holds. And you get to believin' what you dreamed was fact and pass it on as such. And of all the wild tales told, the wildest by far hinges around Zion Jore."

Tensely, the stranger said: "But you believe them?"

The answer was long in coming. Then: "I . . . I'm afeered to," faltered old Dad Peppin. And his face, as scarred and still

15

and brown as the adobe wall behind him, was shadowed with more than the day's dying. "The spirit of ol' Jerico, without his sense of responsibility. . . ." A chill ran through the old man. "Friend," he cried somberly, "you'll hear of Zion Jore!"

The stranger would.

Hushed, as though he had already heard, he sat looking at the great cup against the darkening sky, thinking of the misery it concealed, wondering what would happen to those it held. The sun was down long since, faded, its flush. Weird shadows played among the crags. A cloud hung over it — sullen, black, as if it were the slow-gathering smoke of the impending upheaval that would shake the state.

"But about the golden horse," startlingly Dad Peppin spoke, "I don't believe that."

"What?"

"A horse whose yellow skin is marked with just a jet-black wing! A Thoroughbred stallion that kings it over the mustangs in that basin. Worth a king's ransom, they say. But let to run, unbranded, untamed, and unclaimed. That's the story that goes the rounds. But it's too much for me to swallow."

Too much for Dad Peppin to down, credulous as he was to all pertaining to the Jores; too much for the stranger to down, for he laughed. And yet one man outside that basin knew, from his personal and incredible experience, that it was true. This man had actually defied the Jores' guns and set foot in the forbidden land, and he could have told Dad Peppin that the beauty of Eden lived up to the promise given; that the occult powers of Revel Jore were no legend; and — what he feared to know — that the irresponsible Zion had all the spirit of old Jerico!

This man had also seen the glorious wild horse of the Picture Rocks. His knowledge of it ran four years back — back to the night when Sahra, favorite racer of the nationally known horse-breeder, Luke Chartres, had escaped her pasture at his Val Verde ranch, over the Navajo country, and with her young foal, Black Wing, been swept into a wild horse stampede, and was never seen again. This stampede, by the way, gave every sign of having been engineered by human brains.

For this man, Race Coulter — an ex-jockey, "gone heavy," but who followed the ponies as race-track gambler and tout — had been entrusted with delivery of a newly purchased horse to the Val Verde stables and was a guest at the ranch the very night Sahra had disappeared. He had ridden with Chartres and his cowboys in hot pursuit of the mare and foal. The chase brought them — after days of hard riding — into the wilds of the Montezuma Mountains to the very foot of the great dome, where, just as the scent was hottest, Chartres suddenly, inexplicably, definitely called the chase off, ordering his cowboys home and following them, with no word of explanation. Nor had he ever made, so far as Race could hear, any subsequent attempt to reclaim the mare.

Why hadn't he? How could he possibly abandon to the wild the great Sahra, and her son, Black Wing, in whose veins ran the blood of the mighty Crusader? That question tormented Race Coulter, gave him no rest, until he resolved to find out for himself, and, if possible, for he hadn't a scruple on earth, salvage that fortune in horseflesh.

Bent on this, he had returned to Arizona in the spring and, hiring riders for a wild horse hunt, had led them straight to the pass at Sentry Crags and into the guns of the Jores — only to be turned back with a warning grim enough to curb his greed for four long years. He believed, then, it was fear of the outlaws that had turned Luke Chartres back.

Last autumn he had summoned courage to try again. Alone this time, he had actually penetrated the basin, unseen by any Jore, he thought, but, as he soon found out, watched all the time by the youngest, fiercest, least responsible of the clan, the wild youth, Zion. Spared by him until he had seen Sahra's son, magnificently grown, and every drop of horse-mad blood in his veins had fused into a frenzy of desire that but increased his dying torture, for he would have died then, but for Revel Jore, that ill-fated, tragic mistress of the outlaw basin, who intervened in the nick of time and saved him. But it was the terror of her prophecy, rather than the Jores' guns, that restrained Race Coulter from a third attempt.

Never, however, did he give up his determination to possess the stallion. Desire, kindled by that single glimpse, was a fever within him, which time did not lessen, nor distance — nothing! At Tijuana, Tampa, Long Island, or Vancouver, wherever "quick-bloods" ran and men bet on them, his brain was forever casting about for some scheme, whereby he might wrest the princely Black Wing from the Jores, and so get him out of the Picture Rocks.

He was so casting this May Day, on the Lakeshore course in Cleveland, when he met René Rand, known to the tracks as the Reno Kid, and, strangely, the way came to him.

Chapter Two

THE PAWN

Race Coulter was watching the closing races from the paddocks and cursing the heavy track that had caused his favorite to be nosed out in two successive events, to the serious impairment of his bankroll and disposition. It was raining, not a rain to drive people in, but a chill, penetrating drizzle that cast a gray pall over the scene, wilting spirits as it did the jockeys' silks, blending the enlivening sounds of running, band-playing, and human enthusiasm into something curiously like a moan — all sounds except the *drip, drip, drip* from the paddock's roof and the monotonous coughing of the young fellow at the fence beside him, who was, many tragic circumstances to the contrary, as indisputably a cowboy, as Race, sleek-haired, shifty-eyed, thin-lipped and flashy, was the race-track gambler.

Annoyed by both sounds and unable to stay the rain, irritably Race broke out: "Confound it, kid, I can't stand that cough."

René Rand looked up. There was a smile on his lips. There usually was — although nobody knew what he had to smile at. "Sorry, Race," he said in his husky voice, "it's the best I got."

Brutally Race retorted: "You've got it bad. Why don't you do something for it? Go some place and cure it. Some high, dry climate . . . out West. Ain't that where you came from?"

"Yeah," René owned, and he wasn't smiling. His boyish face, so tragically thin and drawn, was whiter, if anything. His

19

fine black eyes, by far too bright, were brighter, if that could be, and his frail figure, hunched there against the drizzle, expressive of more than physical misery.

Struck by a sudden curiosity about him, Race asked: "Kid, what brought you East in the first place?"

The young man shrugged: "A horse . . . you wouldn't savvy, Race."

Not savvy? When he'd gone into the very jaws of death for a horse! "It's the one thing I can savvy," Race assured him. Insisting, as the boy said nothing: "Come on, kid. Let's have the story."

Swayed by an impulse he could never understand, for he did not like or trust this man: "It was only a cayuse," the young man began slowly, his eyes with their telltale flame fixed on the slippery track before them, "but the first horse I ever owned. I . . . I thought a heap of Flash. But I left him in the home corral, when I hired out on a roundup one fall. And when I come home, he was gone. My step-dad had sold him to a tenderfoot, who'd shipped him East. Well, after the fireworks, I followed my horse. Two years ago, that was. You see," he smiled apologetically, "I was just a fool kid then . . . nineteen, and plenty stubborn."

Stubborn? Yes! Like Race was about that horse in the Picture Rocks. Eagerly, as though he might find hope for himself in this boy's experience, he asked: "Did you find your horse?"

"Easy," was the slow response, "when I got so I could hunt. I was laid up a long spell first. Pneumonia. Sleepin' out in the wet, I guess, and short rations. You see, I come on a shoe string, and . . . it left me bad. Anyway, I located Flash right here in Cleveland. But Major Reeves. . . ."

"The polo player?"

"That's him. That's why he was so crazy about my horse. Greased lightnin', Flash was. I'd trained him. He could turn

20

on a dime and give you change. So the major, he wouldn't give him up."

Leaning toward him, Race demanded harshly: "What did you do then?" He had to know what other men did when they ran against a stone wall — just as he'd run against the fortified walls of the Picture Rocks.

"Oh, I hung around, where I could see Flash now and then, and workin' for a stake to go home. Workin' in a roller mill down the Cuyahoga. And the dust . . . I got no better fast. They let me out. Said it was against health regulations to hire a man with . . . what I got."

Dismally the rain dripped. The young fellow coughed dismally. But no longer conscious of either sound, Race quizzed: "Why didn't you go home then?"

There was pain in every line of that young and wasted form; pain in the eyes lifted to the overcast sky west and then dropped as from something eyes may not look upon; pain in the low evasion. "I like it here, Race . . . on the tracks. I pick up a little work with the horses. When I get a tip, I bet my nickel's worth, and get by fine."

Race had noticed how everyone around the tracks fell for this sick Western lad. That's why he had struck up an acquaintance with him — in the hope of having a live tip relayed to him. He could see now why it was. Something about the kid *got* a man, made you want to help him. The pitiful look of him, that game grin, could get him into anything, might even get Race. It came to Race, then, in a white-hot flash of inspiration. It might even get him into the Picture Rocks Basin!

Mastering his excitement, warily feeling his way while details of his inhuman scheme took form. "You may get by," he told René Rand, "but you won't get well. You won't last a year here."

"Six months," was the cheerful correction. "The doc's held a stopwatch on it. It's the gallopin' kind . . . that's one consolation. Six months, unless . . . ," his voice trailed off.

"Unless what?" Race pressed.

"Unless I do what you say . . . go West."

"Well, why don't you? What's holdin' you? Not that cayuse?"

The young fellow denied this. "I give Flash up long ago. The major treats him fine. He's livin' off the fat of the land. He's made a name for himself. I couldn't drag him down to a common cow horse."

"Then," probed Race, "what in the name of . . . ?"

Passionately, René whirled on him, pleading: "Oh, for the love of peace, Race, shut up! Shut up about home! When I can't even think of it, broke and down!"

Ignoring this appeal, going more surely toward his goal: "Wire your step-dad," suggested his tormentor. "He'll come across."

"When he sold my horse?" flashed René furiously. "When I know he'd sell me, if he could! When he always put money ahead of even his own flesh and blood! Worships it, like most men worship their gods! I'd . . . I'd die first! I broke clean, when I broke with him. And if I don't see him till the Resurrection, it's plenty soon." Then, the strength of hot anger spent, he fell weakly against the fence, trembling, coughing.

Certain of his ground, Race bent over him. "Listen, kid. What would you say, if someone offered to pay your way?"

The young fellow replied fiercely, choking over the words: "I ain't takin' charity!"

"Sure not. I don't mean that. But suppose some man showed you how you could earn your fare to Arizona, and earn your keep till you got well, and . . . well, a mighty big stake from there? What would you say then?"

The young man drew a sharp, rattling breath. Tensely he cried: "I . . . I'd say my prayers to him."

Moved as he never believed he could be moved, gloating over the young fellow's emotion, thinking how it would have affected a more susceptible man than himself, Race said self-consciously: "We'll dispense with the prayers, kid. But all the same I'm hirin' you to go home."

Callous as he was, Race felt a sense of shame at the speed with which the rapt light died out of the young fellow's face, at his hopelessness. "Yeah? What's the catch, Race?"

"There ain't none, kid. Nothin' you need to balk at. But there's risk. You'll earn all I'm givin' you. You may be killed. But you'll go out quick and clean, like a man. Not by inches like you are here. Listen."

There in the drizzle, time and place forgotten, Race told the sick fellow of the Picture Rocks Basin, of that stronghold of the Jores, which few men had ever seen, battalioned by mountains that shot into the heavens, rent by rugged cañons, embracing wild forests, of the lake it wore upon its breast, blue, with the blue of fathomless depths, the purple blue of the signal rims, the blue of the eyes of the girl named Eden.

Awesomely telling how the blue waters of this lake lapped the foot of a stupendous cliff, on the sheer face of which a people, long vanished in antiquity, had crudely painted in eternal red, brown, and blue scores upon scores of gigantic, life-like figures of warriors with bows and spears — a mighty host that struck awe to all beholders, so that the very rocks of the land were in league with the Jores.

Of that fortune in horseflesh going to waste, he told him; and of his two attempts at salvage; his two defeats at the Jores' hands; trying, utterly failing, to describe the stallion.

"I can't put him into words," he raved, memory lifting him

to poetic heights and bearing the sick fellow along. "There ain't words for him. But if there's a heaven, and horses in it, he'd be king of them. He's like a horse you'd dream. Black Wing, that's how he was registered at birth. But he ain't black. He's white . . . no, for white's cold, and he's warm, warm as sunshine. Pale cream, you'd call him. With just that little black wing on his hip, the mark, kid, that's been on every colt of the Crusader strain to upset track dope.

"And he's runnin' wild. Not a mark on him. You know the law of the range? He belongs to the first man to put a brand on him. The Jores . . . I can't savvy it. But they've left him run. If I can get a rope on him . . . get him out of that basin . . . he's mine. But I can't even try for him. The Jores would shoot me on sight. But not you, kid. You. . . ."

"Ain't worth their lead?" Bitter the smile on René's lips.

"You're sick!" cried Race, exulting in it. "They might take you in. You ain't anything to be afraid of. See?" Oh, he made it very plain. "Your weakness is my chance. You might get in, when nobody else can."

Dropping his voice needlessly, for the last race was run, the crowd gone, and the track left to them, the mud, and the rain. "There's a secret pass into that basin," Race rushed on. "It ain't guarded. No need to guard it. Nobody'll ever find it from the outside. Pat Dolan's made one grand try. He's the sheriff. A smart guy, with ambitions. He'd do his part, if the pass was found. For he can't get the Jores as it is. Even if he was to get by Sentry Crags, they could slip out the secret pass. But if . . . listen, kid.

"Show me that pass, and I can work it slick. I know where I can hire some mighty tough riders, handy with their guns. I'd slip them in the basin to hunt that horse. Meanwhile, the sheriff is tipped off, and follows us with a posse. He'll take care of the Jores, while we round up the stallion."

His voice dropped another octave. "See why I'm payin' your fare West? To find that pass! Go out there, get thick with the Jores, worm your way into their confidence, find how a posse can get in, and then. . . ."

"Play the Judas." The young man smiled his scorn.

"Well," countered coldly the race-track man, "ain't your life worth it?"

Ask any dying man what life is worth. Yet René Rand resolved not to do it. If he listened, it was for the thrill of hearing someone speak of the Far West — home. Thrilling to the red history of Jores, dead and living, because they were of home, he yet listened, untempted, to Race Coulter's tempting — "Life, if you win! If you lose, a quick out!"

His heart quickened at Race's talk of Eden, Joel Jore's girl — "a mighty inducement. She'll be sweet to you, kid, for she'll pity you. And you know what pity is akin to."

He was even fighting back the fury of tortured pride to prolong this talk, wondering at the terror in Race's eyes as he told of Eden's mother, Revel — "a Thoroughbred, gone wild herself. They're all afraid of her. She's got second sight! Savvy? Something guides her, so she can pick up the Bible and open it to the very line that tells you what is to be. And she told me. . . ."

A shudder went through him, remembering. His small, pale eyes held the glitter of fear. "I'll never forget it!" he cried shakily. "They had me, the Jore men, and that devil, Shang! I thought my time had come. Then she come, walkin' through the trees. Walkin' like she was in a trance. She made them free me. And she took the Book out of her dress and read."

He swallowed hard. "I've had my fortune told with cards, the stars, the lines on my palm, what they see in crystals, and everything. I don't lay much store by it, although some of the things they told me . . . but Scripture, kid, you can't get away from it. And she . . . she read. . . ." He licked his thin, parched lips.

Breathless, René cried: "What, Race?"

"This . . . 'And I looked, and behold a pale horse! And his name that sat on him was Death, and Hell followed with him!' "

Although yet to learn in agony how true this prophecy, the young fellow was awed. "Race, the pale horse was. . . ."

"Black Wing?"

That night, alone in the stable room, that wasn't charity because he kept an eye on things, René Rand knelt over the one bit of home to which he'd clung, the one thing to which any cowboy clings although he lose all else, his saddle. There on his knees, through a sudden mist that quenched the raging fire in his eyes, he looked at it, battered and service-scarred, coated with dust, the killing dust of peopled places. Lovingly his wasted hands passed over the horn, creased deep that time Flash sat back against a steer at the rodeo in Winnemucca; over the furrow cut deep in the skirt the day he and Flash rolled into the cañon when he was running mustangs; over the scratches inflicted by years of happy, healthy cowboy life; each tear and dent evoking a memory and memory acting as a magic carpet.

For the low ceiling seemed to rise above him, high as the stainless Western sky. The four walls spread from horizon to horizon. The close, damp air became a dry, warm wind, whose only burden was the invigorating tang of sage and pine. And the joy of living coursed through all his being, as he seemed to feel the lift and rhythm of a horse beneath him.

Then a paroxysm of coughing seized him. When it passed, he lay crumpled on the dusty saddle, confined by walls and roof again, the taste of blood upon his mouth, and in his heart, mocking its mighty longing, the awful conviction that this chance had come too late. He couldn't get well.

"But" — with piteous effort his lips smiled the cry of his heart — "I could . . . die there!"

Chapter Three

STOLEN THUNDER

Old Dad Peppin's memory wasn't what it used to be. "War a time," he'd boast wistfully, "when I could recollect and greet by name every man who ever stopped at Trail's End. But faces slip me of late, and the names and facts concernin' 'em. And I git my dates mixed. Ask me what day of the month the Fourth of July comes on, and I'll tell you the seventeenth of Ireland, like as not."

But it was no trick at all for him to recall the face, name, and facts concerning the man now signing the register, a flashy, horsy *hombre*, Race Coulter. He had stopped there last fall, a short visit; something fishy about it. He had asked where he could hire a riding outfit, had hinted he was going to prospect, and rode off toward the Montezumas; out just two days and came tearing back, looking like he'd struck a vein of pure trouble; checked out right after.

Even as these reflections passed through his mind, Dad was amazed to see Race's face taking on the same expression it had worn when he checked out of Trail's End. His pen had barely scratched the sheet, dated May 7th, when, suddenly, he stopped and stared, as if he'd hit the mother lode of dire calamity.

"What's wrong?" queried Dad curiously.

Without lifting his eyes, Race pointed to the last signature, harshly demanding: "He's stoppin' here?"

Nearsighted, the old man bent to the page. "Luke

28

Chartres?" Honest pride fired his face. "He is. He allus stops with us when he's in these parts. Which ain't often. Not as often as we'd wish. Still, there's little to bring him to Big Sandy. His interest is racin' in a big way. Luke's produced some of the fastest horses in the West on his big Val Verde ranch. You've heard of him? One of Arizona's best known citizens. Fine, old family. The Chartreses hailed from Louisiana originally. Southern aristocrats . . . like you read about. And Luke. . . ."

Rudely interrupting what promised to be an unabridged history of the Chartres family, with which he was perfectly familiar, Race asked: "What's his business here?"

"Dunno." Dad's wry smile took the edge off the rebuff. "But it's his, I reckon."

"Sure." Race achieved a grin.

But, once in his room, he cursed the fate that had brought Luke Chartres on the scene at just this time. What business could he have here except to reclaim the horse he had lost? Not Sahra! Even if she had survived the rigors of wild life, the years would have made her valueless. But Black Wing? Why, after all this time? What circumstance had changed? If he had come for the stallion, how did he plan to get him out of the basin? This Race must find out, and soon. He had two days before René came — lucky he'd thought to come on ahead to get everything ready so the kid could get out of town without attracting too much notice. Now, he'd just lay low and find out what the game of Luke Chartres was.

Possessing a singular talent for ferreting out information, Race soon discovered that the business of Chartres seemed to be entirely with the sheriff's office. This bore out his worst fears. Pat Dolan's one ambition was to raid the Picture Rocks. If Chartres had come for the horse, he would naturally

29

join forces with the sheriff. Just as he had planned on using the law when René found the secret place into the basin.

But this didn't prove anything. He had to know more, had to be sure. If Chartres was after Black Wing, he must find some way of queering his game. So he shadowed the race horse man, but without success until the morning of the day René was due. Then, by sheer luck in which his sleuthing played no part, he got it all in one stunning earful.

He was at breakfast in the Trail's End dining room, when the two men most in his thoughts walked in. One, tall and stern, with a jaw that shot out, cheeks that sunk in, and, from under his broad-brimmed hat, a white forelock showing that was in striking contrast to his black mustache. He wore a star on his calfskin vest and a holstered six-gun at his hip. Pat Dolan, sheriff.

The other was also tall and stern. But there all similarity was at an end. He was as different from the sheriff as a Thoroughbred is from a range cayuse. His face, darkly handsome beneath a costly white Stetson, was remarkable for its breeding. His black eyes were memorable for their verve and fire, their pride, likewise, pride that was further expressed in the very way he carried himself. He had the air of a man used to having his own way without any fuss; Val Verde rancher, Luke Chartres.

Passing Race without so much as a glance in his direction, they took a table at some distance, gave their order, and leaned forward toward each other, continuing their conversation at a low pitch. But Race's ears, trained to catch the vaguest whispers in the years when his living depended on stray bits of information, easily picked up this — "No, Pat," — in the low, courteous voice of Chartres — "we can't rush this thing. A false move now might spoil everything. I've worked a whole year to get this opening, and you can be sure

I'll keep it moving. My time is valuable, too."

"Too valuable, I'd say" — in the sheriff's blunt speech — "to warrant spendin' a year of it for one horse. But I'm mighty glad you did, Luke. I'd give anything to raid that nest!"

Hot blood roaring in Race's ears drowned the rest. When he got control of himself, the Val Verde man was saying: "This won't make you popular with your county, Pat."

The sheriff admitted it. "But," he pointed out, "it will with the state!"

"That's right. And with you out for Congress next fall, that's what counts. Well, if we pull this off, you won't need Big Sandy's help. It gets me, Pat" — and the tone of Chartres held a note of personal enmity that Race would long wonder at — "how this town can uphold the Jores."

"It's natural. Big Sandy's grateful to the Jores for puttin' it on the map," Dolan said. "Proud of the black luster they shed over it. Then, too, the old-time spirit survives here. Plenty of old-timers, like Dad Peppin, who remember Jerico Jore. Naturally, they make a martyr of him and heroes of his sons. I doubt if I can rustle a posse in this town, when the time comes. But to the rest of the state, they're outlaws. And if I can put them behind bars, I'll. . . ."

"You can" — Chartres was curbing him again — "if you don't get in too big a rush. Remember, Pat, I don't know where that pass is myself yet. We'll just have to wait."

"Luke, I'd give a heap to know who's workin' with you."

Race's ears were keen to the last pitch. But all he could catch was: "Sorry, Pat, I'm pledged. But I'll pledge you this, when the time comes, my man will lead us through that pass into the basin without a Jore knowing it. And that time must come soon. I can't stand this waiting."

"That's easy to savvy, with the Caliente handicap comin' up in September, and you with no entry. Well, Luke, I never took much stock in this golden horse story myself. But if half of what I hear is true, you'll have a horse that will give Saval's Meteor dust plumb around the track. And I know how much that means to you."

Chartres studied him. "Do you?" His voice was strained. "I doubt it, Pat. Nobody does. Nobody could! Why, it means so much, I . . . I'd sell my soul for such a horse! That's what I'm doing. Going against all sense of honor, of common decency. Oh," he said, shrugging, "you wouldn't understand." And tensely, after a time, he went on: "Saval beat me in every race last season, Pat. That's all right. It's all in the game. But when he makes every victory a personal insult! You don't take any stock in that golden horse story. But I know! That horse has the blood of racing kings. If I can get him. . . ." He rose to go then, abruptly.

Not daring to risk recognition when they passed him, Race got up and, as unobtrusively as he could, sauntered out.

Once in the street, his casual air vanished. He had a million things to do, and not much time to do them in. The scheme he had outlined to René had fallen through, at least for the present. But already he had another. Every detail necessary to put it in operation must be attended to when René's train came in at three that afternoon.

So energetically did Race go about this business, he was at the station a full hour before time, impatiently pacing the platform, worrying about the outcome of his scheme.

But when the train pulled in and the young man descended, his spirits shot up. For René looked far worse than he had a week ago on the tracks. He could barely stand, weaving, as Race greeted him, still feeling the motion of the train, the roar of the wheels still in his ears, the platform, the little cow town whirling by him, as a whole continent had whirled in the last five days.

"Gee, kid, you look fierce." It was impossible for Race to hide his ghoulish exultation. "That's the stuff! Anybody'd swear you wasn't but a jump ahead of the ol' man with the scythe."

"I sure feel like it, Race." Dim, but game, the smile on the young fellow's white face. "But I'll be jake, when I get some rest."

But jake was the last thing Race desired him to be. Already he had him by the arm, dragging him down the street, raving: "No rest for you, kid! Things has happened here. Chartres has stole my thunder. Somebody's promised to show him that pass. He's workin' with the sheriff. They've doped out about the same spread we had. Our scheme's shot!"

René's heart lifted, eased of a tremendous burden. Then he wasn't going to that basin to double-cross the Jores, should they befriend him, to betray a girl named Eden. "You mean" — he must hear Race say it — "you've give up?"

"Not much," was the grim retort. "I didn't risk good money on this race to be left at the post."

"But," panted René, breathless from the pace Race set, "if Chartres wants the horse and is takin' the sheriff. . . ."

"That's where you come in." Race's step quickened. "You're goin' up to that basin to warn the Jores about this. To fight with them. Outlaw yourself, if you must. Do any and everything you can to keep Dolan and Chartres out of the Picture Rocks. Because" — he made plain his selfish purpose — "just as long as Luke Chartres wants that horse, there's just one place he's safe . . . in the Picture Rocks, guarded by the Jores."

That was Race — using the Jores' deadly rifles, as he banked on using human qualities in them which he did not himself possess; as he was using this boy's misfortune; as he would use any weapon he could lay hands on for Black Wing.

33

"But," the young fellow cried, "I thought Chartres had given him up!"

"That's what I thought!" Race cursed. "I was a fool to think it! No man in his senses would give up a colt of the Crusader strain . . . not if he knew what it had. If ever he sees Black Wing like I seen him, he'll. . . ."

"But Black Wing belongs. . . ."

"To the first man to get him out of that basin," Race cut in grimly. "And I'll be that man! When Luke Chartres bats his patience out against the walls of the Picture Rocks, we'll have our innings."

Stopping abruptly, he caught the boy by the arms, searching his pale face with eyes that were steady for once. "Kid," he said tensely, "I brought you West. I staked you to this chance to live. This change of plan don't let you out. Go up there, like I told you. When you get in, *if* you get in. . . ." The terror his eyes betrayed, then, was not for René, not terror lest the boy be slain by the guards at Sentry Crags, but a sudden realization of how slim a thread his hope of Black Wing hung on. "If you get in, tell the Jores about Dolan. Then use your own judgment. You know what I want, that horse, first and last. This warnin' should make you solid with the gang, but. . . ."

He held the reeling form up. "Get this, kid. Don't figure on that passin' you in. They'd never fall for it. Remember, you're a tenderfoot in Arizona for your health, roughing it, drifted up there by accident. You heard this talk in town. Got that? Fine. One other thing. This Reno handle's out. It's a dead giveaway. You're René Rand, see?"

The boy looked at him strangely. René, again? That's what he'd always been until the race track crowd tacked Reno on him. Well, it was just one lie less he had to tell the Jores.

They had turned into the willow grove on the outskirts of

town, where Race had secreted the two cayuses bought that afternoon, one saddled, the other bearing a pack.

"Here's your outfit," Race told him. "Get goin'."

René couldn't believe Race meant right then. And, although his heart failed at the task before him and what strength he had seemed to forsake him, his white lips smiled the promise. "I'll go, Race. But I gotta rest first. The trip . . . I'm all in. I couldn't catch a pig in an alley like this. Give me a week."

"And let you git tanned up! Let you lose that graveyard look, the one chance to land you in the Picture Rocks. Not by a. . . ."

"Just a day. Honest, Race, I'm in no shape."

"The worse shape you're in the better." — was the heartless answer. "Hop on!"

For the first time in his life René Rand required help to mount. Once in the saddle, however, he seemed to gain strength.

Yet, looking up at him, seeing his young, ravaged face in the pitiless glare of the sun, Race had one sharp qualm, not of shame at the unspeakable advantage he was taking of him, but of the danger he knew, as no man knew. One he had escaped by a margin so slight that the very memory made his flesh creep. No, nothing like this troubled Race Coulter, but fear lest this boy never reach Sentry Crags. However, and he was cheered by the thought, men like the Reno Kid died hard.

"Remember," he charged, putting the lead rope in René's hand, "you owe me your life. And the debt ain't paid until I get that horse."

Chapter Four

NOT A HEALTH RESORT

Out of town, out beyond the last straggling valley ranch, René rode toward the gaunt, black range looming west. His strength was gone. But he was borne up by a belated sense of homecoming, by the wild hope gathering in his breast, that maybe it wasn't too late, after all.

Maybe this was what he had been dying for — the miles and miles of sage in purple flower, so sweet that the very dust kicked up by his cayuse and pack horse was perfumed. For the mountains — Dear God, how he had longed for the mountains! — for these great stretches with nothing in them, not a fence, nor building, nor human being; just hush, so deep it blotted the roar in his brain; for this sky hung over him, not just a stingy, unfriendly strip that looked as if it didn't care if a fellow got well or not, but a big, blue one that spread itself all over everything, smiling, like it wanted to help; for air like this — so good he couldn't get enough; air that would bring a dead man to life, he thought.

But it made him dizzy. All the peaks and cañons in the mountain range ahead of him had joined hands around the great dome and were playing ring-around-the-rosie. That was altitude, he guessed. Folks got drunk on mountain air till they got used to it. It was one on him, all right. He'd been so sure one whiff of it would set him up. And here he had a whole lungful — well, half a lung — and he had to hang onto the saddle horn with both hands to keep from falling off.

Anyhow, he was riding. *Not like I used to,* the sick fellow owned. *Me and Flash . . . we used to go gallopin'. All the time!*

No! Not riding like that now — here on the Picture Rocks trail. Instead, his thin figure was swaying, the pallor of death was on his pinched face, and every atom of grit his soul possessed set on holding out until he reached the Picture Rocks. He could see its mighty barriers up there, deceptively near in the clear air. He had to go up there. For what? He forgot.

Oh, yeah, he recollected, *that horse . . . like sunshine.*

He owed Race a debt. Race had staked him to this chance — one in a hundred he'd get past Sentry Crags, past the Jores or Shang Haman. Shang might be guarding the pass. Shang who was a devil.

If I've got to face the devil, he thought with grim humor, *I'll take my chance . . . with the one at Sentry Crags.*

Then he was too faint, too weary, too far gone to think. He just hung on, while slowly the westering sun sank, and the trail lifted him high above the sage plains into the foothills. Soundlessly his horse's feet fell on a springy carpet of needles cast by fir and pine, that locked green arms above him, singing a song so soothing that his head fell forward, his eyes closed, and a great drowsiness overcame him.

A paroxysm of coughing roused him, and, when he had fought it to a wan Waterloo, when he could lift his head again, he saw that he was riding at the very foot of the great dome.

Its massive, majestic rims loomed over him. Their shadow fell blackly upon him; fiery, the sky above them, as if the basin were, indeed, a volcano spouting flame. Sharp and gleaming as bayonets, its peaks stood up, piercing the sky and dripping sunset's hue, like bayonets plunged in living red; and between the sharpest, reddest, splitting that thousand-foot cliff like a sword-thrust, the narrow gap through which no man might pass — Sentry Crags!

Slowly his burning eyes lifted to the heights, where, like a lonely eagle, a sentinel was said to watch. He saw no one. But he felt eyes on him. And desperately he strove to pull himself together to meet, to challenge, to tell the story as Race had coached him. But will could carry him so far, and no further. Suddenly, will failing, blackness closed around him, and he felt himself falling, falling. . . .

As he fell, there rose from the red rims up there a strange figure, strange enough to grace the weirdest myth ever woven about this land of which men knew nothing but said much — the slight, pliant figure of a young fellow of perhaps nineteen, clad in tattered buckskin and tightly clutching a Winchester.

His frayed buckskin hunting shirt was worn over soiled trousers of the same material, its fringed hem striking midway between knee and thigh and confined at the waist by a weighted gun belt. Buckskin moccasins were on his feet. He wore no hat. And his long black hair, whipping back in the breeze that always blew up here, revealed a face singular for its contradictions — one instant, all but feminine in its sweetness; the next, wholly masculine in its ferocity; and eerie always, for a strange restlessness of expression.

Eerily restless were his eyes, likewise. Now the deep, warm blue of a summer sky, then the sullen purple that presages a storm, or flame-shot black, as when the heavens are ripped open and lightning flashes from them.

Lightning had flashed from them this last hour as, crouched up there, he had watched this strange rider coming — as last autumn he had watched another man approach the basin. And he had gripped the rifle, muttering: "It's him . . . come back for Black Wing."

But as this man neared, he had seen it was not the same man. Nor was it a cowboy hunting stock, who would ride up to the crags and turn off. For no cowboy rode like that — all over his horse. Nor did he look like a prospector, although he trailed a pack horse. He fell into no class. Uncanny was this sentry in all else, but canny in guarding the Picture Rocks. Again fiercely muttering: "It's some one . . . come for him."

Rifle to shoulder he leaped up, a challenge on his lips, but was stricken dumb with amazement as, right in the jaws of the pass, the rider fell from his horse, rolled over in the trail, and, bringing up against a boulder, lay motionless. Long the young sentinel watched, suspicious that this was a ruse. Then, in action swift as the play of light on rifles, he whirled, and in a bound, beautiful in its grace and ease, sprang to the back of a horse tethered in the brush and was thundering down the precipitous cliff at a headlong gallop, leaping fissures and deadfalls, dodging in and out of the broken cañons, outriding the avalanching shale that started with him and swooping out on the level floor of the basin, where he veered sharply between the towering portals of the pass.

Coming to a stop about a hundred yards from where the rider had fallen, he flung off his horse and, swiftly, soundlessly, with the caution of a wild thing whose caution is inborn, glided through the trees to a spot where he could see the figure lying by the trail. The horses had shied from it and were grazing some distance back. And the youthful guard in buckskin shied back a bit and watched, his breath coming fast, his eyes burning with a great curiosity. As moments passed and he saw no movement in the still form, curiosity drew him up, step by step, rifle ready, every nerve alert. Stopping short when, within a few feet of it, his keen eyes made out an almost imperceptible rise and fall of the chest.

Playin' 'possum, he thought. And, as a small boy might do, had he actually met a 'possum in the trail and it played dead, he scooped up a small rock and shied it at the figure, at the same time covering it with his gun. But there was no reflex action, not so much as the flicker of an eyelash. The young fellow stared, puzzled by this.

"He's gone," he muttered, his expressive eyes bewildered. *He's gone . . . and he's left himself behind. They do it sometimes. Some don't come back. Dave didn't when he fell off his horse. I found Dave, too! But . . .* — pain was clouding his wild face — *Dave was shot! Shang done that! They say I'm crazy, and they shut me up.*

But this man had not been shot. Nor had he been thrown from his horse. Curiosity drew him close, held him, gazing down at René's senseless face, his own swept by nameless grief. Not in years had he looked into a face so young, unless some mountain stream gave him back his own reflection; never, in all his life, but one. And that one had been white and still like this when last he'd seen it.

"Shang done that!" he repeated passionately, lightning flaring through sudden mist. "He'll pay for it!"

But as a grieving child is diverted when its interest is attracted, so was this young being diverted by what he looked upon. Everything about René intrigued him. His clothing, the cheap store suit and cap Race had forced on him to obliterate the range stamp and bear out his tale of being a poor tenderfoot health-seeker, ill-fitting, uninteresting as they were, filled this lad with vast admiration, and disdain of his own buckskin. Raptly he studied him as one might a being from a strange planet, and with the same apprehension.

For as René stirred with a moan, his dazed eyes opening, the young fellow's gun flashed up, its muzzle within inches of René's chest, his face a savage blaze, crying out, and only curiosity holding his hand for an answer to his question: "What . . . are . . . you?"

What was he? René Rand tried to think. But to save his life he could think of nothing but what Race had told him he was.

He said weakly: "Nothin' . . . to . . . be . . . afraid of." And he smiled in the face of death — the little, twisted, bitter smile that mocked himself, the smile that got all men, that had made even the hard-boiled, race-track crowd look out for him.

And the smile worked a miracle here, relaxed that finger on the trigger, lowered the deadly rifle, brought a ghost of an answer to the wild, dark face above him.

"I reckon," said the young sentinel in buckskin, "I ain't afraid of anything," adding, as if this would explain all: "I'm Zion Jore."

Zion it was — the youngest, fiercest, least responsible of the clan — who had let Race enter the basin, see Black Wing, then captured him. Not that René remembered this; he was far too sick, scarcely aware of another being standing there, perplexed, really not knowing what to do next.

Zion had let the other man in for excitement, and because it fitted his peculiar ideas of revenge. He had instructions never to do that again. But none of his instructions, comprehensive as they were, fitted this case. He was to scare intruders off; shoot, if they didn't scare; or fire six shots in fast succession, if more men came than he could handle. This one was too sick to scare back. He couldn't shoot him. And certainly he wasn't too much for him.

In his bewilderment he knelt down by René. "What brought you here?"

"To . . . get . . . well," René whispered, desperately rallying his thoughts. "I'm huntin' . . . a place . . . where I can get . . . my health back."

Then he hadn't come for the horse. The fierce light died out of Zion's face.

"You see," said René with tremendous effort, "I was dyin' . . . where I was at. Away off . . . that was. . . ."

With quivering eagerness, Zion echoed: "Away off?" He repeated — "Away off." — sitting down cross-legged in the trail, his brown fingers laced about his knees, his eyes devouring René. "Tell me," he begged tensely, "what it's like out there?"

Amazed, René asked: "Where do you mean?"

"Out there" — tremblingly Zion pointed through the black portals, down over the purpling foothills — "where folks can ride and ride, and not run up against a wall."

René moaned bitterly: "I brought up against one, Zion."

He did not think René would understand. But with strange gentleness, Zion said: "I don't mean that kind. I mean" — he threw his dark head back toward the Picture Rocks — "walls like them! Here . . . I'm always ridin' toward a wall. It makes me crazy. I don't want to stop, when I get goin'. I want to run like the wind that swoops down and rushes on, and never stops or turns around!"

Over his shadowed face swept the brooding gleam René was to know and fear. "Sometimes," he went on in a strained whisper, "sometimes, sittin' up there, it comes over me so strong. I look out and see men ridin'. Nothin' to stop them, 'less they come this way, when I stop 'em plenty quick. Seems like, if I just stood up on that ol' peak and let go, I could float down. Like I got wings. Out there men fly, I hear."

Suddenly, confidentially hitching nearer: "My dad's out there," he told René. "But he's in walls, they say. Smaller than these. A heap stronger . . . they must be. Else he'd come back." His wild face flamed with mutiny. "The rest go out. They won't take me. But I'm goin' soon. I got it all made up. I'll tell you someday."

Struggling to raise himself, René cried: "Zion, you're tellin' me too much!"

"Why?" naïvely the wild young creature asked.

42

"Because you . . . don't know me. You don't know if you can trust me."

Zion's smile was exquisite repudiation. "Knowin' folks," he said softly, "don't make trust. All my life I've known Shang Haman. But" — his eyes gleamed like black diamonds — "I ain't tellin' him nothin'."

To keep his thoughts off the other track, René asked: "Who's Shang?"

"The devil!" said Zion.

Always that description.

There ensued a long hush, broken by the faint crunch of the feeding horses, by the sinister hiss of the wind in the pass. Zion watched René, lost in thought. René watched Zion, realizing that his fate depended on the outcome of that thinking, and was relieved when Zion began to think aloud.

"You could get well in the Picture Rocks. It never made nobody sick. Nobody ever died . . . 'less they was shot. And Mother, she's got the healin' touch. Ain't seen a thing she can't cure yet. But nobody's let in." That seemed to bring him to a decision, for his face hardened. Then, as this expression melted before his low-voiced longing: "There's things I'd like to be a-hearin' about . . . out there."

René promised, stretching out a hand: "I'll tell you, Zion."

Hungrily seizing that hand in both his brown ones: "And you could be my pard?" Zion dreamed aloud wistfully. "I ain't had none since Dave was shot. He was cousins with me. Shang done it!" — this with a wild ferocity that sent a chill through René. "My folks might stand for you . . . when they know it's just for health. But Shang . . . he'd do for you, like he done for Dave!"

Before the words had fairly left his mouth, he had leaped up, clutching the gun, crying: "No! Shang won't! If he touches you, I'll blow him to kingdom come!"

Loving him, then, as he would through everything — to the bitter end of the red trail this Jore would run — René cried: "I won't go, Zion! I won't get you in trouble. If he's a devil. . . ."

Piercing his heart came Zion's triumphant laugh. "There's a pair of us! Look!" His eyes darted down the trail, fastening on some object about a hundred yards away. "See that bluebell?" He pointed to the blossom, swaying beside the trail.

René had trouble seeing it for the light was dim. "Yeah," he said wonderingly, "I see it, Zion."

The rifle flashed up, and Zion fired, taking no aim, it seemed, and the flower fell, sheared from its stem. While René watched, speechless at this feat, the boy dropped the rifle and, pointing to another bloom, said: "See that lupine?"

At René's nod, he jerked a six-gun from his belt, firing in a single motion, clipping this flower as neatly as the first. Then, turning back, he said, in no spirit of show-off, but as simple truth: "I'm the best shot in the whole world, I guess. I can shoot rings around Shang. He don't know it . . . yet. I practice all the time. I've got to kill him. He pesters Eden. The men don't see . . . but she tells me." He sprang forward toward René, who was sinking back to the trail, entreating with wild concern: "Pard, don't go away again!"

But René had gone. When he came back, he was conscious of a motion painful to him, of being on a horse again; not the mangy cayuse Race had supplied him with, but a big black that showed Thoroughbred blood. Two bare, brown arms were about his waist, holding him up, bringing back Zion and their talk. And, wearily lifting his eyes from the trail and the horse and the two brown arms, he met a scene as wild and grand as the eye of man ever looked upon.

He saw a long and narrow lake, a shimmer of silver in the twilight. He saw, across the silver shimmer, a stupendous cliff, upon which was painted a host of hostile, savage figures that seemed to live and move, advancing on him, striking awe to his heart — the Picture Rocks!

And he saw upon the near shore, where the singing cottonwoods dipped their feet in the rippling water, a row of cabins, sheds, barns, and corrals; cabins built of unbarked logs, and connected by covered courtyards, from which a pack of dogs had started, with hideous uproar, but were called back by men — by three men, leaving the biggest cabin, advancing, their spurs *whizzing* in their angry stride, as hostile and savage as the painted figures. Jores! For they had the same deep, blue, piercing eye of Zion, without its wandering; the same resilient, quick-moving form; the same reckless hardihood of speech and action.

Cold and grim, one demanded: "What's this, Zion?"

René felt the arms about him tighten, heard Zion pleading: "He's sick! He's huntin' health in the Picture Rocks!"

And from behind him he heard a laugh, Shang's laugh, for it was devilish. "The Picture Rocks ain't a health resort!"

Chapter Five

THE GUIDE

Ever afterward when René saw Shang Haman, he was reminded of Race Coulter. The outlaw was similarly
small-boned and over-fleshed. His small, yellowish eyes had,
at all times, the same lusty gleam; his tight, hard mouth, the
selfishness of Race's at its worst — of Race's when he was
thinking of Black Wing. He was, likewise, as showy in appearance. His high-heeled, filigreed boots, his tight-fitting black
trousers, his heavy belt with its ornate buckle of silver, his soft
white shirt, black silk bandanna, and silver-mounted sombrero were all in rich contrast to the rough attire of the Jores.

But to René then, upheld in Zion's arms, Shang was only a
voice, as were the Jore brothers, Yance and Abel, grim, inimical voices, wrangling over him. The one thing of substance in
the glimmering twilight was the slight, taut form supporting
him — Zion, whose wild heart throbs he could feel against
him, in whose eyes black hate clouds had piled thick at that
laugh, whose slim, brown hands about his waist had flexed on
the rifle they held, so that its muzzle quivered up to rest fully
on Shang Haman's breast and remained there, as his gaze, for
once unwavering, held Shang's gaze, while he told the Jores
how he had found René at Sentry Crags and brought him in.

"He . . . he can't hurt nothin'!" Zion's appeal flung into
the ensuing silence. "He just wants to get well. Help me get
him down, Uncle Abel."

Surely the Jores had some heart, for instinctively Abel Jore

46

stepped toward the black to receive René in his arms.

But Shang Haman, who had no more heart than a rattlesnake, coldly intervened: "Strangers is barred from this basin. Why's the bars down for him?"

Zion cried fiercely: "You keep outta this, Shang!"

Paying him no more heed than he did the dogs, yapping up at the limp figure in the saddle, Shang demanded again: "Why's the bars down for him?"

It seemed too obvious for explanation. But Abel Jore vouchsafed one: "What else can we do?" he asked, exactly as Race had hoped. "The feller's sick. We can't drive him out."

"Zion can dump him back at the pass where he picked him up," Shang proposed. "I warned you not to put that fool on watch!"

Dangerously the Jores fired up at that slur on their imprisoned brother's son. Abel warned in a steely drawl: "Don't forget you're talkin' of a Jore!"

Cowed by that tone, but stubbornly standing his ground, Shang argued: "I'm a Jore, too! I've throwed in my lot with you. I follow your lead in everything else. But when it comes to takin' outsiders in, it's as much my business as yours!"

The Jores admitted this. But they balked at leaving René at the crags.

"He'd die out there," said Abel Jore.

"That beats lettin' him die in here," was the callous answer. "For he'll have folks somewhere. They'll be investigatin'. They'll say we killed him. If" — with a hard glance at René — "he ain't shammin'! If he ain't a spy for Pat Dolan!"

Mercy fled at the mere suspicion. Sheriff Pat Dolan had robbed a Jore of freedom, caged him, like a wolf, for life. Dolan, they had Shang's word for it, had shed Jore blood, had killed Dave Jore, the only son of Abel. He had sworn — innumerable reports had reached them — that he would move heaven and earth to exterminate them.

Reluctantly Abel Jore gave in. "Reckon you're right, Shang." He added coldly as he swung about: "He'll have to go, Zion."

"And quick!" ordered Shang, stepping up on the black. "But I'll tend to it! I'll put him out so. . . ." He froze in his tracks as that rifle twitched, eager for utterance.

But Zion throttled its rapacious tongue to shout a shrill warning: "Keep back, Shang! You don't touch him! You don't kill him like you done Dave!"

"Shut up, Zion!" thundered his Uncle Abel.

But the young fellow defied him. There was something awe-compelling in his wild, passionate face, working in grief and rage. "I tell you he killed Dave! He lays it on the sheriff. But I know! He was afraid of Dave! Dave knowed something! Dave told me. . . ."

"He's crazy!" screamed Shang, a note of terror in his voice that drew the alert eyes of Abel Jore and brought an ominous gleam to them. But the gleam died in an instant, and Abel Jore said heavily: "He ain't responsible, Shang. So keep your shirt on. We know perfectly well that it was the sheriff. He saw Dave outside the basin. It was his chance to pick a Jore off, an'. . . ."

Zion's wild, young laughter was unearthly. "Shang saw his chance to shut Dave up. Dave knowed too much. Dave knowed he. . . ."

Murderously Shang lunged toward him, roaring: "I'll shut you up!" Then, he stiffened in his tracks again as the hammer of the rifle clicked down under Zion's thumb and the black hate in Zion's eyes was ripped by lightning. In Zion's face, now as white as the face of the slight figure in his arms, dawned a resolve there was no mistaking.

"You took Dave," said Zion quietly, suddenly, fatally so. "Dave was pards with me. This one, he's pards with me, too. You ain't goin' to take him. You're goin', Shang. You're goin' out, and you ain't comin' back." His finger bent to the trigger.

In that instant, while the Jores stood powerless to avert the tragedy, while Shang Haman looked into the face of death, there came a low, clear call from the direction of the cabins, riveting Zion, riveting them all in their attitudes of horror: "Son!"

Dimly René was aware of a woman running down the trail, a woman all in black, with a face like white marble and with eyes of fire, a face that was still beautiful, although graven on it was the story of a broken heart and ruined life. And he knew that this was Revel, who as a girl had chosen Joel Jore from all men — and had lost him — who had renounced high position for the Picture Rocks Basin.

Slowly she came up, gazing from one tense face to the other. No one explained the situation to her. They believed all things were known to her. So did René believe it. From first to last, his faith in Revel Jore was absolute.

As she slowly approached the horse, fear such as Race had felt when she came, walking through the trees to his deliverance, struck the heart of René — fear that became a panic of guilt, when, putting one hand on Zion's gun to deflect its aim, she placed the other on the shoulder of the black, and strained up, subjecting René Rand to such a scrutiny as he had never known. For he believed that nothing was hidden. He waited for her to tell them that he had come for Black Wing, the horse whose rider's name was Death.

Instead, she told them in a low, rich, thrilling voice: "He's sick. Take him to the house."

With more gentleness than René had thought him capable

of, Abel Jore denied her. "He can't stay, Revel."

"Can't stay?" echoed the woman blankly. "He's in no condition to turn away."

With a glance at Shang, who was wiping the cold sweat from his face with a soft, white sleeve, the brother-in-law rejoined firmly: "We ain't responsible for his condition."

Then the woman, on whom that glance had not been lost, declared: "You will be, Abel Jore, when he dies on the trail. You'll be responsible for his murder."

One charged instant of silence she surveyed them with heaving breast and flashing eyes, then — "For shame!" — she cried with ringing scorn. "And you call yourselves men! You were . . . when Joel was here to lead you. Have you sunk so low, following your evil star?"

Furious at this thrust, at the interference, at the effect of her words on the Jores, Shang cried hotly: "That's another thing I'm kickin' about right here! This petticoat rule! The way you let her twist you around her finger! The way you listen to her drivel! Go by it . . . like it was law!"

"We've been sorry, when we didn't, Shang," said Abel Jore. "She told us about Dave, and if we'd listened. . . ."

"Yeah," Shang cut in with a nervous glance at Zion. "She told you about Joel, too . . . and she told you wrong! She said he'd come back. And he's up for life!"

"He'll come," said Joel Jore's wife.

Fierce eagerness illumined the dark faces of the Jores. Seldom did Revel speak, never through persuasion, and but once before on this subject. Months and months they had prayed for some word, but she had kept silence.

"Joel will come?" cried Abel hoarsely. "When?"

In suspense they waited, watching the woman; in suspense Shang Haman, ashen, was in stark dread of Joel Jore's return. Even René, fighting off the blackness again closing in and with some premonition of the part he would play in that homecoming, waited in suspense and watched as tensely and breathlessly as the rest the outlaw's wife, who, still as a graven statue, was staring into purple space. It was as if they all stood on the brink of some great gulf which only she could see across. They saw her whole being lift and her tragic face illumine, as with joy of what she was seeing. They saw her shrink, her white hands clutch and twist the black dress at her breast, in agony that shook her frail body. And they heard her moan: "Joel will come in snow and ice and storm. But one of us who stands here will be gone."

Something struck each heart then like the passing of an icy wind.

Completely in her spell, swayed from Shang to her, they asked guidance in regard to this stranger.

"The Book!" cried Yance. "We'll go by it."

With dazed compliance she took a small Bible from her dress, opened it blindly, and blindly marked a passage. Then, bending her eyes to it in the gloom, read in a tone dead to all emotion, but affecting them as no accent could, just by its cold text, for it was Scripture — you couldn't get away from it: " 'Depart from me, ye cursed, into everlasting fire . . . I was a stranger, and ye took me not in; naked, and ye clothed me not; sick and. . . .' "

Zion's queer, choked cry broke into this edict. His eloquent eyes were triumphant as he saw the hot red of shame leap to his uncle's cheeks. Shang, too, saw it. With a curse, unintelligible save in its threat, but deadly plain in that, he swung on his heel and stalked off. And Revel Jore, firm as a statue that, rocked by a mighty tremblor, has righted itself, steadied René, while Zion slipped to the ground and drew the collapsing form into his strong, young arms.

Chapter Six

EDEN

So René was admitted to the Picture Rocks, over Shang Haman's protests, against the sober judgment of the Jores. But there was no sense of victory for him, although he had taken a first long step toward the repayment of his debt to Race, a debt that must be paid before he could call his life his own. His was scarcely a sense of living. He was vaguely aware of being carried into one of the cabins and laid upon a bed, of being disturbed in this, his first chance to rest, by the frantic insistence of one he knew to be Zion: "He'll die inside! You shut dead things up. Live things crawl to the open, where they can breathe. Where the wind can touch 'em. Where the sun won't have to hunt them."

René felt himself picked up again, borne into the open, and gently placed upon a bunk that was mattressed deep with feathery fir boughs, so freshly cut, even his failing senses rejoiced at the sweet, resinous tang of their crushed needles. Here, on the porch that overlooked the lake, he lay for three days, aware of little else. When he felt at all, it was as a dead stick that is cast into the fire. When he thought, it was with a curious detachment, as if all this were happening to someone else. He had no interest in what was going on, and less about the outcome. But one experience was sharp enough to leave its impress firmly in his mind.

In the dead of that first night — moonless, and so sable-hung that the whole universe seemed steeped in sadness — he was aroused by the light and heat of a candle held close, and saw a face bent to his — a face luminous with such tenderness as he had known but once before. And he cried, his lips trembling in a glad smile: "Mother!"

Soft as a breath — "Yes." — she had answered — "Yes." Then, so softly it might have been the night wind's whisper in the cottonwoods: "For what you will do for son of mine . . . yes!"

Then the light was gone, and the face with it, and all was black, although with a radiance which the light on her face seemed to have imparted to it. He remembered that his mother was dead. She had died when he was seven years old, and he knew that this was Zion's mother — Revel, who had interceded for him.

Other nights he felt her near, felt upon his hot face the cool caress such as only a woman can give. Often, when the climbing sun had found him, she would rouse him to force food upon him — food which he had not the slightest desire for, but ate to please her.

At these times, looking into her haunted eyes, that were filled with anxiety always, with tears often, he dully recalled her promise to be a mother to him. For what? He knew he ought to ask her about that. But he did not. He just gave up, just lay there in that volcano, secure in the blessed sense of being cared for, lulled by the lapping of the water, while three times the sun-gold of morn splashed on the mighty cliff beyond, three times dusk's amethyst veiled the figures on it, and three times big, yellow stars blazed out above its rims.

Hour after hour he would stare at the pictures on the rocks with no wonder at how they came to be there — just accepting them as a part of this wild background, as much so as the painted butterflies that fluttered by the porch or the jar of wild roses on the railing, or the great wolfhound, Capitán, that crept to his side, licked his hand, and, with many turnings, lay down to share his durance, the same speechless adoration in its solemn eyes that had been in Zion's.

Hour after hour he would watch the lake, blue with the blue of fathomless depths; blue as the eyes of the girl named Eden, whom he had not seen yet, nor thought about. Nor did he ever think of Race Coulter dodging Luke Chartres in Big Sandy, consumed with his desire for Black Wing; nor even thought to warn the Jores of the law's probable invasion; just drifted — like a dead leaf on the lake that dallies with the tide.

But, waking from a sound sleep on the afternoon of the fourth day, perceptions long slumbering awoke with him. Suddenly all the grandeur, the peace, and the beauty broke upon him. It seemed heaven. But almost instantly he realized that this was the Picture Rocks Basin; was suddenly aware that it was he, René Rand, lying helpless there; that the murmurs that reached him, along with the nicker and stamp of horses in the corral out front, were the voices of dreaded outlaws — Jores, of Shang Haman, who had murderously opposed his entrance.

Jerked to full consciousness, he heard a step, light as a falling snowflake, and, turning his head on the pillow, he saw a girl on the trail. As he first saw her, he never forgot her, but carried in his heart forever the picture she made then, framed by the quivering green of the cottonwood leaves, her slim, girlish figure, outlined against the shimmering water, imparting grace to the simple blue dress she wore.

Her short hair, like black silk, was brushed straight back, intensifying the slenderness of her face, chiseled fine and true as a cameo, but warm with youth's rosy flush; a face memorable for a haunting sadness that was of no passing mood, but there even in her smile, as truly a heritage as Zion's restlessness as were her eyes — amethyst, under long, black lashes —

Jore eyes. To René she seemed the living spirit of this wild and lovely place.

Fearfully, as she came up the steps, he searched her eyes for some reflection of the pity Race had said she would have for him, shrinking in dread of it, steeling his heart against her. But there was no pity there, and — he loved her. She didn't pity him because he was down. She knew he was man enough to get up again.

"You're better," she said in a voice that seemed tuned to the music of the water, and he knew that he had heard her voice in those numb hours; knew that her hands had picked those flowers. She had been near him often, and he hadn't known it — a dead stick, sure enough.

Tensely he said: "You're Eden. I was just thinkin' I'd hit heaven." Her coloring shamed the roses on the railing, as, dropping to the low stool beside her, she took Capitán's great, shaggy head in her lap.

"Heaven?" she echoed with a little laugh. "That's a strange name for the Picture Rocks."

His dark eyes earnest, René vowed: "Anyhow, it's the purtiest place on earth."

She stroked idly the dog's rough mane. "Is it?" she asked, incurious. "I'm no judge myself. You see, I've never been anywhere else."

"Never been away from the Picture Rocks?" René couldn't credit that.

"Just once . . . to Big Sandy." Her eyes clouded with sudden pain. "And it did seem heavenly . . . getting home. I never want to go again." She trembled as with sudden chill. "It was awful."

"Awful?" cried René, thinking how awful it was to keep a girl like her locked up here.

"So many people to stare and whisper. I . . . I was a Jore.

They'd point me out. Like Jores weren't human. Like we didn't have feelings. I . . . I was in trouble. My father . . . I wasn't going to see him again. They fought to get in the courtroom." Her face quivered. Softly Capitán whimpered. "Oh, I try to tell Zion. But he won't listen."

It seemed to René that she was trying to tell him something. He wanted to help, to assure her that *he* would listen. The words were on his lips, when suddenly he remembered why he was here, and, sick with shame, could only watch her, sitting with dark head flung back, blue eyes steadily fixed on his.

A man going by on the trail paused at sight of the pair, his eyes a wicked glitter. Angrily he took a stride in their direction but, checked by the nearness of those voices in the corral, thought better of it and went on. So, at their first meeting, as at most to come, the shadow of Shang Haman fell upon them.

But, unconscious of him, the girl cried unexpectedly: "I'm glad you came!"

Fervently, for this was one thing he could say in all honesty, René rejoined: "I sure am."

"I'm glad," she said in some confusion, "for Zion. He needs someone of his own age. The men. . . . His youth shuts him out of their confidence . . . throws him on himself. He's alone too much. And he broods about Dave. I'm afraid of what it may lead to. And he . . . he dreams about leaving us. He won't listen to me. He says I don't really know. He won't listen to my uncles. He thinks they don't want him to go. But you. . . ."

Bravely her eyes met his again, and he knew by the appeal in them that this was what she had come to ask him. "With you to tell him what it's like out there . . . that he's better off here. You . . . you have talked to him. You must have seen he wouldn't fit in."

Only thus, with terrible reluctance, did she indicate by word or sign that there was any lack, any difference, in Zion. This was wrung from her by her great love for her brother, a love that would follow him to the very end, an end she seemed to foresee, to be battling with. "Oh, I'm afraid," she whispered. "There's things in his blood." In swift appeal she bent toward René. "If only you'd discourage him."

Gently he promised: "I'll do my best, Eden."

His heart leaped to the swift, grateful touch of her hand, to her joyous: "Oh, I am glad you came! Glad it was you! It might have been someone else who would have lured him away. But now he'll stay. He'll listen to you. He trusts you."

Stabbed by remorse, impelled by something stronger than himself, René raised up. "Do you, Eden?" he asked.

He fell back, white and shaken, at her low-voiced: "Yes."

Her trust was torture in the days that passed. For he had come as a thief to steal a horse, to rob the Jores to pay Race. And he owed the Jores most. Or did he? He owed them everything. But the cold fact remained that, but for Race, he would never have seen them. In his despair to know to whom his first loyalty was due, he wished that Zion had let him die at Sentry Crags. No. For then he would never have seen Eden Jore. And but one thought was more unbearable — that he might have to leave her to bear alone this well-founded anxiety about Zion, with her uncles blind to the black trouble brewing between him and Shang Haman.

This thought made him delay doing the Jores the one service in his power while still remaining true to the instructions of Race Coulter. He couldn't tell them that the sheriff had knowledge of the secret pass and planned to raid the basin without involving himself. Already the Jores were suspicious of him. Shang had accused him of complicity with Dolan. Far from making him solid with the clan, as Race had forecast, it might cost his life. Yet he had to warn them.

Day by day he put it off, although any day or night gunfire might rake the basin, although his debt to the Jores grew hourly. He would think of Revel, who had given him a mother's care, of Zion, who had defended him — who called him partner. Then he would think of Race, bringing him from certain death back East, and that now life was worth far, far more than he had ever dreamed it could be. Thus his debt to Race grew hourly likewise.

Remember, you'll owe your life to me — he could hear Coulter say — *and the debt ain't paid till I get that horse.*

Chapter Seven

DRIFTING

Black Wing might have been a myth for anything René had heard of him since coming to the basin. He didn't want to hear anything — overwhelmed as he was by gratitude to the Jores. He could have at any time, for Zion had no reticence where he was concerned. In their frequent chats he might easily have led the conversation to the stallion. But when the young fellow seemed liable to veer in that quarter, René would divert him with talk of life "out there."

He knew now how justified was Eden's fear that Zion might leave the Picture Rocks. He had come to share it, to see how hopeless it was to discourage him. Oh, Zion listened to him. With hunger insatiable, taut, on the low stool by René's bunk, or prone on the bearskin rug before it, he would listen to René, telling of life outside the basin. True to his promise to Eden, René would strip it of all glamour, emphasizing its harsher aspects, its snares and pitfalls, its complex social order, of which he was — René would smile wanly — a "good example."

But when he was done, Zion would jerk up, eager to give his own version, a version made up of his unbounded imagination, of what he had heard of that dark side of life that had been the experience of the Jores, a version that made René's blood run cold. For to Zion, life out there was one swift succession of violent deeds, hair-breadth escapes, crimes that were not crimes to him, but feats of cunning, valor, enviable excitement.

"But things ain't like that," René protested earnestly one afternoon when the sun and leaves made the cabin a checkerboard of green and gold. "Oh, they happen. But just once in a blue moon. So seldom they cause a really big commotion."

"A big commotion." Zion hugged his knees, chuckling gleefully. "Honest, do they?"

Appalled to see that he was merely firing the boy's enthusiasm, René explained: "Most men are too busy workin'. For every man who holds up a stage or robs a train, a million men is slavin' day in and day out just for a livin'."

"They're crazy." Thus with a shrug did Zion Jore dismiss the workers of the world. "Livin's free!"

"Not out there!" cried René. "Out there you gotta pay."

"I hear that." Zion nodded, eager to agree. "I hear you gotta pay for everything but the air you breathe."

"You bet." René was relieved to think he had made some impression. "Money's what makes the world go 'round."

"I hear," pressed the young fellow in buckskin, his expressive face bewildered, as if he could not believe this, "I hear they lock the money up in banks and places so folks can't get at it."

"That's right, Zion."

"No," slowly Zion replied, "it ain't right. Not when it's to live on. Suppose Uncle Abel, say, or Shang, locked everything to eat away from us?" His wild laugh told eloquently what he would do then.

René looked helplessly at him. How explain property rights to one who had lived as Zion Jore had lived, wild as any mustang?

"Pard, tell me," the young fellow demanded in his hot, fierce way, "what's to stop a man from bustin' in and takin' what he needs?"

René cried, with all the strong force of dread this tameless spirit roused in him: "The law! It would run him down, catch him, lock him up."

"Like Dad," Zion cut in soberly. "But suppose" — his dark face clearing — "suppose he had a horse so fast . . . the fastest horse in all the world, I reckon." In his eyes blazed the sun of some mysterious worship. "Suppose he could shoot like I can?"

A shudder swept René, remembering how Zion Jore could shoot. His problem seemed nothing to the one the Jores would face if ever this son of the house left the Picture Rocks. It seemed to René than even the treacherous part he was pledged to play here might be condoned if only he could prevent that, and he could prevent that only as long as he was here. But if he followed Race's instructions, followed his own inclination to do, now, what seemed a greater service to the Jores, he might not be here. For he couldn't tell them without admitting that he knew he was coming to the basin, and being already suspicious, the Jores would think his collapse at the crags had been a trick to get in. But they must be warned. He would find some way. Time passed, and he did not.

He was able to be up and about, feeling "fine," and looking, perhaps, better than he was. For the constant sun had covered his pallor with a deceptive coat of tan, and rest had eased his cough. He sat at table with the clan, tolerated by the Jore men, openly hated by Shang Haman — a table over which the gentle, sad-eyed Revel presided with a ceremony that brought to mind the high estate from which she was said to have fallen. Now he was strong enough to take short walks beneath the cottonwoods or to the corrals in company with Capitán always, and with Zion, when the young fellow was not off on his solitary ramblings, working with stock, or on sentry duty at the crags. Still René could think of no way to warn the Jores without revealing that he had another motive in coming to the basin.

Had Yance or Abel shown the slightest confidence in him, given him the least opening, he would have warned them, regardless of consequences. But they did not. Although courteous always, they kept up between themselves and their guest a wall of reserve against which René felt powerless.

Times there were, although few and far between, when he could put aside this gnawing insistence, and lose himself in the tranquillity of his new life, could believe that Race's imagination, fired by his craze for Black Wing, had put its own sinister construction upon what had been an innocent conversation between Chartres and Dolan; that, anyhow, there was the well-known slip between cup and lip; even that the whole thing might have fallen through before this.

There were times when he forgot that this was an outlaw's nest. For the harmony that prevailed here, despite Shang Haman, would have shamed many a home not shadowed by the disgrace of a world's ostracism; shamed the home of his own upbringing, which a niggardly, surly step-father had made a purgatory. The big house seemed the furthest thing from a cradle of crime with its quaint, hand-made furnishings, its picturesque litter of wild heads and horns and skins, its shelves of books with yellowed leaves and faded bindings — more books than René's eyes had embraced in all his cowboy life.

"Friends," Revel had explained, seeing his surprise, "old friends, I brought from home."

They were friends she had made her children acquainted with, so that René was constantly amazed by Eden's grasp on things outside her experience, her knowledge of things beyond the range of his. But friends Zion had small love for, except such kindred spirits as Ali Baba and Long John Silver, whose turbulent careers had helped to form his idea of life out there and were about as true to it as the world's idea of the Picture Rocks.

But riding, walking, paddling in the old dug-out canoe with Eden — the shadow of Shang Haman inevitably falling over them — René never forgot. The girl's innate honesty, her absolute frankness and trust, brought home the shameful role he was playing here. And he felt like a traitor — hearing the story of old Jerico, a hero to his granddaughter because he had been so loyal, and she thought loyalty the greatest human attribute. He felt like a coyote — standing with Eden under the lone pine on a wind-swept bluff beside Dave's grave, with its rude cross, a silent monument to the Jores' blood feud with Sheriff Dolan and to Zion's sworn revenge on Shang.

"Unless," she said hopefully, "we can rid him of that notion."

His heart singing, for all its guilty pain at the way she allied herself with him, René asked: "Is it a notion, Eden?"

She looked down at the cross and mound, thinking of Dave, who had been scarcely less dear to her than Zion, whose passionate heart, also, had been set on leaving the Picture Rocks, and who had gone.

"It has to be," she said desperately. "It's too horrible, otherwise. If Shang killed Dave, then Zion isn't safe. Zion's not safe while he thinks it. Shang might do him some harm. That's why I don't dare make an enemy of him."

Feeling like a Judas in poor return for all her confidence, he told her of his existence on the race tracks, stretching out his two years there to embrace all his life, and she was so glad he'd told her.

"That explains it," she exclaimed joyously, "the way you ride! Shang's been telling the rest you're no tenderfoot. I'll put him in his place next time."

Oh, she was loyal to him.

But out on the lake today, a rare June day, three weeks after his coming, he forgot utterly and was happy, drifting with Eden under the painted cliff. Love, long repressed, making itself imperiously felt in thrilling silences and prosaic discussion of the painted rocks.

"How did anyone ever get up there to paint them?" René wondered, his eyes on the figures, because he dared not look at her, prettier than she had ever been, nestling in the old canoe, her smooth, white arms bare to the shoulder, her small, shapely hands holding the idle paddle. "It couldn't have been done from above. They're too far down, and the top hangs over. And they're so high up it couldn't have been done from the water."

From that store of knowledge that always amazed him, she explained that the lake had been higher then. "This whole basin was a lake once, René. See those seams?" she asked, pointing up at the eroded lines that ran across the face of the bluff. "They're old shores. Mother says the rocks were painted by a race that lived here when the lake was at that high-water mark just below the pictures. Long, long ago that was . . . but just a flash of time in the ages water and wind have been slashing and sculpturing these old rims. Think of it." Never had her face seemed to René as sad as then. "Doesn't it make the Jores' little day here unimportant?"

And his. Generations before he came, these pictured rocks had been here, and would be here, fadeless, generations after he was dust. Of what moment was any act of his? Just a shadow flitting across the old cliff's face.

"Shang hates them," Eden mused.

"Hates them?" René was shocked that even Shang could fail to love the old picture rocks.

"He says they scowl at him."

"At first they seemed to scowl at me," owned René. "But now they kinda smile."

"Then you're a Jore!" cried the girl, her eyes like stars. "They only smile at Jores."

A Jore! With what a torturing, self-revealing pang did he stare at her. A Jore! And he was endangering the whole clan by holding back that warning, endangering everyone she held dear. Love had made him blind. But now he saw.

In horror of what he saw he bent toward her, seized the paddle, and sent the canoe skimming along.

"Stop, René!" she protested, amazed, anxious. "It makes you breathe too fast. It will bring your cough back."

He smiled in a way she never forgot: "I've drifted long enough."

For he was resolved to seek out Abel Jore and tell him what Race had overheard that day in Trail's End.

But when, nearing shore, he saw Shang Haman's shadow on the water, saw Shang, dapper, devilish, actual, watching them from the trees with that in his eyes which brought back Zion's cry — "I've got to kill him . . . he pesters Eden!" — he couldn't deliberately do something that would put him beyond the power to help her and Zion. And so he put it off again.

Bitterly, while life lasted, René would regret it; would always think that, if he had gone to Abel Jore there and then, that which happened might never have been. He never had another chance. For that night, in the most unfavorable night, it all came out.

Chapter Eight

ON TRIAL

They were at supper in the big house, all except Yance, who was at the crags, when Abel Jore, eating in thoughtful silence at the head of the table, suddenly put down his fork.

"Rand," he asked out of a clear sky, "how long were you in Big Sandy?"

Though startled by the abrupt query, René managed: "Two hours, more or less."

"Hear any mention of us?"

Realizing that he had drifted into a snag that had ripped the bottom out of everything, René said: "Yes."

An absolute hush fell upon the room. Every eye turned on him — Abel's piercing his very soul; Eden's wide with apprehension; Revel's unreadable. Zion's, fiercely loyal, darted from René to Shang, whose beady eyes reflected his venomous satisfaction at this most surprising turn.

"Uhn-huh," drawled the outlaw. "You would. A crow couldn't light in Arizony and not hear what scalawags we are. Hear anything particular?"

"I heard," René said steadily, "that the sheriff's goin' to raid the Picture Rocks . . . that he's got information about a secret pass."

"What?" Abel Jore sprang up violently, but Shang held his chair as if glued there.

"What's this," Abel demanded grimly, "about the pass?"

"I didn't get much," said René, as Race had coached him,

"just the drift. The sheriff was talkin' in Trail's End with a man, that big race horse man, Chartres." A cry, articulate only in its horror, drew his gaze to Revel. Her black eyes were riveted upon him, her hands outspread as if to ward off some monstrous thing. "It seems," he went on slowly, "somebody's promised to show Luke Chartres the way in."

"It's a bluff!" Shang was on his feet then, drowning René's voice with his blustering. "It's a bluff! Nobody knows where that pass is but us!"

"Dolan don't make loose talk," said Abel Jore curtly. And, turning back to René, his face as hard and expressionless as rock, he asked coldly: "So you knew where you were comin' when you headed up here?"

It was the question René dreaded. "Yeah."

"And you didn't come for health?"

"I sure did!"

"And what else?"

With a hesitation that went against him, the young fellow said evasively: "To warn you, for one thing."

"You sure took your time! You've been here three weeks. Why ain't you spoke up?"

"I was afraid to," René owned with that game grin. "You'd accused me of bein' a spy for Dolan. I was afraid you wouldn't believe I was with you. Afraid you'd make me go."

"And you liked our society so well you risked us all? That's flatterin'. Just what's the big attraction?"

Reddening at the biting sarcasm in Abel's tone, René's eyes involuntarily sought Eden, white, stricken at this cross-examination, at his damaging admissions. That glance told the story. In fury, Shang turned expectantly to Abel Jore. But the outlaw seemed to be beyond the power to do then whatever it was Shang expected of him, and dismissed René with a gesture.

The young man went out and, with a deeper sense of isolation than ever the Jores suffered from a world's ostracism, sat down on his cabin steps to await the verdict. It was easy now to realize that he was in an outlaws' nest; in the hands of the Jores, against whom the whole state warred, whose greatest weapon was the dread their name inspired, and who survived the unequal conflict only by reason of the fact that they would never let that weapon grow blunt, but kept it keen by striking unhesitatingly and with all their savage force at any invasion of the basin, as any free-born citizen defends, to the last drop of his heart's blood, an enemy's intrusion of his home. They had let the bars down once, had dared to hesitate, had showed human feeling. And they might have paid for it with their lives, or with what they valued more, their freedom.

Well did René realize, sitting there alone, with the big hound's nose thrust consolingly beneath his palm, and purple twilight falling, that the Jores were deciding what to do with him, and that mercy would be excluded from that decision. Nor did he blame them. He was a stranger, and they took him in, sick, and they. . . . Killing was too good for him. Through his black sense of shame but one bright ray shone. The Jores were warned in time, and would be prepared for whatever came. So far he had done what Race had asked, although from now on. . . .

"Well," he said to Capitán, shrugging, "there won't likely be any 'from now on.'"

A chance for life the stakes had been, or a quick exit. A quick exit, then. He had lost, but he had won — had won weeks of real living back in God's country, where the wind blew clean and the sun didn't have to wallow through clouds of dust and smoke to get to you, and a man had elbow room. He had lived more in his three weeks here than in all his twenty-one years before, had lived to love Eden Jore.

68

What was she thinking of him? Did she understand why he had risked them all? She thought the best thing a man could be was loyal. Did she know how hard it was sometimes to know to whom to be loyal? Did she know that he had kept silent because he wanted to repay her and Revel and Zion? For what?

Into his worried thoughts broke a light footstep. Lifting his head, he saw Zion coming up, his face as wild, as perplexed as when he'd seen it first at Sentry Crags, his weird blue eyes probing as he sat down beside him, twisting the fringe of his buckskin in painful doubt about something.

Zion suddenly laid an uncertain hand on René's sleeve. "Pard, you mean that . . . about bein' with us?"

Hot tears stung René's eyes. He gripped that brown hand in his own. "Yes, Zion."

The cloud passed in an instant. "I knowed it! All along I knowed it . . . in my heart. But they say you can't trust hearts."

So that's what they were saying in there.

"They say Jores mustn't have hearts. They say heads is what . . . ," Zion broke off, heat-lightning flashing in his eyes as Shang Haman burst out of the big house and tore down the corral trail.

A moment more and both, listening with unconscious intensity, heard him galloping away. *To the pass,* René thought.

"He's goin' to town!" blazed Zion with that dangerous hostility he always displayed toward Shang. "He's goin' to try and get something on you."

Going to Big Sandy, where a dozen people might have seen Race with him. "But how can he?" cried René. "Dolan will arrest him, if he shows up in Big Sandy."

Zion laughed bitterly. "Not Shang! They got nothin' on

him. He's too slick. Shang's the only one who's free to go and come. He. . . ."

"Zion!" Abel Jore was now loudly calling.

The young fellow left, and René sat on alone. He saw Zion saddle and ride off toward the crags. Before long Yance Jore galloped in. He could hear Yance and Abel heatedly discussing something in there, but, lacking Race's trained hearing, no syllable reached him. He sat on, while night spread over the basin, layer upon layer of velvety black, and great silvery stars pierced it; still sat — a time as long as all the time since the Picture Rocks had been — in suspense, waiting to know his fate. But he was not to know it that night.

One by one the cabin lights went out. The Jores slept. René slept, by fits and starts, hearing, toward morning, a horse coming in, dogs clamoring, and a voice cursing them. Shang was back.

Breakfast time came. But René couldn't go in. He couldn't eat the Jores' bread, when they felt like this about him, but if he didn't go, they'd think he was afraid to. Well, he'd risk that. He'd fix his own breakfast out of the provisions in his pack. He was undoing the straps, when Revel came in. She saw his intention at a glance.

"No," she said sorrowfully, "you'll breakfast with us."

Silently he went into the cabin with her.

Shang was already in his chair. He didn't look like a man who had spent the night in the saddle. He looked as dapper as ever. His pale-gray shirt was guiltless of speck or crease. His jowls were blue from a recent shave. His "silverware," as Zion contemptuously termed his heavy belt buckle, filigreed boot-tops, and other glittering niceties of costume, was as bright as if he'd spent the night polishing them. His eyes, however, had no gleam, but the filmy look of an animal feasting, and he seldom took them from René.

René was making a brave show of eating, although every morsel choked him, watching the door for Eden, wild to see what she was thinking of him, and painfully aware that Yance and Abel, the only others there, thought even less of him than at supper. They were courteous still, but with a deadly quality, the ominous politeness of an executioner toward the condemned. He knew they had called a truce until this meal was at an end. Impatient to have it over, he pushed back his chair.

As if this was what they were waiting for, Abel rose. "Now," he instructed Shang, "tell him what you just told us."

In a vicious, explosive breath, sinister as a rattler's hiss, Shang flung at René: "I've been to Big Sandy!"

"Yeah?" coolly René rejoined.

"Yeah! And I learned all about your little game! Oh, it was a slick one, shammin' sick to get in here for Race Coulter!"

Strange the fire that name struck from the flinty eyes of the Jores. What had they against Race except the attempted theft of a horse? A horse they let run like any mustang, and didn't value enough to brand.

"Rand," Abel finished what Shang seemed unable to do through the very excess of his desire to, "Shang says Race Coulter met you at the train in Big Sandy. He says Race bought your outfit. Is that true?"

The young man replied scornfully: "Shang says so."

"We've heard Shang," said the outlaw quietly. "Now we want to hear you."

Something told René he could deny it and the Jores would believe him. He was cruelly tempted. But he said, although it might sign his death warrant: "It's true."

Hardly had the words left his lips, when he realized it was not. Not all that Shang had accused him of, not true he'd been playing sick. And he cried: "It's true Race staked me, but. . . ."

"That's plenty," said Abel Jore.

"But I can't leave it there!" the young fellow insisted wildly. "You've got to know. . . ."

"That's plenty!"

They weren't giving him a chance to defend himself. They thought he was low enough for that. Furious at this injustice, René swung on his heel and left the room. He went out into the bright sunshine of early morning, his soul crying out against the accusation that he had shammed his condition. He was in agony lest Eden and Revel think that, after all they'd done for him.

Down at the corral he hung around, hoping against hope that Eden would see him and come out so he could tell her what little there was to be said on his side. When she didn't come, he was sure she thought . . . that.

As if running from that thought, he saddled his cayuse and galloped up the lake trail, riding furiously, aimlessly, for a while, bringing up by Dave's grave beneath the pine. Finding himself here, a spot hallowed to him for moments there with Eden, he slipped down and, breathless from the exertion, flung himself in the grass beside the cross, his dark eyes on the pictured rocks, his black thoughts far off on a muddy race course, with a man asking him what life was worth.

"They don't know," he moaned, "the fix I was in."

Then wild hoofbeats on the slope jerked him around to see Eden galloping toward him, a distracted figure, her black hair wind-tossed about her face that was robbed of all color.

He leaped up, as she reared to a stop beside him, and put out his hand to help her down. But she waved him back.

"I can't stay, René. They'll miss me. I . . . I sneaked away. I couldn't let you hear it first from them . . . that way. I had to tell you myself. They . . . they. . . ." But the tears came, and she couldn't tell him.

Gently he said to help: "I know, Eden. I'm to leave the Picture Rocks . . . by this route," — laying his hand upon the cross.

She flinched as from a blow. "Not that!" she cried, tears in her eyes. "No. But they say you've got to go. They say" — the wet blue eyes flashed indignantly — "you're able to."

"I am," said René smiling, although this sentence seemed the harder to bear — to live and be banished from her. "I'm as good as I was when shiftin' for myself on the tracks."

"Mother begged them to let you stay" — her nervous gaze was on the trail — "if only for a few weeks more. She told them you might have a relapse."

"I won't, girl."

"They say" — distractedly as she shortened rein — "they don't dare let you stay, when you admit you came from Race Coulter."

"Eden."

She wheeled her horse away from him. "I want you to know, René, I don't care about that. I don't care what was in your heart when you came to the Picture Rocks. I know it's been true since. I know if there was any kinks in it, you've got them straightened. I . . . I. . . . Oh, good bye."

She would have dashed away, but he caught her saddle, holding her. "Eden" — his dark eyes burned with intense fire — "you trust me still?"

"Yes," she said, and again, "yes."

Mad with joy at this, at something else in her lovely face, René's voice sang out: "I'll go, then, but . . . I'll come back."

Mad with terror at that, she pleaded: "Don't, René! Don't try it. Promise me! You'd never get in again. Shang. . . . Oh,

René, don't think of it even. Forget you've ever been here. Forget us all."

Forget her? "Eden," he said tensely, "there's things I'd like to say, but I can't. I ain't my own man. I ain't even a man . . . yet. But I will be some day. And when I am, I'll come. These rims, guns, all the Shangs this side of Halifax can't keep me out."

And to give him strength till then, he put up his arms and drew her down till her wild heart beat on his.

"I'll come," he whispered huskily. "I'll come . . . as sure as the ole rocks stand."

Then, with her kiss upon his lips, intoxicated with joy, his soul sweeping the very clouds, he watched her riding down the trail, watched until the green leaves that had framed her in his first conscious glimpse of her had swallowed her again. He little guessed how like a dream all this would seem when next he saw her, dreaming now how quickly he'd get well with her to live for.

He woke with a start to hear another set of violent hoofbeats on the slope, to see the black that had carried him into the basin pounding up with Zion on its back. He was holding the big rifle in his hands, and in his eyes there was a savage blaze. That resolve there was no mistaking.

Zion was crying: "I'm huntin' Shang!"

Chapter Nine

BLACK WING

Zion's vengeful gaze was scouring the bushy slopes. "I'm huntin' Shang!" he blazed. "I'm goin' to kill him . . . dead! He's up here . . . some place! He tagged Eden!"

Then René knew that in their last meeting, as on the first one, the shadow of Shang Haman had been over them. Shang had seen their farewell. His heart stopped, overcome by a terrible fear for Eden, and he cried hoarsely: "What's Shang done?"

"He's talked 'em down on you!" Zion flamed.

In his relief René could have laughed. "It's all right, Zion." He tried to soothe him. "Eden told me. They're just goin' to send me back."

"Back?" It had anything but a soothing effect. "Back . . . where you was dyin' at?"

"It's all right." René held that gaze by his very earnestness. "You see, I got a start here. I can get well anywhere. I had to go sometime, you know. As well be now."

One instant Zion pondered this. "Yes," he mused then, "of course, you'd be goin'. Nobody'd stay in this basin 'less they had to." Undergoing one of his startling transformations, his dangerous mood was replaced by one of wild enthusiasm. "As well be now!" His voice trembled with eagerness. "And I'll go, too! I'll go out there with you!"

Terrified by this decision, the last thing he could allow to happen after his promise to Eden, René insisted: "I can't take you, Zion!"

Shocked, hurt by this refusal, Zion looked at him. "Why not?" he asked then, his lips quivering.

"Because," desperately René offered every reason he could think of except the real one — that Zion wouldn't fit in, "you couldn't stand it, raised like you've been. You saw what it done to me. It might do worse to you. You ain't felt walls till you feel a city. Walls like a house . . . that close. Even when you're outside. Pressin' on you. Smotherin' the very breath."

"I won't stay in them places." Zion was again all eagerness.

"You might have to!" cried René out of his bitter experience.

"I'll ride away from them so fast," Zion said, and laughed, "you can't see me for dust." And he slipped his rifle in its scabbard in readiness for travel.

"There's other things." René racked his brain for them. "The law that keeps you shut up here. There'll be a thousand Pat Dolans out there. Every place you go, there'll be one . . . watchin' you, anxious to see you slip, so they can say they caught a Jore."

"Will they know?" Zion's eyes sparkled. "Honest, will they know me out there?"

"Zion, you don't savvy the danger."

Talking of danger to a Jore. "Pard" — Zion underwent another baffling change — "I want to show you something. Get your horse and come along."

René shook his head. "I can't. I got to go back. They'll think I'm hidin' out. They're just waitin' to send me now."

"Let 'em wait," Zion entreated. "It won't hurt. They ain't told you yet. They don't know Eden did. Please, pard. I want to show you something. I'll bet you'll say I can go then."

Impelled by the young fellow's excitement, ready to do

anything he asked but take him out of the basin, René went with him, wondering what Zion had to show him, his wonder growing as Zion kept on beyond the north horn of the lake. Then, turning west, they began a steady climb of the sun-flushed slopes, taking them farther into the basin than he had ever been. And ever the strange fire in Zion's soul blazed higher, so that his lithe figure strained forward in the saddle, even while he held it back to a moderate pace, remembering that René couldn't ride as he could yet.

Up they climbed, and still up, toward the fluted edge of the great cup, coming out finally on a high mesa where, it seemed, they could go no farther. Sharply across their path reared that great rock barrier, the wall that ringed the basin, the wall that Zion was always riding into, when he wanted to run — like the wind that swoops down and rushes on and never stops or turns around. Now he had ridden into it again.

Pulling up beside him, René was amazed to see all his fire gone and his wild face overcast by some strange doubt — doubt that flickered in his eyes, fixed on René with strange intensity, and trembled in his voice as he asked in pitiful uncertainty: "We're pards, ain't we?"

With assurance René rejoined: "We sure are, Zion."

Instantly Zion kindled again. "It's all right, then. Pards don't keep things." And before René could speculate on what he meant, he flung an arm out at the cliff, excitedly confiding: "There's the secret pass."

Stunned by the unexpectedness of this, René could only stare at the rock wall, seemingly unbroken anywhere, unscalable, rocketing hundreds of feet into the air, where it split up into pinnacles.

"You ain't lookin' right," Zion shouted with boyish laughter. "Look down. Here! Between these rocks. Can't you see daylight?"

77

Then René's eyes fell on the mound of shattered rock at the foot of the cliff — remains of pinnacle that, wearying in the ages of standing up there, had fallen and been dashed to bits. And he saw an opening in it. It looked like a tunnel, worn through the wall of the ancient crater by the action of water in the ages when this basin had been a lake, and running completely through the rim, for he could see, if not daylight, at least a faint gloom, as of light that has survived a long, dark, and tortuous journey.

Long he stared at it, trying to grasp the astounding fact that, thus, with no preparation, no conscious effort, he was seeing the pass for which the whole state sought. This was the pass the Jores were said to use on their lawless excursions. This was the pass Luke Chartres had spent a year of his valuable time to find. And Sheriff Dolan had. . . .

"Why's it left like this?" he asked jerkily of Zion in alarm. "Right now a posse may be headed toward it. I warned your uncles. Why ain't they guardin' it?"

"It's guarded, you bet," said Zion, and laughed at René's bewilderment. "We guard it from Sentry Crags. We can see the country outside this pass from there. If any one drifts this way, we send a man over."

So they watched both passes at the same time. "But at night," cried René, thinking of Pat Dolan, wild to raid the basin, driven by the sharp goad of ambition, and with so little to stop him. "You can't watch it after dark."

"No need to," smiled Zion, canny in all pertaining to the Picture Rocks. "The outside openin' is high on a shelf, covered with rocks like this. Horses can't get within a mile of it no time. And men has to climb to it hand over hand, hundreds of feet. It's risky in daylight. They couldn't do it at night, even Jores." He plucked eagerly at René's sleeve. "Let's crawl through. I'll show you."

But René didn't want to know any more of the Jores' secrets. Already he knew too much, when he was leaving the Picture Rocks and going out where Race was.

"If this is what you wanted to show me," he said wearily, "let's go back."

"This?" The blue eyes flashed scorn. "This ain't nothin'. This just happened to be on the way. Wait till you see!"

In ten times his first excitement he wheeled his horse and was off again, so wrought up that, for long stretches, he forgot to wait for René, and remembering, would dash back all contrition, insisting that René rest. Then, unable to endure the delay, he would race on again, leading the way along the great hogback that bisected the basin. Coming at last to its highest point, a timberless knoll where René, halting to rest his steaming horse and his own fagged self, forgot fatigue, forgot Zion, who was whirling back to wait for him, forgot that the Jores were waiting — everything — in the panorama spread before him.

On his left the hogback dropped off into a jumble of forested mountain and cañon, wild as on the day of creation. On his right, by more gradual stages, it rolled down to the level floor of the basin, where the lake flashed in the noon glare and the cabins nestled in the green trees on its shore, and, awesomely, over him and all around, the age-scarred, iron-stained rim — of the very world, it seemed. It stretched without a break, save that thin split at Sentry Crags and the washout at its foot that had been so long a secret, but with many a break on its top, rags of crags, like tombstones to the world that was.

"Come on!" cried Zion with fierce impatience, tearing off at a gallop down where the wildest jumble was.

Trees rose above them. Grass brushed their stirrups. René wondered at another change in Zion. He was even more tense, but alert and cautious, his restless eyes questing, now studying the ground, now searching the crests, now scouring the cañon pockets. Suddenly, jerking up at the foot of a low, green ridge, he implored silence with a finger on his lips. Then, slipping from his horse, he motioned René to do likewise. And with a soundless movement René found impossible to emulate, he crawled up the brushy ridge to the summit, where he dropped flat, parted the grass, and looked down.

René, creeping up, to drop breathless beside Zion, did the same. He saw below them a little valley of unearthly beauty, luxurious with grass and wildflowers, and a spring that bubbled up to overflow its ferny banks and flash away in a mad little stream. Nothing more. Nothing to account for the way Zion was trembling against him.

"Hush," said the young fellow. "They're comin'."

Coming? Who? René looked the question. Tingling through all his being at Zion's thrilled whisper: "Wild ones."

Then his heart leaped as over the green slope beyond, down to the spring, streamed a band of wild horses, the finest he had ever seen. Then it ceased to beat as his rapt gaze fell on the one in the rear, a glorious stallion — creamy skin glistening in the sun, mane and tail like spun gold, swirling about him, like nothing he'd ever seen, like a horse you'd dream about.

"Black Wing," whispered Zion.

Chapter Ten

BREAKING AWAY

Then, suddenly looking at Black Wing, René knew vast pity for Race Coulter, felt complete sympathy with his desire, understood all his mercilessness. There wasn't much a man wouldn't do for such a horse — for Black Wing. There weren't any more like him. There were creatures out there men called horses. But this was what the Creator had in mind when he made the first one — this royal, fiery thing, poised near the spring, his feet in the wind-stirred ferns, his head high, vigilant while his subjects drank. He pitied all men who hadn't seen him, was angered that such a horse should be hidden.

Anger shook his whisper: "It's a crime he's wild."

Zion laughed softly. "He ain't, pard." And quickly, to repress René's outburst, he went on: "Oh, he's wild enough. But just because I let him be. Because I like him that way. He's broke . . . though. I broke him. I been a whole year doin' it. Nobody knows but me . . . and you, now. That's all right, ain't it?"

Right then, with Black Wing in his blood, René didn't know whether it was or not.

But Zion knew in his heart. "Watch." Pride flamed in his eyes. "Just watch. I'll show you."

Noiselessly, moving some distance from René, he put his fingers to his mouth and whistled. Instantly the wild band broke into flight, vanishing over the opposite slope, all but the horse like sunshine that whirled and stood, himself quivering, tossing his proud head up and sending a silver whistle back. Zion repeated the call. Black Wing circled back toward him, passing from sight beneath the slope. René was sure his eyes had tricked him. Sure he had dreamed Black Wing.

Then he caught the soft thud of unshod hoofs on grass, and before his incredulous eyes, quite close, burst the golden horse, starting at sight of him, but held by the white magic of the young man in buckskin, who was slowly approaching, murmuring endearments.

While Zion slipped a light rope from the front of his shirt, quickly fashioning a hackamore to fit that slim nose, the stallion swung, and René saw, on the satiny curve of one creamy hip, that jet-black wing — the mark that had been on every colt to the Crusader strain, upsetting track dope.

Spellbound he watched. He saw Zion's brown arms flash up, saw his dark face press that golden cheek. On his brain forever was seared this picture of the wild young creature and the wild horse, in the full flush of their untried strength, their tameless, fearless spirits sorely tried by the powerful urges that were their heritage.

As Zion lightly bounded to Black Wing's back, René wanted to stop him, to scream that the rider's name was Death. But he remembered that Zion must have ridden him often, and that the prophecy could not apply to him. Nevertheless, terror chilled his rapture in the stallion's grace of motion, as it whirled and danced before him, controlled only by the light hackamore and the pressure of Zion's knees.

He could have sobbed with relief when, riding close, the young fellow slipped down and stood with one arm flung over Black Wing's neck.

"Tell me," earnestly he appealed to René, "are there many out there can beat him?"

"None in the whole world, Zion!"

The young fellow nodded. "That's what I reckoned. Else folks wouldn't come in for him. A man did once, you know. A man who knows horses, they say. They say he. . . ." A wild light flared in his eyes. René knew he was thinking of Race. Fiercely he proclaimed, his arm possessively tightening about that golden head: "He's mine!"

René felt a mad desire to dispute it, to tell Zion that this horse belonged to the first man to put a brand on him. He even knew an insane longing to be that man.

"There's others out there would claim him, if they could," said the young fellow moodily. "Dad told me so . . . before they locked him away. Black Wing wasn't born here. Dad stampeded him in with his mother, when he was little. He had a right to her."

What right had Joel Jore to the racer of Luke Chartres, the mare Sahra?

"Dad always watched him close," Zion went on. "He said Black Wing was worth a dozen caches, like they got in banks and places. So does Uncle Abel and Yance say that. They say he'd make us very rich, if we had him out of the Picture Rocks."

So the Jores knew they had a fortune in horseflesh. Then why did they let him run?

"Zion," René asked, "why don't you brand him?"

"Brand him?" echoed Zion blankly. "Why?"

"So folks will know he belongs to you. So they won't try to steal him."

"But there's nobody to steal him, pard. Shang might. But he wouldn't dare try it."

"Outsiders, I mean!" cried René earnestly. "You Jores ain't safe, while he's let run. You couldn't hide a horse like that so news of him wouldn't get out. So men wouldn't risk

83

their necks to get him. Brand him . . . to stop outsiders from breakin' in.' "

"We stop 'em at Sentry Crags. One man got in . . . but just because I let him. I wanted him to see what he was missin'. You couldn't believe Black Wing unless you seen him."

Nor even then.

"Black Wing," Zion mused wistfully, "is like I am. Walls weary him. He wants to run."

Crusader's son craved a clear track for the release of inborn urges just as the grandson of old Jerico must have for the universe.

"Pard," cried Zion, his wild face glowing, "I'm goin' with you! And I'm ridin' Black Wing!"

Riding Black Wing out of the basin, out where Luke Chartres could claim him, could command all the forces of wealth and law to enforce that claim — away from the Jores, the only safe guards for him. For once René had no doubts to whom to be loyal; for once the interests of Race Coulter and the Jores were identical. Black Wing must stay here.

"You see," Zion was saying, "you needn't be afraid for me. I can ride away from anything."

Away from anything? Little he realized that there were honest men who would band against a Jore, run him down, kill him, for his misconceived ideas of life out there. A stillness crept into the day like the stillness of death. And through it there pierced a girl's voice, sharp with dread: *I'm afraid . . . there's things in his blood!*

"No!" René cried harshly. "You can't go! I won't let you! I won't be responsible for you!"

His words seemed to hang in the stillness, to ring in his ears as he looked down the valley, because he dared not look at Zion. Expecting some outburst, argument, or reproach, and, hearing nothing, he feared he had hurt Zion too deeply for speech. But, forcing his eyes to look at him, he saw to his intense amazement and relief that the young fellow was unaffected by this ultimatum. Other thoughts seemed to engross him. Accustomed now to his changing moods, René believed he had changed his mind about going.

In terror lest he revert to it, he leaped up. "We'd best be getting back," he said gently. "They'll be wonderin' about me." René had to repeat it. "We'd best be gettin' back."

It was as if Zion had gone a long, long way from him and was reluctant to return. Even when René's voice reached him, he stood a moment, eyes full of dreams, fingers twisting the stallion's golden mane. Then — "You go on." — he pleaded, his gaze dropping. "I'm goin' to run . . . on Black Wing. I've held it in all I can."

In a flash he was on the stallion and gone — down the slope before him and over the slope beyond; gone like an avenging demon; gone from sight before René, enthralled by Black Wing's running, realized that he wouldn't be seeing him again — that he had let Zion go without saying good bye to him. Then he called: "Zion! Zion!"

But Zion didn't hear him. With a new ache in his heart, René went down to where his cayuse waited beside the black, that must often have waited for Zion like this. Mounting with ominous weariness, he rode back to face the Jores and be cast out of the Picture Rocks.

Chapter Eleven

OUT OF THE WALLS

All the rough miles back René rode hard, pursued by the fear that Zion would change his mind and follow. A hundred times he looked behind, half expecting to see Zion and Black Wing racing after him. He resolved to leave the basin the instant he got back, whether the Jores were ready to send him or not.

But, loping through the trees on the lake trail, he saw that they were. A horse was tied to the railing before his cabin, the pack horse Race had supplied him with. His pack was in place, loaded just as heavily as when he'd left Big Sandy, not one article removed. As he got down, too disturbed by the meaning of this to take any notice of Capitán, joyfully springing upon him, Abel Jore rose from the step. He was no more hostile than he had been, but the iron rims were not more rigid.

"Rand . . . ," he began.

With a smile that cost him more than any smile in his whole life before, René anticipated him, suggesting: "Here's my hat and what's my hurry? Is that what you mean?"

The outlaw nodded curtly. But something in the young fellow's face, as white and hopeless, as full of pain and strain as when he'd first seen him upheld in Zion's arms, must have touched him. For he yielded a bit.

"At that," he said gruffly, "you're lucky. There was votes cast to keep you here permanent. Savvy? But we decided you'd done no damage yet." After a pause, with still more gruffness, he went on: "Us Jores can't do as we'd like always. It's dog eat dog with us. And some things go ag'in' the grain, so . . . *adiós!*"

"Thanks!" Somehow there was a painful thickness in René's throat. And the little cabin that had been home for three weeks — more nearly home than any place on earth had been — blurred in his sight. So did the painted figures on the old bluff across the lake, although smiling yet, as if they knew he was a Jore at heart. But when he looked toward the big house, praying for one last glimpse of Eden, for a chance to say one word of thanks to the sad-eyed woman who had been a mother to him, everything ran together.

"There'll be no good byes," said Abel Jore.

Nevertheless, René bent to say good bye to the big hound that had been so faithful to him. Then, groping for the lead rope, he swung up on his cayuse and rode off, spared, in his total blindness, the sight of Shang Haman, posted at the corral to gloat over his departure.

When he rode through the soaring corridor of Sentry Crags, his vision had cleared. High in the spires he made out the lone figure of the sentinel. It was Yance. René waved to him, but got no response.

So he rode again under the frowning rims, under the murmuring pines that locked green arms above him, and down the Picture Rocks trail, up which he had toiled a few short weeks before; down over the golden foothills, over the flat sage wastes — gray now as ash, their purple glory gone — wondering how this had ever seemed beautiful to him. It was drab, desolate, after the basin, as he thought any place must be, compared to heaven. He thought of the shape he had been in then, and by contrast felt strong — strong enough to turn about and fight back to Eden. But he couldn't do that yet.

Not until he was a man — his own man — again. And far, far off that day seemed.

Black depression sat heavy on him when, late that afternoon, he wound between the straggling valley ranches, with Big Sandy looming beyond. For Race was there, under that red-tiled roof of Trail's End; Race, who would raise the roof at his failure to stay in the Picture Rocks, to hold the confidence of the Jores. Race wouldn't be discouraged by this. He'd figure out some new scheme to get the horse. And René would have to do just what Race asked.

"But," he vowed through set lips, "it will be in the open. I'm done coyotin' around. After all is said and done, a man owes himself something."

Having vowed this, he felt better, and dared to dream of Eden, to hope that whatever he had to do for Race would be forgiven.

"Because," — he clung fast to this — "I done what she asked. I kept Zion in the basin."

He didn't ride straight into town, but stopped a mile short of it, where the road bridged. Placer Creek. There, where the willows were dense on the creekbank, he made camp. Never, until he was finally well, would he confine himself within walls again. Stripping the burden from his pack horse, he staked him out and spread his blanket roll in a secluded spot. It would be dark, when he got back. Already the sun had set. Shadows filled the low places.

When he rode out on the highway and pulled up to look back at the great cup against the sky, he saw it, red in the sunset's afterglow, the bright red of life's own tide. Red that seemed to well up from within, clear to the rims, and splash over them, gleaming up there in the whole world's sight as if the very heavens had turned a searchlight on the Picture Rocks.

Sick with a presage of he knew not what, René rode on to seek Race at Trail's End.

He was far too weary, too absorbed in his own problem, to note the unwonted activity in Big Sandy, but, getting down before Trail's End, it did occur to him that the hotel was doing a rushing business. The street before it was filled with saddled horses. The wide verandah was jammed with men — a rough-looking lot who broke off in their low-toned talk to stare hard as he milled among them, seeking Race. Failing to find him out there, he went inside to inquire of the grizzled old-timer who was standing behind the desk.

"Race Coulter?" Dad Peppin repeated the name with frank disfavor. "He's out. Nope, can't say when he'll get back. He's onsartin in his movements. Here today and gone tomorrow. Oh, sure, he's still stoppin' here. You can leave a message. I'll see he gets it, when he does come in."

René hesitated. He might write a note. Let Race know the worst and cool off before they met. But no. What he had to say wasn't safely written.

"If you'll just tell him I'm down at the bridge camp."

"Who'll I say?"

"René Rand."

"Stranger here?" Dad's old eyes took frank appraisal.

"In town, yeah," smiled René.

"Thought so." Dad warmed to him strangely. "Though faces slip me. But" — with a black glance toward the verandah, from whence came a low-pitched hum, sinister as the rasp of hemp through a hangman's knot — "there's a heap of faces I won't fergit. I'm makin' it my business to. . . ." Suddenly breaking off, he seized René's arm, peering close into his face. "Didn't come with them, did you?"

Wild to get away, René replied: "No."

Dad nodded sagely. "Thought that, too. You wouldn't

have no truck with them, a fine, clean, young man like you."
He glanced back at the verandah, his eyes lit with a fierce
glare. "Buzzards! That's what they are. Buzzards that's flew
in from all parts to feast here. Let 'em flock on my porch so
the boys could look 'em over. Plague take 'em! We don't aim
to fergit none of them!"

Swiftly his passion subsided, and, as if the mere harboring
of it had wearied him, he dropped René's arm, sighing.
"Waal, drop in ag'in, son. If I can find anything fer you, just
holler. Allus glad to help a stranger."

Little dreaming how soon, how desperately, he would
need Dad Peppin's help, René thanked him and rode back to
camp through the gathering twilight. There, after a meal of
canned beans, bacon, and coffee, he sat by the fire, waiting
for Race in growing uneasiness, as if the tension in town was
being communicated to him at last. Nervously he jerked up as
every horse crossed the bridge, and scores of them did. But
they all went by. Finally, giving up hope of Race's coming
that night, he turned in.

So exhausted that he slept long after daylight, he slowly
opened his eyes to find the sun high in the willows, a bird
chorus going strong to the creek's sweet accompaniment, and
someone sitting beside him.

Zion had followed him, and there he was, cross-legged in
the grass, a big rifle on his knees, laughing at René's conster-
nation, forestalling his objections. "You didn't bring me. I
come myself, see?"

As he lay there, speechless with horror to see Zion here,
the young fellow sprang up. "Gee!" he cried rapturously,
throwing out his arms as if to embrace the earth, but in
despair of it hugging himself. "Gee, it's like I just been born.
It's like I been dead all along and just come alive this mornin'.

We run and run, and there wasn't a thing to stop us. We'd be goin' yet, but we seen your cayuses. Nothin's goin' to stop us again."

We? Us? In twice his first horror, René gasped: "You brought Black Wing?"

"Sure thing."

All excitement, Zion lifted the green boughs behind, revealing the stallion, glistening in the morning sunshine, as vibrant with the zest of life as Zion. "You didn't think I'd leave him behind?"

René had no thought yet beyond the terrible fact that Zion Jore and Black Wing were here.

"You think I'd let you get away without sayin' good bye, if I didn't know I'd be seein' you again?" Zion came back to him, chuckling. "I was laughin' up my sleeve all the time. I had it all made up in my mind. You know where me and Black Wing run? Straight to the crags! I hid him up there. I knowed I'd be on watch last night. And when Shang came up to take my place at daylight, I slipped out. They won't miss me till night, anyway. They're workin' in the hills . . . Uncle Abel an' Yance, I mean."

"What at, Zion?" René could think of no work that would take the Jores in those wild hills.

"I don't know. But they'll be gone all day. I heard 'em tell Shang. Shang don't know what they're doin', either . . . for he asked me." Swiftly, then, his face changed, its joy consumed by the fires of old wrongs, and he stated passionately: "They don't trust me. They'll wish they had someday. They don't think I know much. Someday they'll see!"

Whipped to his feet by that, René said: "Zion, you can't stay here. You must go back."

"I'd die first!" He was wholly mutinous.

"But your mother . . . and Eden."

This had some effect on Zion. His expression softened. "Oh, I'll go to see them. Not soon, though. Not for a long time. Someday when. . . ."

Planks drummed to a wild gallop. Whirling about, René saw a rider on the bridge, saw with horror that it was Race Coulter. Race was coming here, and Black Wing so near.

Quick as thought, he seized Zion by the arms. "It's that man," he panted. "That man you let in. Hide! Get Black Wing out of sight. And keep him quiet . . . as you're my partner."

In a flash Zion snatched up the big gun and slipped into the brush where the stallion was hidden. As the screening green dropped into place, René stepped out to meet Race.

Chapter Twelve

"I'M ZION JORE!"

René had expected Race would be furious at his leaving the Picture Rocks, and was prepared for it, in fact, but not for the frenzy in which Race was pulling up. Yet, the terror that filled the young man's heart was not of Race's wrath, but lest Race see Black Wing; lest Race sense his nearness and some instinct tell him he could almost reach out his hand and touch the horse he had coveted so long; lest Race hear the rustle of leaves, the snap of twigs, that broke on his ears like cannon shots.

But Race's ears, trained to catch the vaguest sounds, were filled with his own raving. "What are you doin' here?" he foamed at the white-faced, young man he had brought West. "I sent you up there to watch that stallion! Why ain't you on the job?"

Striving to keep his gaze on that heated face, René said steadily: "They run me out. They learned that you staked me."

So that was it. Sulphurously Race cursed his luck. It was, he informed the green grove and its environs, a pretty kettle of fish. "I hang around here for weeks, and nothin' happens. But I drift over to Solitaire one night to break the monotony and ride home to find you back and a posse pullin' out to raid the basin!"

"A posse?" René almost forgot Black Wing.

"Thirty of the toughest *hombres* I ever laid eyes on. Outsiders. Dolan couldn't rustle men in Big Sandy. The town's sidin' with the Jores. So he called in all the rag-tag and bobtail of the country, picked out thirty-some, and is holdin' 'em."

The buzzards I saw at Trail's End, thought René.

"They're fixin' to start this minute!" Race fumed. "Luke Chartres is on deck with a raft of his Val Verde cowboys. All set to round up that horse, when the posse breaks into the Picture Rocks. Say something! Don't stand there star-gazin'!"

It wasn't stars René was seeing, but those mighty rims, the two small rifts in them, and the intrepid sentries with their fast guns. He said, with a conviction that cut through Race's jealous passion: "They won't get in."

"Are you sure?" Greedily Race snatched at that. "You ought to know. You've been up there. Are you sure?"

"As I'm standin' here," vowed René.

"Do you know who sold the Jores out? Who Chartres was workin' with?"

"Who, Race?"

"Shang Haman."

René had no sense of shock. It seemed as if he had always known it. He recalled Shang's alarm when he told the Jores someone was telling the sheriff about the pass, his hurried trip that night.

Oh, Race had been busy. "Shang rode down night before last and told Chartres to have men ready."

Then Shang hadn't made that trip just to get something on him, but to hurry things up.

"And this mornin' he rides back to lead the posse to the Picture Rocks."

Shang had been in Big Sandy when he was supposed to be on watch, when he knew the Jores were in the hills and would be all day. Then — and René's brain reeled with this — there was no guard at Sentry Crags! Instantly the whole devilish scheme flashed to him. Shang had sold out to Chartres, intending, first, to lead the posse through the secret pass. Now he was seizing this unexpected opportunity, when there wasn't a Jore within miles, to take the posse straight through Sentry Crags.

"René," cried Race again, seeing his agitation, "are you sure, now you know it's Shang? Would he be takin' a posse up, if he knew it couldn't get in?"

Fired by a plan to defeat Shang Haman, thrilling to the memory of a horse's running, of a rider like an avenging demon, René assured: "They won't get in."

Race seemed to slip a mighty weight. "Kid" — he was hoarse in his relief — "it's worth a million to hear you say that. I've been scared stiff Luke Chartres had me beat to that stallion. But now . . . well, let 'em go, if you're sure the Jores can handle 'em. Mebbe they'll kill each other off someday and leave a free path to. . . ."

Down the road from town thundered many horsemen!

"The posse!" Race yanked his horse around. "Reckon I'll trail along and see the fun."

He started off. René's eyes sought the brush. But Race pulled up.

"See you here after the battle, old son, and we'll figure out something. Rest up all you can. You don't look like it's done you much good to come West. You look like a ghost. Save your strength. I'm goin' to need it."

With this characteristic charge he spurred out to join the posse, now thundering over the bridge. At its head, glittery-eyed as the snake he was, galloped Shang Haman. On his left, a stern, determined man, with a gray forelock and black mustache — Pat Dolan, the sheriff whose ambitions rose above the star on his breast, who was out to take the Jores, dead or alive, that he might use them as stepping stones to higher office. On Shang's right, there rode a noticeably fine-looking man in a white Stetson, Luke Chartres, bent on retrieving a horse at the cost of life and freedom to the Jores.

Curiously, as they swept past, something in the face of Chartres struck René as familiar. Yet he would have sworn he had never seen it before. Then, vividly, his mind flashed to that scene in the big house night before last, when he told the Jores the sheriff was working with Chartres — to the face of Revel Jore, riveted on him in nameless horror. Chained as in a dream of horror, he saw the rag-tag and bobtail of the country kicking up dust behind the three, all heavily armed.

Then, jerked from that spell by the terrible necessity for action, he turned to the brush where Zion had hidden, to send him back to the Picture Rocks, back to guard Sentry Crags. He wouldn't refuse this call to duty. On Black Wing he could easily beat the posse. But when he tore through the thicket, wildly calling his name, both rider and horse were gone. He thought Zion had overhead Race tell of Shang's treachery and had gone already, but, following Black Wing's tracks down to the creek and up on the opposite bank, he saw them turn into the road and point toward town.

Running back to camp, he saddled like a madman, sickeningly aware that every second might mean life or death to the Jores. He was almost crazy when, pounding up the road to Big Sandy, he found that the posse had wiped out Zion's tracks. There was no clue now to his whereabouts save to seek him where the most excitement was. And this was hard to tell.

For the town was in a turmoil. Citizens, many of whom, like Dad Peppin, remembered Jerico Jore and considered him a martyr, roused by this unprovoked roundup of his sons, stalked the boardwalk. Coldly they marked for future discrimination and present animosity — as they had the posse —

the riff-raff of the country that had flocked here in the hope of being in on the kill, but not numbered among Dolan's picked thirty, were now hanging around town for the morbid pleasure of seeing the Jores brought in.

Forcing his way through the throngs, René could find Zion nowhere. But as precious moments passed and he was almost in despair, shouts of coarse laughter drew his eyes toward Trail's End. Up there a crowd was gathering. He lashed toward it, sure of what he'd find; so sure that he wasn't shocked, when he saw the golden horse of the Picture Rocks champing at the bit in the shrubs beside the hotel. In the turmoil, the stallion had been overlooked.

René rode on until, over the massed heads of the mob, he saw the core of excitement — a young fellow in buckskin, with a big rifle in his hands, looking with pitiful uncertainty at the score of rowdies making cruel sport of him.

As René flung down, frantically trying to push in, he heard the ring leader, a big, red-bearded, plaid-shirted man, insultingly chanting: "Oh, it's Yankee Doodle come to town! Yankee Doodle Dandy!"

"I ain't Yankee Doodle," declared the young fellow, eager to be friendly, to meet the world halfway, but not sure that this was friendship.

His simplicity made the crowd howl with mirth. Flushing painfully, he tried to go on, but the red brute stopped him. "Wrong ag'in, huh? Waal, then it's Kit Carson."

"I ain't Kit Carson!" His eyes faintly flared, as of lightning over the horizon.

Brighter it broke as, elaborately apologetic, his tormentor taunted: "My mistake. Excuse it." Then, appealing to his audience, he said: "Name it, boys, and you can have it."

"That's Hank Farley from the Verde," an appreciative bystander told René, who was caught in the jamb. "Good as a

97

circus when he gets goin'.' "

"It must be Daniel Boone!" Farley was going strong now, sending the mob into gales of merriment. "Why, shore, it's Daniel! I'd know you anywhere by your deerskin and long ha'r. Waal, Daniel, how'd you leave things back in ole Kaintuck?"

With mock cordiality, he struck that slight figure a blow on the back that made him reel. Catching him again, he held out a dirty paw as if to shake hands. But, instead, reached up and brushed the young man's long black hair in his face, holding him in a grizzly embrace while he rubbed it roughly, as a bullying boy washes the face of a smaller child in snow.

But this young fellow's spirit would brook no such indignity. With a pantherish twist he wrenched free, and, leaping back against the adobe wall of the hotel verandah, confronting them all, face as white as the snow which, it was predicted, would lie on the ground when his imprisoned father came home, he jerked the big gun up, shrilling: "Let me be or I'll tell you who I am!"

This threw the mob into convulsions, and, spurred to greater histrionic heights, Farley made another grab for him.

It was all over in an instant. Before René could utter one cry of warning, the big gun belched flame and smoke. Sodden as a log with a rotten heart, Hank Farley crashed to the walk, a stain overspreading his checkered shirt, bright as that which the sunset had painted on the Picture Rocks.

Into the hush that followed the roar, awing everyone, the spirit of old Jerico Jore rampant in him, the young fellow told the world he had so yearned for: "I'm Zion Jore!"

Chapter Thirteen

MAD PURSUIT

So, as the careers of other Jores bid fair to end, did that of the youngest, fiercest, least responsible of the clan begin. He seemed not to realize it yet, standing there, stunned, a smoking rifle in his hands, a dead man at his feet, and, rising all around him, a vengeful muttering that broke into a horrible snarl at a cry from one of the dead man's friends: "He's killed Hank, that whelp of a Jore! Killed him! Do you hear? Why don't you do something? Where's Dolan?"

But Sheriff Dolan was miles away, and riding fast in his determination to "do something" about those other Jores. And, barred from that affray to which their blood was leaping, this remnant of the riff-raff of the range around rejoiced that a Jore had fallen to them. They'd had nothing against the Jores when they rallied here to hunt them down, but were, as many men are beneath the strata of restraint that civilization imposes, savages, and just as ready to kill with the sanction of the law or some legitimate excuse to give them a loophole. They had it now. They had something against Zion Jore, something that lay there and never stirred, yet, by its very immobility, lashed them to higher frenzy than any words.

Frenziedly one of them roared: "We don't need Dolan! There's just one system for Jores! The old vigilantes had it!"

"A rope!" another ruffian yelped. And the pack took it up.

A rope seemed to leap to every hand.

Zion Jore, looking in dazed bewilderment at the savage faces that glared upon him, came to life as they pressed forward, came to that lambent life that would be his until its flame was forever snuffed out. Menacingly he swung the rifle, covering every man in that half circle, his eyes glittering like points of steel above the barrel, his voice the dangerous, steely drawl of the Jores.

"Keep back!" he warned. "I'll shoot! And I can't miss!"

The rush was checked. But René, watching in horror, saw a man who had worked around partially behind Zion raise a gun. There was no time to warn him, no time for anything but what René did. Before the man could pull the trigger he snatched a gun from the nearest holster and shot. The man screamed like a wounded wildcat, grabbing his wrist. His gun rang to the porch, and the mob, looking to see who had taken the part of a Jore, saw a man scarcely older than young Jore — a youth in a cheap suit and cap that did not obliterate the range stamp. Pale and frail he was, yet the spirit that blazed in his dark eyes daunted them.

"Stand back!" He waved the gun. "Back! Clean away from him!"

As they wavered, he cried to the young fellow, praying that he would understand: "Run, Zion, for Sentry Crags! Shang's double-crossed you! He's left it open! He's takin' a posse in! They got a long start, but you got Black Wing!"

His heart turned sick as Zion stared at him one dazed instant. Thinking he didn't comprehend, he cried wildly: "Go, Zion!"

Zion understood. Swift and clear came his answer: "With you, pard!"

"Don't think of me!" shouted René, although he thrilled to it. "I'm all right! Don't think of nothin' but beatin the posse to the basin! Don't let 'em see you! Circle 'em! Run . . .

like you always wanted to run!"

He dared not take his eyes from that hostile press to watch. But he knew Zion had gone. He heard the rush of hoofs that were not shod. Saw wonder and awe leap to the angry eyes of the mob, when they saw the horse that Zion rode. Then René thought of his own escape, and knew it to be hopeless. The instant he turned to seek his cayuse in that horde of horses, a dozen men would shoot. Nor might they wait for that. Savage, frenzied faces glared at him, and their snarl was rising horribly.

"I'll cover you, son," a metallic voice rang down.

René looked up to see the grizzled old-timer he had talked to in Trail's End. He stood in the open door, upright, militant, a .44 in his hand, his seamed old face aflame with the spirit of other days, when life hung by the flame of a six-gun and was as sweet then, perhaps sweeter, for you weren't sure of a tomorrow. Those days seemed to be repeating themselves.

"I'll cover you!" cried old Dad Peppin. "Go . . . and the *hombre* what tries to stop you better look out!"

Whirling, René ran toward his cayuse, and was vaulting on when Dad stayed him.

"Hell, no! You need a hoss! That bay, nighest the rat-tailed roan . . . he's a good 'un, and belongs to a white man. Take him with my compliments, and . . . good luck."

In a bound René hit the saddle, and the bay was plunging down the street of Big Sandy. Yes, he would need a horse. Before he reached the outskirts he heard the pack howling in pursuit, as rabid to take him as Zion. Well, they wouldn't get Zion. There wasn't a horse in town could keep in sight of Black Wing.

He blessed Dad Peppin's judgment, for the bay was a good one. Bent low over him, thrilling to the speed and power in his smooth stride, pounding over a bridge and flashing past his camp in the willows, he thought that, if he were half as good as his horse, he would give that pack of wolves a run before they got him. For he had no doubt, then, that they would get him in the end.

But racing past the valley ranches, out over the sun-fired ranges, the bay's running inspired him with the hope that he, too, might get away. Hope stimulated him so, that, for a time, he rode as he used to ride on Flash, before he knew what being tired was, before he had ever gone East or met Race. He rode as he used to, whether there was any call for it or not, now with desperate need for it. For his life wouldn't be worth a plug nickel if he were caught. So he rode lickety-split, straight for the Picture Rocks.

His direction was instinctive. He had outlawed himself, was in need of a refuge, and the basin was the nearest thing to home. Skimming the sage-choked flats, he remembered that he couldn't go to the basin, even if Zion got there first and let him in. The Jores had banished him. Nor could he go in any other direction until he learned just what happened to the Jores from Zion.

Looking back, he saw that he had put a lot of distance between himself and his pursuers. Looking ahead, he saw the posse. It was far up in the foothills, fewer by half than when it had started out. He saw why this was. The sheriff's men had split into two bands. One was on the Picture Rocks trail, the other veering south to circle the mountain and so to the secret pass. They would cut off the Jores' retreat should they attempt to escape through the pass when the rest invaded the basin at Sentry Crags — as they would unless Zion beat them to it. Could Zion do it? Could even Black Wing overcome that handicap?

Tensely, in that vast panorama of sage flat and foothill, he

102

sought for Zion, but could not see him. He was glad of it. Zion had understood. He was keeping out of the posse's sight. That low ridge to the right — a mountain, ages since, but now worn down to a line of broken buttes that ran up the foothills, almost to the crags — it was likely that Zion was behind it, burning the wind. Vividly René envisaged the golden horse running, as he had seen him yesterday, across a marshy green valley.

Casting his eyes along that route, straining on the gaps between the buttes, never letting his own horse slacken, his heart bounded to a fleeting glimpse of what he had seen — Black Wing as he flashed across a gap, with Zion flat on his neck. The Jores were safe with Black Wing running like that. Although the posse was far ahead and riding hard, it did not know a guard was racing them for Sentry Crags. Unless they saw him first, Zion could easily get by them and cut in ahead to the pass, where his shots would bring his uncles.

His mind eased about the Jores, René thought of his own predicament, of how he could shake off pursuit. It wasn't close enough to be a menace. A half mile behind, at least, down in the wastes of sage. Nor had he exhausted the horse Dad Peppin had told him was a good one. It was his own strength that was going — the strength he had stored up in days of rest in the basin, and in the last twenty-four hours so recklessly drawn on.

A dozen times in the last fast mile he had clutched the horn of his saddle. Now he dared not relax his grip on it. For an overpowering weakness was stealing over him, a dizziness such as he had known the first time he had ridden this trail to the Picture Rocks. Again the peaks and cañons in the black range were dancing. The great crater up there spun like a top. The white ships that sailed the blue main above it revolved as if caught in mighty whirlpools. And he knew he couldn't last, that he must ride fast, if he was to ever shake off the men behind at all.

Turning toward the ridge that hid Zion, he gave the bay its head, feeling it flatten and strain, conscious of the sting of wind in his face, its whine in his ears, the clutch of chaparral on his legs, its clash on his stirrups. Catching another longer glimpse of Black Wing almost opposite the posse and forced to run a hundred yards with no cover, he was in terror lest the posse see, also, but it did not stop. Breathing again, he was about to swing behind the first butte, when he saw that which made him forget the men behind, the men before, and clamped him in the saddle in the cold vise of fear.

Beyond the posse, madly galloping toward them, was a rider, a rider so small as to be almost invisible, just a bright splash upon a plunging horse.

René knew, with shock surpassing that which he had felt when he awakened to find Zion beside him, that it was Eden. She was out of the basin, where she had been but once before, out in the world she found so terrifying.

She hadn't seen the posse. It was in a deep depression banked high with mesquite and sage. Nor would they see her until the trail lifted them out of it. But someone saw her besides René.

For René's eyes were drawn to the buttes beyond, and a groan was wrenched from his lips. There, in a gap, not flashing, but standing, poised so all could see, was the glorious cream-white horse. Zion had seen his sister. He must have had some wild idea that she was in danger, for, to René's despair, he cut straight across to her, running with all the unbelievable grace and speed of which Black Wing was capable. He was out in plain sight of the posse, as well as Shang Haman, who would recognize the rider and horse and reveal them to the rest — Luke Chartres, on whom the sight of the stallion would be as flame to powder, and Race Coulter, who would know at last that Black Wing was out of the protective walls of the Picture Rocks.

Even as these thoughts flashed through his mind, the posse saw Zion. For they stopped, consulting with many gesticulations, then swung toward him, lining out like hounds on a fresh scent.

Desperate at this fatal twist when all was won, René cried wildly, hopelessly: "Zion! Zion!"

But the wind whipped the cry from his lips, strangling it before it had gone a hundred yards. He remembered the gun he had snatched from that holster in Big Sandy, and was reaching for it, hoping that a shot would attract his attention, when he saw Zion had already sighted him. Black Wing was slowing, losing precious seconds, and Zion was waving to him.

Jerking off his cap with his free hand, René swung it madly, crying, even though it were useless: "Zion . . . go back!"

The young rider stopped, uncertain what he meant, but ever ready to do anything that his partner asked.

"Back!" René motioned toward the buttes. "Go back!"

Zion wheeled and raced for the gap. But the posse was hot on his heels. With a vague impression that Eden was reining in and bewilderedly looking after him, René dropped to lower ground and lost sight of what went on. But he imagined everything — imagined Pat Dolan, seeing this chance to pick off a Jore; imagined Shang Haman seizing this opportunity to shut Zion up about Dave. But none of his imaginings, terrible as they were, was more terrible than the fact that Zion was cut off from the pass.

But he heard no shots. If Zion kept out of gun range, they wouldn't get him — not on Black Wing, although Luke

Chartres and his cowboys would run him to the world's end. But the sheriff cared nothing about the horse. Nor did he know Zion Jore had killed a man. Soon he would swing his posse back to complete their grim task at the Picture Rocks.

Then René's foaming horse raced out of the swale, all but colliding with Eden's as she would have dashed into it in pursuit of Zion. But René blocked her trail.

"Eden," he cried huskily, "what are you doin' here?"

He never forgot the despair in her answer: "I'm after my brother."

He tried to hold her, to tell her.

But she held her sweating horse in to tell him: "You lured him from us . . . for Black Wing! For that is Black Wing, although how he comes to be broken, I don't know. Perhaps you do. You know so much. For a horse, you let your friends run him down like a wild beast. Oh, you . . . you traitor!" The quivering, struggling passion behind her words held René white and mute.

"We took you in and cared for you like you were one of our own. We trusted you, and you struck at us through the one who was helpless. You wouldn't do that to your own kind. But we're Jores, free game. But bad as they paint us, not a Jore on this earth or beneath it would do what you've done."

Chapter Fourteen

A SPLASH OF COLORS

He looked at her, scarcely hearing, scarcely able to believe that this was Eden, this unstrung, suffering girl, so small up there on the big black, so charged with feeling, her throat pulsing above the careless knot of her crimson scarf, whose ends whipped angrily in the wind, as if sharing her opinion of him, her eyes flashing purple fire beneath her sombrero. Yet those eyes had never looked at him any way but friendly, had looked love but yesterday — looked hate now, hate that was absolute.

"My friends?" René said, stabbed to the heart that she could think that. "Eden, I'm not with them."

"No?" Her red lips smiled scorn. She tried to ride past him.

But he plunged his own horse before her. "Eden, you've got this all wrong. That's Pat Dolan and his men. Shang's bringing 'em."

Her laugh was half crazed. "Shang's at the crags!"

"He's not." Desperately René tried to make her understand as he had Zion. "Shang came into town this mornin' for the sheriff. It's him that promised to help Chartres. Girl, it's the raid I warned you of. You've got to believe me . . . this once."

His deadly sincerity forced her belief. Such reason as she was capable of in her present state bore him out. Shang hadn't hailed her, when she left the basin, and he hadn't been in sight, although she had looked for him, fearing he would protest her going.

"Oh," she moaned, with a hopelessless that pierced René's breast, "isn't there anyone we can trust? The raid. And Zion."

"They'll never catch him on Black Wing," René stated. "The horse don't live that can. I've seen him run. Zion showed me before I left the basin. Showed me how he'd gentled him."

"Oh, you played the game well."

"Girl, I swear. . . ."

Suddenly erect, her eyes fixed on something behind him: "Is that," she asked, pointing back, "more of the sheriff's men?"

It was Hank Farley's friends storming over the rise with faint, fierce cries as they sighted him.

René said with a twisted smile: "It ain't Jores they're after."

Something flicked her eyes then. Could it be fear for him? No, for she said coldly: "What did you do to them?"

"I helped Zion." Pain tortured the truth from him. "He followed me last night. I didn't know he was comin'. He shot a man and . . . ," he broke off, horrified at his words.

Quietly, fatalistically, with the sorrow that was her heritage, corrected Eden: "He killed a man!"

"But it wasn't his fault." René was anxious she should have that comfort, even though the mob was pounding close, with fierce shouts no longer faint. "He was drove to it. He's safe for the present. But Dolan's sent men to the other pass. And your uncles. . . ."

The blue eyes widened in awful understanding. "They're in the hills. They think they're safe. They think Shang's on watch. They'll be trapped, if Dolan's men get by the crags."

Seizing her bridle, René swung her horse around. "We'll stop them, Eden! Come!"

She hesitated but one heart's beat, her eyes turned in the direction Zion had gone. Then she was racing with him up the winding trail, under the somber rims, with the pack baying after, seeing, just as they dashed between the dark portals, far over the slope to their left, the posse coming back.

"We can't stop them!" Suddenly she remembered this. "We've nothing to stop them with!"

"I've got a gun," the young fellow promised. "It's got five shells in it. I'll hold them till you bring rifles from the cabins."

But she was slow about going on — although that would take long, although the rims about them wildly rang with the iron song of horses galloping.

René shouted bitterly: "You can trust me!"

She cried in far more bitterness: "I've got to!"

Her forced trust tortured him as she raced on. But he was thankful for it. Through it he might win the old trust back.

Half falling from his horse, he staggered to one of the boulders that all but blocked the narrow pass. The very rock beside which he had fallen on that first trip to the basin, and from which Zion had taken that first cautious, curious look at him. He must not fail this time. He must fight off this weakness. He must hold the pass. One man could stand an army off. *Then*, he thought, with that slow grin that mocked himself, *I oughta handle a squad like this.*

One man could hold the pass? Yes, he could — from the crags up there, with the full length of the narrow aisle to operate in, with high-powered rifles and no lack of ammunition. But what could he do down here, his view obstructed by rocks that could be used as advantageously by his foes, with only a six-gun and five shells?

Crouched behind the boulder, René saw the first horse

burst around the trail. He aimed at the rider — the big, red-eyed hoodlum who had knelt over Hank Farley's body at Trail's End, frantically imploring somebody to do something. Now, red-eyed, reckless, taking the lead himself, he dashed into the pass, unconscious of the bead drawn on his breast.

René didn't want to kill. He only wanted to prevent these men from taking him, from blazing a trail into the basin for Pat Dolan. He fired high, wasting a bullet in warning. With a startled oath the rider whirled his horse in the startled faces of the other riders, that, whirling, stampeded with him.

But the warning didn't hold them long. Their blood was too hot for caution. Spreading out the width of the pass, they plunged toward him, yelling, guns blazing, still led by the big hoodlum. Again René leveled on him, again he couldn't kill a man, but brought the man's horse down, sending him scuttling for cover as wildly as the rest. René was victor of this skirmish, but with only three bullets left.

Spent and shaken, he sagged against the boulder, waiting. He could see nothing but shadows, rocks, and the dead horse. He could hear nothing but his own hard heart throbs, the labored breathing of the bay, standing by, gallant under fire, and the wail of the wind that always blew up here. There was a lulling sound that induced a strange drowsiness. But he fought it off to see the reckless leader, not so reckless now, but as bent on vengeance, crawling from rock to rock in an attempt to get above him and pick him off. René's bullet kicked gravel in his foe's face, and, rolling to shelter, the man worked back to figure out another move.

Then for René there followed more silence, more suspense, more trying to fight off the blackness. He was roused this time by a mighty drumming as the rims about him amplified in wild alarm the beat of many horses, running. Louder it swelled in volume, rolling up to a grand finale at the mouth of the pass, where René heard an authoritative voice sternly demanding what was going on, and wolfish voices yapping that the Jores had murdered one man and wounded another in town. They had run one of the killers down and had him cornered in the rocks here. Jores? Zion Jore, was the reply, and his partner. This one was the partner.

He heard Shang laugh contemptuously. "He ain't a Jore. He's nothin' but a sick tenderfoot."

Then the official voice again, Dolan's, railing at them for butting in on his game. The Jores might hear this shooting and be warned. No, they couldn't get out, but they could hole up. He couldn't waste time on this tenderfoot. There was one of him and fifty of them. Altogether — rush him.

Desperately René braced himself as they came — fifty determined men, led by a sheriff who was grimly determined to reach the halls of Congress through this pass. That star, flashing in mad gallop, made a fine target. But he couldn't use it. Just the same, he had to make them think he would. He had been something of a dead shot before he went East. He prayed he still was, waiting until the sheriff was a scant twenty paces. Then his gun blazed. The bullet lifted Dolan's hat. It raised his respect, likewise, for this tenderfoot Shang had so belittled. For he yanked back into the rocks, ordering a retreat. Then, maneuvering around the bend, he went into conference with Shang.

Crouched there, listening, René heard their voices plotting. How long would it take them to concoct something? How long before Eden would return? She'd just about be to the cabins now. He had to hold out till she got back — a long way for one shot to go. But a smile curved his white lips — a shot had gone around the world once. Anyhow, it was heard around the world. Whose shot was it? He couldn't think. He knew only that it was fired by an American for liberty. A Jore, maybe. Jores had fought in every war there was, Eden had told him one day. Every time their country's liberty was at stake, the Jores had fought for it. Now the Jores were fighting for their own liberty, and. . . .

He jerked up suddenly, hearing shots from within the basin. One, two, three, four, five, six, he counted. Six shots in fast succession. That was Eden, giving the signal that more men were at the crags than the guard could handle. The Jores would come too late — too late even for Eden to get to him. For they had finished plotting.

Tensely he watched, braced for another rush, wondering how to turn his last shot to best account. Then the very rock he pressed shook on its base. The earth shuddered beneath him, and a muffled roar ran 'round the rims, as if all the guns on earth rolled into one had been fired off on the other side of the world, as if the old crater were erupting again. He wondered what had happened? Whatever it was, would it hold Dolan back? And then he wondered at the sudden stillness.

For over the pass had settled a deep, unnatural hush. The very wind had ceased its wail to listen. René's heart stood still while he waited. His every nerve shrieked danger. The smell of danger was in the very air.

Suddenly he was conscious of the soft brush of cloth on rock, a muffled breath, more felt than heard. Someone was creeping up on him. Glancing wildly around, he saw no one. Then his eyes, drawn to the rocks above, looked into the big, black bore of a gun trained squarely on him and in the hands of one who knew this pass far better than René Rand — knew this safe route to him — Shang Haman!

Right then, seeing his doom, René had a fierce urge to kill. His last bullet would be well spent, if he could kill Shang. He had to do it, remembering how Shang had looked at Eden, and that his own passing would open the way for Sheriff

Dolan to take the Jores, leaving Eden unprotected in the Picture Rocks. He jerked his gun up, but even as his fingers tensed, Shang's gun roared.

As the bullet crashed against René's breast, Shang yelled with hideous triumph — "Got him!" — retracting, however, almost in the same breath, dodging back, cursing, scrambling for cover as René's bullet ricocheted from the rocks, a scant inch from his face: "No, by the powers!"

But he had. Although shot through, possessed by pain, the fellow remembered they must not know it, and held out to shoot. Now he lay stretched on the ground, his white face to the pass he must defend, his nerveless hand clutching an empty gun, a smile on his lips, because, far above, almost out of his consciousness, there poured a torrent of shots, as if the very heavens had opened to pour molten death. And the pass was jammed with riders in mad flight — *out!*

Laboriously his failing eyes climbed the black walls to the splash of color in the spires — bright, like sunset on the Picture Rocks, like the color that had made one tone of a checkered shirt at Trail's End, like the bright little river running from him, like Eden's scarf. There was a guard at Sentry Crags. He could rest.

So deep his rest, nothing broke it — not the plunging hoofs that later stopped beside him, nor the ring of hoofs as they hit the ground, nor the broken cry of a remorseful man: "He ain't shammin' this!"

Again in a Jore's arms, he was borne into the Picture Rocks.

It never disturbed his rest.

Chapter Fifteen

ABEL'S STORY

Back in the basin, but it wasn't heaven. It was just the opposite — a black pit filled to the brim with worry about Zion. They did not know what had happened to him; if dead, how he had died? — or living, how he lived? Imagination filled the gaps, and worry gnawed ever at their hearts, although they seldom spoke of him.

That first week, lying on the porch, between death and life — dead to the beauty of green leaf, blue water, to the painted rocks' somber grandeur, but cruelly alive to this worry about him — René never ceased to speak of Zion, deliriously babbling the story of the shooting a thousand times to Zion's mother, so patiently caring for him, telling her that he had tried to keep Zion in the basin. Calling on his own dead mother to witness.

"I know," Revel would say in a dead voice. "Hush."

But René could not, wildly insisting: "He'll tell you so, when he comes back!"

Her haunted gaze would go far from the things that were, fixing on things beyond the range even of fevered vision. Silent tears would flow down her pale cheeks, and she would repeat: "When he . . . comes back."

"Tell Eden," he would implore pitiously everyone who came near him. "Tell Eden. I can't . . . she don't come."

René knew that. Although he felt like a dead stick that is cast into the fire, he would have known her. But she never came.

114

Growing strong, with that June behind eternally and the hot days pushing halfway through July, he realized that there was something between Eden and him far blacker than the shadow of Shang Haman.

From the day Abel Jore had carried him home, shot through the chest — a high, clean wound, but so dangerous that his life was despaired of — she hadn't spoken to him. She seldom spoke to anyone. She was seldom at home, for she couldn't bear the big house, filled as it was with Zion's trophies — the head and horns of a mountain goat he had trailed to the sheerest rim, now hanging above the fireplace; the pelt of a huge silvertip he had brought down for a couch covering; a hundred things to remind a worried heart of his recklessness and hunting skill. Often René saw her riding in from the direction of Dave's grave, where, he knew, she had gone to think of Zion, or from the crags, where she had been watching for him.

His heart bled for her. He knew how she loved her brother. She had been closer to Zion than anyone else, and in her deeper knowledge of his wild nature had more to fear. Zion was gone, and she blamed him. Oh, he knew what she thought. She had told him — he had lured Zion out for Black Wing. She thought — in his wretchedness René supplied this — that what he had done at the pass had only been for himself. For she knew that mob was after him, and even a cornered rat fights for its life. He didn't blame her for what she thought. He didn't see how she could think anything else. But deep down in his heart he wished she didn't.

Back in the Picture Rocks, his position was reversed. Before, the Jore men had barely tolerated him, and Revel, Eden, and Zion had been his friends. Now only Revel was the same. Zion was gone. Eden hated him. While Yance and Abel couldn't do enough for him, couldn't blame themselves enough for having listened to Shang, couldn't pile enough praise on him for what he had done for them.

"It was the nerviest thing I ever heard of," Yance put it huskily. "You . . . holdin' that posse back with nothin' much but grit till Eden could get on the crags. But for you, me and Abel . . . waal, we might be twangin' harps! We won't forget. We count you one of us."

One of them.

"I ain't," René told Capitán, again keeping faithful vigil by him. "I can't be. Even if they do think I am. Even if I do look like a Jore in this buckskin."

For they had taken his bloodstained garments from him, and Abel had brought a suit of fringed buckskin like Zion's.

"You'll be needin' things," the man had said in a trembling voice, "so I'm givin' you Dave's." Giving him his dead son's things.

"I can't wear 'em," René had insisted, in far more pain from shame than Shang's bullet had caused him. "I ain't fit to."

For this life, on which he got a stronger grip each day as new blood was built up to replace what he had lost and his old trouble ceased to trouble, as if it had run from his veins at Sentry Crags or been burned out by the fever his wound set up — this life belonged to Race, until Race got Black Wing.

All those weeks, lying on the leaf-roofed porch, watching the painted figures, that seemed to wear a broader smile, as if they, too, accepted him as a Jore, he wondered if Race had the horse. Or had the prize fallen to Luke Chartres? Then and after, when able to be in the saddle, riding the bay Dad Peppin had given him — Stonewall he called him, from the way he had stood by him — he would see the wild horse running with a vengeful world behind. In his mind's eye, also, he would see the wild, young creature who had no sense of wrong or right, who could shoot as only Zion Jore could shoot, laughing at the big commotion, raising the big gun; rider and horse, hard-pressed, running for the one sure haven, only to find it barred to them.

René shuddered, for the pass at Sentry Crags had other guards now. Camped just outside were many grimly determined deputies. The Jores were locked in the Picture Rocks. Zion was locked out. For there was no other pass.

That roar René had heard at Sentry Crags had been the echo of a terrific blast that had destroyed the secret pass. That's what the Jores had been doing in the hills, planting dynamite, stored in the basin for just such an emergency. They hadn't told Zion or Shang. And, warned by Eden's signal shots, seeing men climbing to that pass, they had set off the blast and raced for Sentry Crags. Tons of rock had closed the opening. And Sheriff Dolan had sealed the Jores in the basin until he could find some way to take them.

"And whatever it is," Abel told René this sultry day, when the young man rode up to the pass where he was watching, that must be watched, now, every moment of the day and night, "whatever it is, it'll likely be taps for us. Dolan means business. And we can't hold out ag'in' the odds he'll be able to throw ag'in' us."

Amazed by this pessimistic note, the first he had ever heard a Jore strike, René said: "Why not? You've held out a good many years now. They can't get in any other way. And it would take an army."

"Then Dolan will bring one," said Abel grimly. "Oh, we ain't fooled ourselves none. We've known all along that even a hide-out like the Picture Rocks couldn't hold out long, if they really wanted us. But the sheriffs up till Dolan ain't wanted us bad. It wasn't policy to. We've got altogether too many friends in the county.

"But Dolan don't give a hoot about local votes. He wants to dangle our scalps at his belt. And he wants the glory for himself, which is why he ain't asked for outside help. Anyhow, it wasn't much use, as long as we had the other pass. While they was comin' in here, we could crawl out there. Shang rung our knell, when he told where the pass was. Dolan knows that. And he won't quit till he has Yance and me under lock and key. He'll call in the state militia, if he has to. But not till he's dead sure he has to. And," Abel added grimly, "by that time there'll be plenty more charges ag'in' us."

Soberly René looked down at the shadowy pass, of which every tortuous inch was visible from here — from the tents of Dolan's camp, pitched near the opening, to the barricade constructed near the very spot where he had fallen, from which point the pass was watched at night. He could see armed men lounging about, breaking the monotony now and then by firing at the crags, on the long chance of picking the sentry off. And for the first time they really struck him as a genuine menace.

"However," said Abel, shifting his position, but never letting the rifle out of his hands, "I ain't thinkin' about Dolan. What's worryin' me is Zion."

His dark face turned to René, the sunlight starkly revealing the deep grooves worry had cut. He cried, almost in appeal, a revelation of his love for his brother, whom Dolan had imprisoned: "How'll I answer to Joel for him . . . if Revel's right, and Joel comes back?"

Hard on that thought, another thing that worried him, he asked: "How'll I settle with Shang Haman?"

While René sat mute, awed by this revelation of hate, Abel said, his face hard and set: "I can't settle till I know how much I owe him. If it's as much as I'm thinkin'. . . ." From under his

118

jet-black brows shot the cold gleam that spelled doom in a Jore's eyes.

Vividly, in the pulsing silence, a rude pine cross flashed between René and the shadowy pass he watched, the cross that marked the grave of Dave Jore. Somehow he knew that cross was set up in the man's mind as well.

With strained calm, Abel broke out, hungry to talk, to share the thoughts stored in the long and lonely watches: "I reckon you're wonderin' how a snake like Shang got in with us."

René was. He had wondered that from the first. But he couldn't ask. Now Abel was telling him.

"Joel brought Shang in nigh on five years ago. Joel run across him on one of his trips out. Helped him out of a tight jam of some kind. Shang didn't have no place to go, so Joel brought him home. Can't say as I ever liked him. But he was handy. We couldn't go outside . . . open. And he could. He was our ambassador to a hostile world. That it put a noose on our necks and the rope in his hand did come to us now and then. But we trusted him. Now I'm thinkin'. . . . Joel went out to Rocky Run to meet Shang, the night he was caught. Dolan ambushed him. He never had a chance. It allus struck us queer Dolan knew he was to be there at just that time. Joel wasn't one to advertise his moves."

"What did Joel think?" René asked tensely.

"We never saw him after his arrest. He didn't talk on the stand. And he didn't have a chance to talk alone with Eden, when she went down to the trial. Zion says my son Dave accused Shang of double-crossin' Joel. Zion says Dave was goin' out to try and talk with his uncle, when he was killed just outside the basin. Shang swore Dolan's men shot him. Zion swore it was Shang. Dave was gone. So it was Shang's word ag'in' Zion's. And we had to take Shang's, for Zion wasn't responsible. But now," — again his eyes flashed that cold glitter — "I ain't so sure."

"But what was Shang's object?" cried René. "Why would he double-cross Joel?"

Abel said shortly: "Eden."

Eden? "But I don't see," insisted René. "Joel was her father."

Briefly the outlaw explained: "Shang had been shinin' up to her for some time. Joel didn't like it. Zion says Dave overheard him callin' Shang for it . . . just before he was caught. It's comin' to me that Shang tipped Dolan off to get Joel out of the way. And that he wanted to get rid of Yance and me for the same reason.

"You see, son, after Joel was sent up, we stood in the light of a father to her and watched mighty careful. Not so long before you come on the scene Yance had occasion to tell Shang plain that Eden wasn't for him. I think that's when he decided to squeal on us. Likely Chartres got hold of him about that time and made it worth his while to. And he figgered with Joel and us out of the way. . . ."

Starved for an audience, he resumed talking, and hungrily René listened. "Joel's kids," Abel mused, his brooding eyes on the long drop, "has mighty good blood. Oh, not the Jore blood, although it's good enough. But Zion and Eden are . . . waal, something extry through their mother. Joel didn't think much about it when they were little. But as they growed up, he worried a lot. He seen what a crime it was to keep them in the basin, especially Eden. He wanted she should have her chance. He asked me and Yance to help . . . to do nothin' that would call attention to the Picture Rocks till he could take his family and my boy out to some far place, where they could start life fresh under a new name.

"And that" — with scarcely a break in his voice, he raised

the rifle and fired a warning at a man straying too near the pass — "that's why he let Black Wing run. The horse was only a colt then. Joel was just waitin' for him to grow to his full size and power to make the break. For he was countin' on the fortune Black Wing was worth to make a new start when he left the Picture Rocks. He watched the horse close. Wouldn't let a rope be throwed on him . . . lest some accident happen. 'It ain't a horse,' he used to say, 'but a dream of heaven.' "

That's what he had pledged himself to steal for Race, thought René, *not just a horse, but.* . . .

Through René's horror ran Abel's laugh, a brittle thing that broke in his throat. "Dreams!" he laughed again. "Dreams ain't for folks in our fix. Oh," he owned, as if it were a crime, "I had mine. Long as I can recollect. I wanted to be a cattleman. I dreamed of ridin' through my herds, a free man that it was a credit to know. I never even dreamed of inflictin' myself on the world outside. Right here in the Picture Rocks was good enough. I tried it. But even with friends outside to help, it was too hard to sneak my stock to market. But I got start enough to help Joel's dream. For my cattle's kept us goin' these last five years. Goin' till I learned better than to dream."

Again he ceased. Both stared into the pass. Clouds scudded over their heads. The wind wailed through the spires. Then, again, desolate as its mourn, Abel's voice spoke: "A man don't dream for hisself. He's got to have someone to hitch his dreams to. I had Nance, then . . . my wife. She died when Dave was small. Died on the trail. I was takin' her out to a doctor. Kind folks buried her. I . . . I could just kiss her dead lips and smooth her brown hair the way she liked it. In a loose braid around her head, she allus wore it, with soft little rings peekin' out. I could . . . just kiss her and smooth her hair and. . . . Then I had to hunt my hole, one jump ahead of the law. But I had Dave. My dreams died when I laid him in his grave."

The pass and everything in it swam in René's eyes. His dark face working, Abel muttered: "When I think how Joel's dream turned out . . . with him in prison, his wife eatin' her heart out for him, and now Zion. . . ."

Mockingly, as if it were the expression of the world's indifference to a Jore's feelings, a bullet smacked the crags above them.

"An honest life for a Jore," Abel stated. "A pipe dream, sure. A Jore couldn't be honest. At least, nobody would believe he was. Oh, I ain't kickin'. It's the way things is. We have been honest for five years. And that" — pointing the rifle at the brown tents — "is the wages of honesty."

But, as if he must be honest with himself, he took it back. "No! It's the wages of sin we're payin'! And you know what that is?"

Fatefully to René flashed: "The wages of sin is death!"

"Us Jores," Abel's face was deadly earnest, his piercing eyes veiled in thought, "are payin' for a lot of sins that ain't ours. It's a habit to credit sins other folks walk out on up to us. But what's th' odds? Our father paid for his. But they tacked 'em on me and Yance. As ours will be tacked on Zion, and so on, as long as there's a Jore."

He seemed to grow resolute again, to be strong and grim as the rocks about him. "It can't go on! It's got to stop right here. Me and Yance has got to pay in full, so they won't come back on Zion. He's runnin' up an account of his own. God only knows how high it's run. But they'll see he ain't responsible. They won't hold him to account, even if he is a Jore. Not," he added, with worry shared by René, "if they wait . . . to see that."

If. . . .

★ ★ ★ ★ ★

For two days René brooded over this talk. Two days of shame that seared his soul as the fierce heat scorched and browned the green of the basin. Abel Jore had shown him his heart, a good heart, with nothing bad to be seen, when it lay wide open, bleeding. But he had kept his own locked on its black deceit. He had vowed that day, riding back to meet Race Coulter, that he would come out in the open. What was his vow worth?

This afternoon, down by the lake with Capitán, he lay in the grass, staring out at the water, hating himself. The heat was almost unbearable, the air so still, the glassy, glaring expanse before him was unmarred by a ripple. A storm was brewing. He wished it would come and get over with. He saw Eden, riding in from somewhere. He heard Abel come out on the porch of the big house and call to her. From that direction came a sound that made the big hound whine, a sound like a woman crying.

He lay there, thinking how a man's life was ruled by circumstances; seeing life as a trail on which a man set out with every intention of going straight, but was turned aside here and there by little obstacles, deadfalls of destiny, until he had swerved completely out of his intended course — got lost, so to speak.

No. Circumstance was a rope that life threw on you, dragging you into things — as the Jores had been dragged into outlawry before they knew what it was, as their father, old Jerico, had been dragged into crime by a civilization that made criminal his normal existence, as he himself had been dragged into crooked work for Race. He couldn't go on like this, letting the Jores tell him things which he might have to use for Race. For he owed Race his life. He couldn't get away from that.

Oh, he felt the rope, then, binding him to treachery, strangling every bit of decency in him. In sudden rebellion he sprang up, his arms outflung, as if to tear the invisible fetters from him.

"I can't stand it!" he cried to Capitán, his dark eyes aflame. "I've got to tell them! I won't be a traitor no more! I'll tell them everything. Then I'll leave here. They'll think less of me for it. They'll think I'm goin' because Black Wing is gone . . . that I'm goin' after him. But I can't help that. I'll be square with myself."

Chapter Sixteen

LEAVIN' THE BASIN

His resolution firm upon him, René hurried to the big house. He had mounted the steps and was crossing the porch to the open door, when suddenly Abel Jore bulked there.

"You, son?" ejaculated the man with surprise that seemed strange. "I was just goin' to hunt you up. Come in." He moved aside for the young fellow to precede him. Odd it seemed now that he had ever spoken of dreams, or ever harbored a dream, towering there in the door, hard-eyed, lean, his dark face strangely set in its careworn seams.

With vague apprehension René stepped past him into the room, but stopped at sight of Eden and Revel on the low couch by the window, open to admit any possible breath of a breeze from the lake, but letting only heat in and the fierce glare of the sun that outlined them, throwing their features in shade. Yet René felt that a storm had raged here, that it wasn't over, for the air was charged still, and that Revel had borne the brunt of it.

She lay back on the cushions, white, spent, her tragic eyes with their beaten light fixed on Abel. He had crossed to the dead fireplace, which occupied the corner and was flanked by windows, so that anyone sitting on the couch before it could watch red flames leap up its black throat or the shimmering lake, as one chose.

Often, in the weeks of René's first stay in the basin, he and Eden had made summer rain an excuse for a fire, that they

125

might sit here and talk, while the flames crackled and the storm lashed the waters. Now it was choked with the ashes of dead fires. Abel was staring at the ash, and Revel at him, and Eden anxiously watching both of them.

Eden, whom he hadn't talked to since that day at the crags, didn't speak to him now. After the first startled glance, she looked away — as if she couldn't bear the sight of him. A traitor, she'd called him. Now she would know what he was. He'd tell her so. He'd tell them all. Hot words rushed to his lips.

"René," Abel spoke first, "we're leavin' the basin."

That blunt announcement killed every thought of confession. "You're givin' up the Picture Rocks?" cried René.

"No," Abel said slowly. "Yance and me is goin' out to find Zion and bring him back home, that is, if you'll. . . ."

But Revel stopped him. A moment before she had seemed beaten. Now she was on her feet, facing him, crying: "No! No! I tell you. . . ."

"There, Revel," Abel said gently. "We've gone over all that."

"But I tell you," she panted, beside herself, "you must not. I told you what would happen, if you went out. The Book said no! It said" — she could only whisper it, but they heard — "it said . . . 'Let the dead bury the dead.' "

His heart aching with nameless grief, the young man looked at Eden. She lay against the pillows, her face in her arms, her slim form shaking.

"But you ain't always right," Abel reminded the woman steadily. "About Black Wing, you always were afraid of him because the Book said death came to the man that sat on him. But now you see. . . ."

"Oh, it will come," she moaned. Then she was clinging to him, pleading: "Wait! Wait till Joel gets home! It won't be long. Snow comes early on the rims!"

It didn't seem possible to René that anyone could resist that plea. But Abel did. With a sorrowful shake of his head, he said: "We can't wait. We don't dare wait. We don't need no prophecies to tell us what Zion's doin'. We've got to bring him back before it's too late! Please, Revel, try to get a hold of yourself. Don't make it harder for us."

A long moment she searched his face. Then slowly released him and sank down by Eden with a calmness that frightened them, a numb resignation, more heart-rending than any pleading. Abel Jore went on telling René what he had been hunting him up to tell him.

"Me and Yance is goin' out to find Zion. I can't say how long we'll be gone, but not a second longer than we can help. For we've got to get back before anything breaks . . . before Dolan figgers out his move. Sure, lad, the Lord must have sent you here. For we couldn't go, if you hadn't come. But we know we can trust you to keep Dolan's men out of the basin, and. . . ."

"You can't!" In terror of such a trust, René threw up his hand. "You can't trust me any more than Shang! The Lord didn't send me here! It was Race Coulter! Lissen! Shang told you Race brought me West and bought my outfit. He told you straight! You know what Race wants! He'd give his soul for Black Wing! He'll give mine, too! For I've promised to steal the horse from you!"

He paused for breath, and the shameful words seemed to ring in the room. He felt Eden's eyes turn to him, felt the intensity in them, but, unable to meet the scorn he was sure they held, kept his own on Abel's that were too hard to show feeling.

"I didn't know what I was promisin'," he rushed on. "I thought Black Wing was just a horse that could run races. I

127

didn't know I was stealin' Eden's and Zion's chances. I didn't know how good you'd be to me. How much I'd owe you, too. No," he begged, as Abel seemed about to speak, "don't stop me. I tried to tell you once, and you wouldn't let me. I've got to tell you why I done it. Why . . . I'm a traitor. I . . . I've always been on the dead level with everybody before."

There in the big living room, Dave Jore's sombrero clenched in his hands, the sun's glare in his face, his lithe figure taut in its earnestness, backed by the gold-and-brown bindings of books that spoke of Revel's life before she married a Jore, surrounded by the heads and skins of wild things slain to adorn the den of the Jore she had renounced all for, René told them how he had followed his own horse, Flash, East and given him up when he found him, because he was "makin' a name for himself" as a polo horse; how he had worked then for a stake to get home, but took sick, and it was all he could do to pick up a living around the race tracks; how the doctor had given him six months to live, unless he went West.

"Then I met Race." With a helpless gesture, he broke off. "Oh, you don't follow how homesick I was for the West. That was half the matter with me, I guess. Seemed like I'd rather be dead and be here, than live back there. You can't see the fix I was in, when Race put it up to me."

Oh, they saw it — stark naked, terse, as he told it. For they had seen him when Zion carried him into the basin. Now they saw him like that, under sentence of death, on the gleaming track, in the cold rain, with a man tempting — "Your fare West, if you'll get into the Picture Rocks and get me that horse."

"I told him I wouldn't play the Judas. He asked wasn't my life worth it? I thought it was then. I know now it ain't. Life's worth just what you can do with it. I'd sooner not have it than do this. But I've got it, and it belongs to Race. He staked me to a gamble. I won. I'm honor-bound to pay him."

Soft in the hush: "Yes," said Revel Jore, "you're honor-bound. You've got to pay."

She savvied. She would. She was made that way. "Son," crossing to René, Abel laid a hand on his arm, "you ain't told us much we didn't guess. We figgered you'd come for the horse. We knew Race Coulter was holdin' some kind of a club over you."

Abel savvied, too. Hungrily, René's eyes sought Eden's. But she had turned to the window again.

"So you see," he said, in white misery, "why you can't trust me. You could some . . . before I told you. There was some things I couldn't do even for Race . . . livin' with you like this. But now I'm leavin'. When I get out there, I'll have to do whatever Race asks. Anything, but take Black Wing from Zion while he's out of the basin. I promise you I won't do that."

"I'd have gambled on it," Abel endorsed heartily. "But about leavin' . . . you don't savvy, son. You'd be arrested and tried on serious charges. You helped a Jore escape. You wounded a man doin' it. You fought for us at the pass. The world classes you with us. I'm mighty sorry that had to happen, but it's facts we're facin'. You couldn't do Race no good in jail. And it won't be workin' ag'in' him to watch the Picture Rocks till we bring Zion and Black Wing back."

René saw this. Race had said himself that the only safe place for the horse was in the basin, guarded by the Jores, until Luke Chartres gave up the chase. Again the interests of the Jores and Race were the same.

"I'd like to stay," said René wistfully, "if you still trust me."

"Fine." Abel wrung his hand. "It's goin' to be a tough job for one man. We hate to ask it, but it needs must be when the devil drives. There's plenty of ammunition. And Eden will spell you off."

"But you and Yance?" René's fears were all for them. "You'll be takin' your lives in your hands. How'll you get past that camp? They're watchin' for just such a break."

"We'll have to risk that. We know every inch of the pass . . . every rock and bush, no matter how dark it is. If we're seen, we'll run for it. There ain't many horses in these parts can beat ours."

Nevertheless, he admitted it was a dangerous mission. And the gravity of it weighed on them with the worry and heat. They were leaving that night. Revel and Eden went out to prepare a cold supper for René, so he could go right to the crags and relieve Yance, who would need to catch a few hours' sleep before the start.

The meal over, René stepped out on the porch. Abel stood there, eyes scanning the sky. Black clouds were rolling over the rims.

"Looks like ol' Jupe Pluvius is with us," he grinned. "If the storm only holds off till dark, we'll make our break when it gets goin' strong."

Down at the corral, cinching his saddle on Stonewall, René looked up to see Eden standing beside him. "I've put you up a lunch," she said, holding it out to him. "It will be a long time until morning."

He took it and thanked her. His smile was a happy one. Eden had spoken to him. True, her voice didn't say anything. He might have been a total stranger to whom she'd made some comment on the weather. No, for she'd have been friendly then. But she had spoken to him. Now she was going.

Quickly he stepped up to her. "Ain't there something I can say on my side to you, Eden?"

She looked away. "What is there to say?"

"A lot, girl."

"Perhaps," she said, quietly. "But nothing I want to hear. Nothing that will change . . . oh" — bravely lifting her blue eyes to him — "I want you to know I don't blame you for trying to get Black Wing. You couldn't help it. Anyone would have done that. You were just true to the man who gave you your chance. Why, I . . . I'd have helped you steal Black Wing myself from my own folks. But what I can't forget. . . ."

"What, Eden?"

"That you sacrificed Zion for him. When you knew he was . . . when I told you he must not leave the Picture Rocks. You took him from us."

"I didn't do that!" René protested. "It's the truth. I didn't. You must know it, Eden. You do know it, don't you, girl?"

She looked into his face, so earnest, so honest, her blue eyes filling. She looked off at the storm-capped rims, and she cried, in pitiful confusion: "I . . . can't! Oh, I don't know! Zion's gone!"

Zion was gone. The Jores were risking their lives to bring him back, and René Rand was standing guard over the Picture Rocks.

Up there in the spires where, so often, Zion had sat with the spreading world calling, until in his mighty longing it seemed he must just let go all "holts" and "float" down, René now crouched with ready gun, waiting for dark when the Jores would make their break. Far down, he saw the winding thread of the trail up which he had toiled a few weeks before, expecting a challenge from the sentinel. Now he was the sentry, sworn to enforce the strict taboo of trespass; sworn to shoot anyone who tried to break it; to shoot these men camped below him, should they attempt it, although they represented the law, all the things he had ever stood for, still stood for — although he was an outlaw.

The sun had gone down, dragging its light with it. When the dusk got too thick for sure aim, he slipped down to the barricade to watch. Night brought no coolness. Heat seemed rather to increase. The air became more oppressive. The very earth seemed to have caught and held its breath. The storm still threatened. Endless, black hours passed.

Shortly after midnight, René heard a muttering in the south. Rapidly it neared, and, crouched behind that bulwark of rock, tense, listening, he heard muffled hoofbeats coming from within the basin. In a blinding bolt that split the blackness, as the rims resounded deafeningly with thunder, as the wind came in a rush like the breath of the world released and water fell in sheets, the Jores rode up.

"The rain will wash out our tracks," said Abel in a whisper. "They won't dream we're gone, if the lightnin' don't show us up."

Noiselessly they tore a hole in the barricade, and slipped their horses through. Then, before mounting, they turned to say good bye. Yance wrung René's hand in silence. There was no need to say anything. Their actions spoke for them. They had placed their lives in René's hands. For they had not only to get past Dolan's camp but, after they found Zion, must get back in. And they trusted to René Rand that they would return to a refuge and not a trap.

Abel long held the young fellow by both arms, while the wind, the rain, and the thunder crashed about them. "If we don't come back," he said, "take care of her, son." And René saw on his face in the lightning flash a look that haunted him for years.

Then they were gone, in their rash attempt to slip through

the enemy's camp as, in days past, their father had slipped through the camp of the fierce Apaches. Gone, in the crashing blackness, and René listened with his heart in his mouth.

Chapter Seventeen

UNLOOSED

The wind, the thunder and lightning rolled away into the night, but the rain kept up until dawn, a warm steamy dawn. Mists rose from the basin as from a mighty caldron. Out of the mists at sunrise came Eden. She was off her horse and standing beside him before he saw her. Then he had to look twice to make sure. For her short, fawn-colored skirt and blouse blended right in with the dun crags and sun-browned grass. But her face was like a patch of snow against the rocks and her eyes, shadowed from an all-night vigil, startlingly purple.

"They got through?" she asked in a drab little voice.

"You bet." René grinned. "At least, I didn't hear anything to the contrary. And the camp's goin' on as usual."

She took a step to the brink of the cliff and looked down through the crags of rocks. Guards were busy about the tents, nursing a smoky campfire, hunting dry fuel, and spreading out things that had been left out last night and got soaked by the rain.

She turned back to René: "I'll watch, now. Go down, and get some sleep."

He said unsteadily: "Reckon that I had as much sleep as you, Eden."

She gave no sign of hearing and probably didn't, noticing that his sombrero was limp and his buckskin sodden. "And get out of those damp clothes. You'll be sick again."

134

She cared. Transformed by the thought, he told her he wasn't sleepy a bit. He could stay up a year. Besides, this was no job for a girl. He couldn't bear to leave her.

"Don't be silly." She reached for his rifle. "There's no telling how long you'll have to watch. You must keep up your strength."

He turned away, suddenly weary.

Down at the big house, he breakfasted alone at the long table. Revel came and went like a ghost. She had always been silent, but not like this — as if she'd never been anything else. She had got hold of herself, a hold that worried René. He wished that she'd let go, wished that she would cry, anything, but this stoniness, as if the heart had been torn from her breast, as the heart had been torn from the big house, so empty and still now — nothing but a shell, for all its appearance of cozy cheer.

"Come on up to the crags," he begged her, after three hours of sleep, as he was starting back to Eden. "It's lonesome for you down here. Come on up and watch for them."

She didn't then, but in time she did, seeing that he was worried about her. She would walk up and stay with him and Eden, her black eyes bent to the world she had abandoned, but which had robbed her of husband and son. There, she would sit by the hour, her thin hands monotonously plaiting her black dress with thoughts they could only guess.

But for the most part René watched alone. Day after day, vigilant as ever Abel had been, he watched to see that no one came in. Day after day, relentlessly, Dolan's men made sure, as they thought, that no one went out. René would smile to himself, picturing Dolan's chagrin if he had known the Jores were gone. He looked for Dolan among the guards, and, although the distance he encompassed was too great to distinguish faces, he was sure he would recognize the tall form of the sheriff. But he never saw it. Nor could he see Shang. He would grin, imagining Shang's state of mind, if he should learn that the Jores were free to settle their score with him. As for Race and Chartres, he never looked for them. They wouldn't be here, now that Black Wing was gone.

It was, for René, a long and weary grind, but, when Dolan's men tired of the waiting game, others replaced them. The trail was seldom bare of riders, coming or going. Those who stayed had many amusements. René would watch them pitching horseshoes or squatting about a blanket, playing cards, shooting at a target — the crags, often as not — or racing their horses from the tents to the mouth of the pass, a pastime that kept his finger quivering on the trigger of his cocked gun, lest it be a ruse to break in.

For he never forgot that, when the Jores came with Zion and Black Wing, the basin must be sanctuary. Whether they came by day on the run, or at night, stealthily, as they had slipped out, it must be to safety. By day, he watched for them. By night, he listened. They should be back.

"They'd never have gone," cried Eden, one twilight, "if they'd known they'd be away this long."

René worried, too. But, curiously, he seemed to thrive on the strain. For up there, drenched in the hot sunshine, breathing the untainted wind, always in the open, always resting, he made miraculous gains. It was as if he drew strength from the very ground he lay upon. Seeing him there, his slim figure, sinewy and hard-muscled, the sparkle of health in his fine, dark eyes, his young face bronzed, it was hard to believe that this was the pale, thin youth, who had been dying by inches on the Eastern race tracks. René could hardly believe it himself. He felt so good, he could scarcely contain himself. All this new life that sang in his veins rebelled at inaction. He wanted to be doing something real, something that would command all his powers, such as Yance and Abel were doing out there, risking everything, hunting for Zion. And something seemed to be calling him, as it had Zion. It seemed he must drop everything and respond.

Then, this sunset, three weeks after he took up his watch, he came back to the crags, to see Eden flying to meet him, in an apprehension that could mean but two things — Dolan was trying to break in or the Jores were coming.

But she cried, as he swung down hard at her side: "The camp's leaving!"

"What?" René couldn't credit it.

"They took the tents down and have packed everything."

He rushed past her and looked down at the pass. Sure enough, Dolan's crew had pulled up stakes and were riding off. "Oh, what's happened?" the girl appealed wildly to him. "Something must have happened to my uncles or Zion, else they wouldn't be going."

René feared it. But he didn't let Eden see it. "Dolan's give up," he assured her. "That's it. Dolan seen it wasn't any use, and he give up. No, we're all right. They'll bring Zion back, and everything will be like it was."

He succeeded in making her believe what he didn't believe himself. When she had left, the very absence of tents at Sentry Crags, the silence, the loneliness, seemed a menace. That night he watched from the barricade, lest this be a ruse to throw him off guard. But nothing happened.

Dawn found him on the rims again, straining his eyes for sight of the guards returning. He saw no one. But, an hour after sunup, a rider lifted above the sage and turned into the Picture Rocks trail. In suspense, René watched him coming nearer, praying it was a Jore. But it was not. It was Race Coulter.

For weeks René Rand had watched the Picture Rocks,

steeled to take life if he must, to hold the Jore refuge. In all that time no one had tried to enter. Now the one man on earth who would call it treason, if he were refused anything, was coming.

As Race climbed the last steep rise to the pass, René ran to Stonewall, tied back in the brush. For this issue with Race must be met face to face. Mounting, he turned back to scan all approaches to the basin. Certain that no other human being was within miles, he put spurs to his horse, plunging down the steep cliff at almost as mad a pace as Zion had taken that day he came, dodging the same obstacles, leaping the same fissures, outriding the avalanching shale to the floor of the pass.

Here, he dismounted and ran up to the barricade of rocks, just as Race rounded the trail, his roan shying violently as it sighted René. Race started, too, in more than surprise. Long and hard, he stared at the young fellow standing behind the wall, hands resting on it, and steady in them, a business-like Winchester.

"Kid!" he gasped. "Kid . . . is it you, or your ghost?"

René answered tensely: "It's me, Race."

The man drew a long breath. "Yeah," he admitted with a jerky laugh. "I reckon it is. But it's hard to believe. You here . . . fit as seventeen fiddles, when I thought you was dead. Shang swore he'd let daylight through you. And knowin' the shape you was in, I reckoned you'd turned up your toes. Figgered I'd lost my investment, and would have to go this alone. But I see Shang was lyin'."

"No," said René. "Not about that."

"Then," Race laughed, all his aplomb back, "hot lead was the medicine you needed all right. You look great!" He couldn't get over it, his small, selfish eyes appraising the young fellow's physical fitness, exulting in it, as he had in his weakness, because, he explained: "This just doubles my chances to get that stallion."

His face flamed to that lusty gleam that always came over it at mention of Black Wing, but more marked than ever, absolutely unrestrained, wholly fanatical. "I got no chance out there," he confided to René. "No use tryin' to stick to the tail of a comet. So I come up here to wait. Sooner or later that young stallion will make a break for the basin, now the guards is gone. And I aim to be that Johnny-on-the-spot when that happens. So throw down them rocks and let me in."

René's hands tensed on the gun. "You can't come in."

"Can't?" Still Race didn't tumble. "Why can't I? What's to stop me? Not the Jores. I know that."

Did Race know the Jores were gone? Sick with a dread he dare not analyze, René said firmly: "I'm stoppin' you, Race."

"You?" cried Race with ludicrous dismay. "But you're workin' for me!"

"Not on this. I'm holdin' this pass for the Jores. I got orders to let nobody in. And that means you, Race."

Understanding at last, fully alive to the potency of that gun, when backed by the driven intensity he saw in René's eyes, Race's face went livid with rage. "I see." His lips drew back in a sneer. "Horatio at the bridge, huh? So that's the stripe you are? I pick you up back there, out of the gutter . . . worse, just waitin' for the hearse . . . and I bring you West, make a man of you, and you go over to the Jores. You go over to them outlaws, when you owe me. . . ."

"I ain't forgotten what I owe you," René stated. "But I owe the Jores as much and more. And I can pay a little on what I owe them by holdin' this pass."

"And I can whistle, I suppose." Race was furious. "Oh, I've been deaf, dumb, and blind. You've been workin' for the Jores all along. You coulda turned Black Wing over to me that mornin' I was talkin' to you in camp. But I didn't tumble. I even figured, when you helped Zion Jore get away with him, that you'd done it to get him back in the basin . . . away from Chartres. But I see now . . . you was gettin' him away from me. Then, when he got cut off, you sneaked back to watch things, while the Jores went after him."

Pale through all his tan, trembling for all his strength, the boy cried: "How do you know that, Race?"

"Oh, that ain't half." Never had the rims returned a sound more grim than Race's laugh. "What's more, they ain't comin' back!"

"You mean . . . ?" Numbly René stared at him.

"Just that! The Jores ain't comin' back . . . no time!"

There was a heartbroken cry behind. René swung. There in the trail were Eden and Revel. Eden, with eyes dazed and dreadful, coming up to cling to the barrier, and Revel as stony as ever, standing beside her daughter, quietly telling Race Coulter: "They'll come."

The young man saw Race fighting back his terror of her — the terror she had instilled in him that morning long ago, when she made that prediction about Black Wing.

"You don't savvy." Race licked his dry lips nervously. "They can't come. Not unless they bust through steel, reinforced special for them, past a special guard. Pat Dolan captured 'em yesterday in an old line cabin on the Hondo Ranch. He's got 'em both locked safe in jail in Big Sandy."

Sudden darkness seemed to fall over the pass. The wind seemed to wail inconsolable loss. First Joel, now it was Yance and Abel. Every male Jore but one, every Jore but the one of whom Eden was asking. "Zion," she whispered, "have you heard of him?"

Race stared into the blue eyes lifted to his. Then he said, slowly repeating: "Have I heard of him?" His swarthy face hardened, and he cried with a force that buried the words deep in each breast: "I reckon, girl, everyone on this green earth has heard of Zion Jore."

As well then, as when Race was done, René knew what was coming. He would have given anything to keep it from Eden.

But she said in a piteous voice that brought tears to his eyes: "We haven't heard a word since he left us. What have you heard?"

Race threw up his hands in despair of an adequate answer. "Anything," he told her. "Anything that's wild and terrible! Things to raise your hair. Reckless things to make the most reckless feel like a piker. Anything you want to hear. Blood-and-thunder tales. Stories of black art. For there's some as says he ain't human, but something infernal that changes its form into this and that. That's how they account for the way he does his disappearin' act. But I say it ain't him . . . it's his horse that's half human. I tell you, that stallion. . . ."

"No! No!" protested the tortured girl. "Tell us about Zion."

Race frowned. Any subject but Black Wing bored him. "It ain't pretty!" The prelude showed he wasn't totally devoid of pity. "He's killed two men besides Hank Farley. And left his mark on I don't know how many more. But one pretty deep on one of the Chartres cowboys right after they took up his trail out here. They didn't follow him far. Who can follow a shootin' star? And that golden horse. . . ."

"Go on!" pleaded Eden. "Oh, go on about Zion!"

"He got away. Next we heard, he was over in the Navajo country. He'd walked into a restaurant and asked for a meal. When he got it under his belt, he started to walk out. The town marshal happened to be eatin' there, and the proprietor called on him to collect. He did . . . whatever he had comin' to him when he faced it. Saint Pete at the Golden Gate. Zion Jore rode off with half the town on his trail. But that yellow tempest he's straddlin'. . . ."

He went on irritably, as again the girl wrenched from him the subject that obsessed him: "Well, then, he broke out again in Big Sandy. Held up Jake Wheeler's supply store in broad day, and helped himself to grub and cash. The streets was full of people. But he walked out, cool as a cucumber, and ties his loot on that gold . . . that horse. Then he crosses the street to where some raggedy Mex' kids is eyin' goods in a bakery window. He says . . . 'You look hungry.' They said they was. He says . . . 'You needn't be . . . livin's free!' And he gives them the money he'd took from the store. Wheeler took it away from the kids after Zion had gone, but. . . ."

"Oh! What?"

"Zion heard of it somehow, and that night he come back and robbed him again! Wheeler was on watch and tried to stop him with a shotgun. It was the last thing he ever done. Zion made a clean getaway."

"But now," cried Eden desperately, "where is he?"

Race shrugged. "Where is the wind? He's here, there, and everywhere. He'll be seen today in a prospector's cabin in the Rabbit Foot country, and tomorrow there'll be plenty to swear he's showed up in a cow camp on the Verde. He's everywhere . . . raisin' red, white, and blue blazes. Every place, but where they look for him. Dolan got a tip Zion had holed up in that line cabin. He collected Shang and Chartres and an army of deputies, and hid in the loft to wait for him. But Zion smelled 'em. And Yance and Abel walked into the trap. Dolan is still knocked dumb by his luck."

Turning to Revel, immobile as marble through this awful recital, Race told her: "The last part of what you predicted has come to pass. Hell has sure followed that horse."

She never flinched.

But Eden went to pieces then, breaking down and sobbing. "Oh, where will it end? He doesn't realize what he's doing. He doesn't mean any harm. He's not . . . any of the terrible things they're saying. He's just a child, playing a game. But they'll. . . . Oh, God, help him!"

Blindly René tore at the rocks that formed the barrier.

"What are you doin'?" Race Coulter shouted.

"I'm goin' after Zion."

"But you're guardin' the pass."

"No need to . . . after the news you brought. Yance and Abel won't need it. It doesn't matter much who comes to the Picture Rocks . . . till I get Zion back. But nobody'll come. Dolan will draw the line at women." Grasping Stonewall's trailing reins, he led him to the opening.

But Race swung his own horse, blocking the way and blustering: "Are you loco, too? Don't you know Dolan will clap you in jail, if you go out there? What good would you be to anyone then? Wait here, till Zion Jore comes, if you do aim to pay me."

René blazed up. "Quit dunnin' me, will you? There's things more important than Black Wing. Get out of my way. I'm goin' after Zion!"

He pushed Race's horse aside and was leading the bay through, when Revel stopped him and silently held him, her hands on his shoulders, looking at him with those deep, tragic eyes, seeing, he always believed, the horrors that lay before him; seeing him, in that far desert camp with Zion at his red trail's end and hundreds of hostile miles between them and home; seeing him, at that water hole, with Zion, mad in delirium, striking out at him; seeing him win to the very portals of the Picture Rocks, with Black Wing's helpless burden, only to find that. . . .

143

He always believed Revel saw all that was to be, and wanted to make it easier, and that was why she made this great sacrifice. Going up to Race, awing him by the strange force of her nearness, she said: "You must go with him."

Hoarse in fear and defiance, Race rasped: "Not by a. . . ."

"Wait! You say this young man owes you a debt."

"You bet! And I aim to collect."

Stunning them all, Revel Jore said: "I'll pay it. I'll pay his debt, Race Coulter. I'll give you Black Wing. But" — she made this very simple condition — "only if you go with him."

Hot in Race's eyes burned that greedy flame. "You'll give me Black Wing?" he gasped, as if it was too good to be true. And it was. He said harshly: "Black Wing belongs to Luke Chartres."

"No," said the woman, her stony calm breaking. "Black Wing is mine. You'll have a clear title to him. Luke Chartres won't press his claim, when you tell him the horse came to you from my hands."

Her words carried conviction. Race was knocked just as dumb by his luck as Dolan had been. But René's wild protests snapped him out of it in short order.

"Not Black Wing!" René most earnestly begged her. "You know exactly what he means. You know Joel's dream."

"I only know," said the outlaw's weary wife, "that I must do this. And it is done."

"Then," violently Race yanked his roan around, "let's get goin'. I don't want my property rode down . . . ruined . . . crippled up. I tell you they're usin' that horse for a target."

But René was detained again. Somehow, Eden was in his arms. It seemed to him that now her tears washed away the barrier that, so long, had been between them, for the blue eyes flashed the old trust. "Oh, I know," she whispered, as fast he drew her to his breast. "I've known all along. I must

144

have been out of my mind. Don't go, René. Stay with me. I can't lose you, too."

This memory would light the blackest hour for him. He smiled happily: "You can't lose me, Eden. I'll come back, and I'll bring Zion."

Chapter Eighteen

ZION JORE — OUTLAW

Was this the terrible killer who had thrown half a state in panic? Was this the fiend around whom centered scores of hair-raising, blood-and-thunder adventures? Was this, according to the grisly fancy of the superstitious, the inhuman adept in black magic? He did not look it, this young fellow in buckskin, standing on a high butte overlooking Big Sandy. He did not look terrible. He did not look like a killer. But he looked very, very human — standing there, talking to his horse, a tender, whimsical smile on his lips, his long, black hair blowing back from a wild, sweet, restless face that gave no hint of the ferocity and cunning accredited to him. He looked like any young fellow of his own age, but far, far wearier than most.

He didn't look like an outlaw, any more than his superb, trim-limbed, creamy-skinned stallion looked like the king of a wild mustang band. Yet his cool self-confidence, gained in many victorious encounters, was clearly shown in his standing thus, with no sign of nervousness, only half a mile from the town where a determined sheriff, pilloried by an outraged populace, sought his life.

His weird blue eyes, narrowed against the glare of mid-afternoon, were on the town that sprawled below him like "a dark-hued lizard on the dark-hued sand."

"It's sleepin'," he told the stallion, his fingers straying down that high-arched, golden neck. "But we'll wake it up.

We'll sure surprise 'em. They don't think we're in fifty miles of here. We wasn't last night. They think we'd be a-scared to come back here anyway in wide, open day. But we don't scare, do we, pony? We go where we like. Nothin' stops us. When the sun says three . . . we'll go. It ain't much after two yet. We got to wait. We got to time it right. At three. Then, if our scheme works, we'll get Uncle Yance and Abel out of jail, so they can go home. They come out to find us. They thought I couldn't take care of myself. But I can. And I'll take care of them."

Eyes still on the town and softly chuckling, as any child might envisage the working out of a prank. "We'll stir it up, you bet," he assured the horse, that was so tremblingly responsive to every word. "They say nothin' does it like a bank robbin'. Just like René told me, folks is crazy about money. Store it . . . like bees do honey. We'll rob their cache, and they'll do like wild bees . . . take after the first movin' thing. That'll be me . . . and you, Black Wing. Somebody'll git stung. But" — with a wild laugh — "it won't be us!"

The horse stamped as if eager to be off, but young Zion soothed him. "Not yet, Black Wing. Not till three o'clock . . . that's when banks shut up. That's what that prospector we stayed with told us. Oh, he told us a lot about banks. He thought I was a fool not to know. But he'll know who the fool was when he hears. He'll know it was Zion Jore he was talkin' to. He'll feel green, the way he talked about me . . . not knowin' who I was. Tellin' me things I done, stretchin' 'em out of all sense, makin' up some. But we owe him a lot for tellin' us how Pat Dolan got my uncles in that ol' line cabin where I used to stop at. Bet that prospector'll cuss he didn't try to get me and get the reward he said was on me. There's a reward on us, Black Wing."

Strangely, his tired figure straightened, and his dark face

beamed, as if a medal for valor had been pinned on him. "Jores," proudly he informed Black Wing, "always has rewards on them. I'm worth something, too. Mebbe as much as Jerico."

But he was glad the old miner hadn't tried to take him. He'd have had to kill him, and he hated to kill anyone. "But," he told the horse bewilderedly, "I can't live out here, and not. I ain't hurt anybody yet, that wasn't tryin' to hurt me. Trouble is, everybody does, soon as they find out who I am. Lots of ways" — the words were dragged from him — "it was better in the basin."

Almost against his will, his eyes were drawn back to the black mountain range, to the great cup against the burnished heavens, and fixed on it with awful longing, longing that had grown all the endless time he had been running wild, that kept the basin always in his mind. In times of peril — and most times were perilous — he would see the Picture Rocks. In comparative security, sheltered for the night by some unsuspecting host or stretched out with Black Wing in some lonely spot, sleep never brought such oblivion that he did not see the basin.

He would see it all green and glowing in the spring. He would see it all summer-tanned and riotous with autumn colors. He would see it when snow lay on the rims and the naked trees were clothed with frosty rime, all silver desolation. By the sun's light, he would see it, by stars, and moon, and dawn. And when there was no light of any kind, he could see the basin, the blue and shimmering lake that was as variable in its moods as himself, the changeless painted figures. He would miss them and feel they missed him — as if they had the power to feel, the living breath that his imagination had always imbued them with. He would see. . . .

"If I just could see Eden." He faltered to Black Wing,

heartsick for more than the mental image of his sister. "I'd sure listen to her. I'd tell her she was right."

And his mother. . . . "She'd be proud of me, I bet, if she knowed all the things I've done."

Something hot and wet touched his cheek then. Furiously, he brushed it off with a buckskin sleeve. "You can't hardly just ride off," in broken apology to the horse. "Lovin' folks is strings on a man."

Wistfully he thought, waiting there for three o'clock, how quiet and peaceful the basin was. In there he knew every tree and plant and bird, and they loved him. Out here, everything was strange and hated him. There was something wrong with him — some place. He didn't know what it was. If he did, he could fix it. It hadn't mattered in there. You had to think every minute out here. And it made his head ache to think. He pressed his hands to it now to ease the throb. It wasn't fun running — now, he'd got his run out. No fun bein' chased like a rabbit when the hounds got after it.

My pard's in there, he thought. *Somebody held the pass that day. It musta been René. If it was, Uncle Abel wouldn't send him away. I could have fun in there with René.*

A long moment he stood, his haggard face lifted to the Picture Rocks. Then, his lips quivering — "I'll bet you're homesick." — shamefacedly he accused Black Wing.

Responsive to this, as to all else, the horse tossed his sleek head against Zion's breast.

"Well" — Zion tried to restrain his eagerness — "we can go back . . . if you're homesick. But" — he was firm about this — "not yet! We gotta go back with our tails up. We gotta finish our work out here. We'll get Yance and Abel out of jail. Then we'll get Dad out of that prison. Then" — his eyes flashing lightning — "I'll kill Shang! I don't mind that. He needs killin'. We'll do them three things, Black

Wing. Then we'll go home."

Three tasks as great as ever the twelve labors of Hercules, yet of no moment to him. To Zion Jore, it was as if they were already done. He saw himself riding home in triumph, saw the hounds bounding to meet him, saw himself surrounded by those who loved him.

"We'll see the folks," he whispered wearily to the horse, "and the lake, and the ol' paint' rocks. Then we'll just lay down and rest."

Zion Jore would go back to the Picture Rocks. But not like this.

His time nearly up, he inspected the six-gun at his belt, twirling the cylinders, looking at every working part. He took up the rifle, leaning on the rock beside him, and, ascertaining that it was in perfect order, slipped it in the scabbard under his stirrup leather. Then he turned his attention to his saddle rigging and, sure that everything was right, reset the saddle and tightened the cinch.

As he put foot in the stirrup, a transformation took place. All the regret, the dream, the tenderness, vanished from his face. His mobile lips were set in lines of terrible purpose. His blue eyes flashed a savage blaze. He looked capable of everything they had accused him of.

As he bounded to the saddle, the stallion reared like the wild king he was, eyes aflame in transformation as startling as Zion's. Lightly the young fellow's spur touched a gleaming flank. With a half snort, half scream, the buckskin horse, bearing the young fellow in buckskin, plunged wildly down the slope toward town.

Chapter Nineteen

DEAD OR ALIVE

The latest arrival, lounging on the shady verandah of Trail's End, looked at his watch and yawned. Just a quarter to three? Great Scott! Half a day in this burg, but it seemed like a week. He cast bored eyes back to the street. From the Stockman's Bank, a block down, to the county jail, a block up, there was nothing but heat and hush, but so much of both.

Turning on the grizzled proprietor of Trail's End, who was awakening from his *siesta* in the easy chair beside him, he ungraciously blurted: "I don't see how you stand it!"

Drowsily Dad Peppin looked up. "Stand what?"

"This infernal quiet!"

A queer smile quirked the old man's lips. He said feelingly: "We are thankful for it. We've had uproar enough around here to last us for a spell. And we'll have more." He drew himself up in his chair. "You've heard of the Jores?"

"And little else! Every paper I've picked up for weeks has been full of your outlaws. All I've heard since I hit Big Sandy is Jores. I feel personally acquainted with the whole clan. Know their history from the Year One. Wish I could have been here when all the excitement was going on . . . though it's hard to believe anything ever excited this town. And probably never will again, now they've got the Jores behind bars."

"But they ain't . . . not all," was the slow denial. "They ain't got the dangerous Jore. He's still free."

"Zion, you mean? The young fellow they say is crazy?"

151

Old Dad nodded gravely. But his guest failed to extract any thrill out of that. "He won't be free long . . . with a sheriff like you got. From what I read, Pat Dolan must be pretty much of a man."

He was surprised to see that didn't set well.

"Yeah?" said Dad, in his slowest drawl.

"Meanin' that you really don't think so?"

"Waal," Dad's drawl speeded up, "you didn't say pretty much of what kind of a man you thought he was. I think he's pretty much of a bluff myself. I think" — his wrinkled old countenance flushing with righteous wrath — "he's the most graspin', self-aspirin', fame-famished yahoo which it's ever been my misfortune to know."

"W-whew!" That was going some for a hot day.

"And contrary to what the papers said" — Dad's ire boiled over — "it ain't no laurels on Dolan's blockhead that he got the Jores. He couldn't help hisself. Yance and Abel walked right into a trap he'd set for Zion. Somebody give him a tip where the young fellow was stayin'. The Jores must have got the same tip. It was a bad break for them. But fool's luck for Dolan! And he's playin' it up for all it's worth. Takin' credit on false pretenses. Why, he ain't made a move of his own since he's been sheriff. Done nothin' . . . till he got the help of that black-hearted scalawag. Read about Shang Haman?"

The stranger had. "Waal," grimly predicted old Dad, "you're apt to read more, if you watch right close. A pithy little notice . . . all about how he was born, such and such a time, and died any day about now, with his boots on. Plenty of folks right in this town what's r'arin' to give him a send-off."

"Doubtless! A squealer was never popular. But Luke Chartres," asked the visitor, "just what's his interest in this? From what I catch, he'd as much to do with this clean-up of

152

Jores as the sheriff. Seems to me, it's a strange business for a man of his prominence to tangle with."

"Chartres," said Dad Peppin shortly, "wants his pound of horseflesh."

Which was a phase of the case the stranger had missed. A dozen questions rose to his lips. But before he could voice one, old Dad boiled over again.

"Pat Dolan," he said, "has greased the skids for more bloodshed than this country's seen yet. Nobody on earth could have got Zion back in that basin and looked after him, but his uncles. It's all they asked for in life . . . just to get their brother's son home before he caused grief. But Dolan blocked their move. Nobody else has any influence. . . ." He started suddenly. "Unless," he said thoughtfully, "it's that young fellow he calls pard."

"The sick tenderfoot crook who kept the posse out of the Picture Rocks?"

"If you go by the papers," Dad admitted indignantly. "And that's about as straight as the rest of the stuff they print! He was sick, all right. But he ain't no tenderfoot. And if he's a crook, I'm Saint Cecilia makin' music, with angels dropping roses on my halo."

He looked so far from this, that his guest couldn't repress a laugh.

"He's a fine, clean, upstandin' young man," warmly declared the old man. "He come here one night inquirin' for a *hombre,* and I took to him right off. Next day I had occasion to help him. Dolan's dragged me over the coals for doin' it, but I'd do it again." His gaze went from the shimmering miles of range to the Montezumas. After a time he said grimly: "If René Rand don't come for Zion Jore, who can say what'll happen, or when."

Stirred by his tone, but reassured by a glance at the

sleeping town, the stranger said: "Aren't you taking the situation too serious? There's been other badmen, and they all came to one end. It's ridiculous to suppose this looney kid can ride around long, robbing, killing."

He was abashed by the deadly seriousness with which his host took issue with this. "It's ridiculous to suppose in this case. Zion Jore can't be took too serious. There's never been a outlaw like him. Oh, mebbe he ain't got all his buttons. But he's got more of what he has got . . . savvy . . . than lots of smart men. It's what's missin' that makes him dangerous!"

He went on with moving solemnity. "Friend, it's what Zion Jore ain't got that gives me cold chills to contemplate . . . right now, a hundred in the shade. It would make the hottest Jore sympathizers draw a long breath of relief to hear that young fellow had been corralled safe. You've mebbe read, and you've heard more here, but it's plain to be seen that you don't savvy Zion Jore. He's like this."

As he hitched closer to his guest, he continued gravely: "He's likely the best shot with rifle or six-gun ever seen in the West. He's got no sense of responsibility, no savvy about the sacredness of property rights, nor the meanin' of the word fear. The best safeguard around any institution is the knowledge of its protection. But it means nothin' to Zion. He don't know. He'd rush in where the nerviest, willin'est outlaw would balk cold.

"Not ten feet from where you're a-settin'," cried Doc Peppin, "he killed his first man! Nobody blamed him for that. Nobody blames him for anything yet. But he's got to be stopped. Though how that's to be accomplished. . . ."

Then he told of the golden horse he had so long believed a myth.

"And it's more of a myth," he frankly confessed, "since I've seen it in the flesh. For it ain't possible for a horse to run like that horse runs. And bullets don't touch him. He's a devil on hoofs. A wild, yellow phantom."

But the stranger wasn't hearing him. He was staring down the street with incredulous eyes. Could Dad Peppin's description of the horse be vivid enough to cause him to materialize there in the heat and hush — so realistically, that his golden flanks gleamed wet, as with sweat. Was that Black Wing standing down there or. . . . "Is it," gasped the guest, pointing a shaking hand, "there . . . by the bank! Am I seeing things?"

Dad looked, and his eyes almost leaped from their sockets. Wildly he sprang up. "Black Wing! What's he doin' here alone? Where's Zion? Does this mean Dolan's . . . ?"

"A young fellow just got off!" cried the guest. "Or I imagined him! A young chap in buckskin."

He winced at the bite of the old man's clutch. "Where did you imagine he went?"

"In the bank!"

Dad Peppin groaned. His eyes sought the jail, as if to call the Jores from their cells. Then he was plunging down the steps of Trail's End, the stranger hard after him, trying to calm him.

"We may be wrong! He's not the only young fellow wears buckskin! Black Wing's not the only cream-colored stallion!"

But before their racing feet hit the sidewalk, a sharp retort shattered the quiet. And out of the door of the bank down there burst a wild figure — a Big Sandy man, who looked wildly around, then raced toward them, eyes popping, spurred to another admirable burst of speed by a second gunshot!

Meeting them halfway of the block, he seized Dad Peppin, clinging to him as to his one hope of salvation, panting, in a very hysteria of terror. "Zion Jore!" He tried for more, throat working, face contorted with as much pain as if he were swallowing something scalding. "I . . . I was at that desk . . . behind the door, signin' a check. I'd hurried to cash it . . . before closin' time! I saw him come in! And he poked a gun through the wicket, and . . . I run . . . and he shot at me!"

"You're crazy!" Dad tried to jerk free. "What Zion Jore aims at, he hits!"

Then, riveting him, struck an ear-shattering *clang-clang-clang,* as the electric gong before the bank set up a wild alarm, calling for help as with human tongue, seeming to shriek to the slumbering town — "Zion Jore! Zion Jore!"

The buckskin stallion at the curb madly pitched in his terror of it and of the bedlam that broke out around him, as Big Sandy awoke with a bang. Startled faces were thrust from windows. Doors slammed. The street was full of men, wildly demanding information of men, no better informed. Running to the bank, eyes on the bell as if it had done something terrible, while the cry was raised: "Zion Jore's in there!"

With the courage of numbers they were pushing to the very door, when it suddenly swung in their faces, and a young fellow stood there, a weighted canvas bag in one hand and in the other a black six-gun, from which they recoiled as if pushed back by an irresistible force. Coolly pausing to survey the frightened faces in the circle slowly backing away from him, the young man suddenly laughed, a wild laugh that unnerved them and sent them stampeding for the nearest covering.

Old Dad Peppin stood his ground, and he made no move to stop Zion. Any interference would be madness. A word, a sign would result in more blood being shed, more blood on this young outlaw's head. He could only watch, fascinated by Zion Jore's absolute lack of fear, as he sauntered to the curb, soothed the pitching horse with a word and, as careless as

156

though he were upon legitimate business, as though there were no threatening eyes on him, no gong clamoring for more men to come and kill him, no sheriff and deputies bursting down the street with guns drawn, he swung the bag up before his saddle, swung on behind it, and shot like a rocket between the bank building and the grocery store next to it — unscathed by the bullet Dolan sent after him, or by the charge of buckshot from a sawed-off shotgun, leveled on him from a window, or from a dozen shots that rang out from different quarters.

"They're right!" Dad Peppin swore awesomely to himself, seeing man and horse emerge from the alley and streak up the road behind Trail's End. "He can't be human!"

Then he joined the mob now fighting to get into the bank to see what had happened. There were two men in the cashier's cage — one, leaning weakly against the wall, white as paper, lips compressed, while the other applied a bandage to his bleeding arm and gave Sheriff Dolan an account of the hold-up at the same time.

"Me and Chet," the cashier was saying, "was busy makin' up the money. Didn't see him, till we heard his voice. Saw his gun first . . . looked like a cannon to me. He told me to hand out that bag of money. I made to do it. But Chet, here, made a dive for the gun under the counter. Jore got him through the arm, but Chet rolled to the button and set the alarm goin'. He got all the cash in sight. Not much."

It wasn't the money Big Sandy was clamoring for, but Zion Jore. His boldness terrified them. Why didn't the law protect them? What were they paying taxes for? If Dolan couldn't handle this situation, why didn't he say so like a man? They'd elect somebody who could.

"Zion Jore," was the outspoken threat, "or a recall!"

Wouldn't that be something to write up?

"I'll get him," promised Sheriff Pat Dolan, inwardly writhing. "This time I'll bring him in, dead or alive! I want a dozen men on fast horses. And I want a fast horse for myself."

Whirling on the man in a white Stetson who was standing beside him, a fine-looking man, whom nobody touched even in this press, who all now watched with respect, Dolan said: "Luke, didn't you say you'd brought two of your racers up here, so you could supervise their trainin'?"

"Goblin and Mate are here . . . yes."

"Waal, I want one of 'em."

Big Sandy gasped at his audacity in commandeering horses of such worth for a manhunt. They understood, they thought, the awful reluctance of Chartres, and intensely admired the man, as he shrugged and said: "You're the sheriff."

"Then scatter!" Dolan waved at the rest. "We'll take up the trail in five minutes. Meet at the jail."

Grasping Luke Chartres by the arm, he was striding down the street to the barn where the Thoroughbreds were stabled, when a hoarse cry from the bank drew his eyes back. The mob was pointing up at the high bluff behind Trail's End, crying, as with one voice: "There he is!"

Dolan and Chartres looked, and there he was. Up there, in full view of the town, just out of rifle range that wild young being sat the wild stallion, looking down, as if enjoying the commotion he had caused.

"Mockin' us!" huffed the sheriff. "This has gone far enough!"

Zion Jore was still there, when, less than five minutes later, a dozen men, mounted on fast horses, the sheriff and Chartres on two of the fastest in the West, raced away from the jail.

Still there he was, in plain view of the imprisoned Jores,

who had heard the shots, the gong, and the posse rallying. They had divined the rest. In agony, as men and horses swarmed up the bluff, they strained at the bars and cursed their helplessness, and all the while Zion and Black Wing stood out motionless against the sky.

Chapter Twenty

THE RUSE

Still there, contempt and defiance infuriatingly expressed in his every pose, was Zion Jore, when the posse had galloped halfway up the road that wound to the top of the bluff. They thought he was going to make a stand, and, in fear of his deadly aim, some of the riders were slowing when, with a mocking wave of his hand, he whirled the stallion and was gone.

Pounding over the crest, they saw him far down, doubling back around the town toward Placer Creek and the rough hills north.

"He's overreached himself this time!" yelled Dolan to the man on the sleek racer beside him. "It ain't in reason that yellow demon can run clean away from Mate and Goblin! He's got less than a half mile's start. Luke, we've got him!"

He expected equal enthusiasm from the man who had spent a fortune in time and money to achieve that end. Getting no response of any kind, suddenly realizing that Chartres had hardly opened his mouth since he had seen Zion Jore get on his horse before the bank, he shot a glance at him. But the face of Chartres was strained on the fleeing stallion — strained out of all expression, as it had been last spring when he said he'd sell his soul for Black Wing, that he was selling. . . .

"What's got into you?" The sheriff reined his racing mount close. "You've been turnin' this state wrong-side-out for that horse! Why the chill all at once, now you got a chance? Don't you want him?"

The man turned on him fiercely. "Want him?" His voice was strained out of all semblance to the voice of Luke Chartres. "With the Handicap less than a month off? With Saval saying I've stayed out of the racing this season because I'm licked? Because I'm such a poor sport, I won't. . . . Want Crusader's colt!"

His wild laugh seemed the echo of another wild laugh to Dolan. Then what was wrong with him? Sore about using his Thoroughbreds? No. The ends justified the means. Chartres would give every horse he owned for Black Wing. Well, he couldn't worry about Chartres, now that he had a chance to make a clean sweep of the Jores.

More determined to do this than he had ever been to do anything in his official life, the sheriff gave his racer his head. Chartres, on Mate, kept pace with him. The rest of the posse dropped back. Neck to neck, the Thoroughbreds splashed through Placer Creek. Climbing out on the opposite bank, Dolan sighted the golden horse — not heading north, but streaking straight across the open sage flats — and he raved to Chartres.

"He is crazy! Givin' us a break like this! If he'd kept to the hills, he mighta shook us! But he's took to the level. Thinks he can outrun us without any trouble. He don't know what horses we got!" In his triumph, he flung at the fugitive: "Kid, you sure did overreach yourself!"

Had Zion done that? Had he underrated the speed of his pursuers, trusting to Black Wing to run away from them on the level stretches? It seemed so. For the pick of the Val Verde stables, fresh and eager to go, put their best into that race, a best that had won Chartres many a prize; a best that — to the utter dumbfounding of the men on them — brought them steadily upon the golden stallion.

As they splashed through the sage, Dolan roared: "Where's all this speed I been hearin' about? Bunk . . . that's what it is! He's had you-all hypnotized! He's fast alongside common range saddle stock. But he can't run with a real horse! Look how we're comin' up on him. Tough luck, Luke! I don't wonder you're down in the mouth."

He considered the race all but over. He was, in fact, already planning the capture. It was going to be a ticklish piece of work. As soon as Zion Jore saw he was caught, he'd turn to shoot it out. And he, Dolan, couldn't sling lead with such a dead shot. He'd have to fire the instant he got within six-gun range, and pray he was a better judge of that than this young maniac. Only a matter of seconds — he drew his gun.

But Luke Chartres, rising in his stirrups, as if his whole physical being revolted at what was happening, saw they were no longer gaining. On the contrary, the stallion was running away from them, as easily as they had run away from the posse. And he thrilled to the quick of his horse-loving heart by the smoothness and ease and incredible speed of that flight.

"Is that bunk?" he hurled at the sheriff over the pound of their horses. "He's not been running . . . up to this! The fellow's been holding him in, testing our speed. Crazy? Like a fox! And that stallion . . . look at him go! He's not running with range stock now."

Pat Dolan looked and had faith in the golden horse. Luke Chartres watched and envisaged him running from Saval's Meteor, as he now was from the pick of his string, winning Val Verde a glorious revenge.

Yet, as Zion swerved toward the wild foothills of the Montezumas, he told Dolan it was no use going on. "We can't get within miles of him."

But, even as he spoke, he was amazed to see that the stallion was falling back again. Steadily, they gained, almost within range. Black Wing was tiring. Weeks of running were telling, but, just as he decided this, Zion flashed a backward glance and, seeing them so close, bent low over his horse, and again, swiftly, effortlessly, the stallion pulled away from them.

"He's playin' with us!" swore the sheriff, furious. "That cub's made a fool of me long enough."

He drove in his spurs with such suddenness and force that Goblin shot ahead in a terrific burst of speed, regaining the distance lost, but unable to better it, unable to hold it. And, sure of this, Dolan raised his gun and, heedless of the hoarse protests of Chartres, fired at the fugitive — fired again, and again — emptied his gun, reloading at a gallop. There was no result that he could make out, save to increase Black Wing's pace, and he felt, as Chartres had said, further pursuit was useless.

Yet, doggedly, he clung to the trail. The sleek coats of the racers gleamed wet. Their jaws dropped foam but, with the staunch courage of Thoroughbreds, they strained their lungs on the steep pitches that the wild-bred Black Wing took like a bird. In a long mountain run, Dolan would have wished for a good, deep-winded cow pony under him. But he anticipated nothing like this. The chase was leading into the broken cañon country, miles north of the Picture Rocks. His one hope of catching Zion Jore was to do it before he could hole up there. Steadily that hope grew less.

But, just as he despaired altogether, he saw that Zion wasn't riding as he had been. He was riding like a drunken man, crazily weaving.

"Hurt, by heaven!" he screamed. "One of my bullets landed, all right!" Wildly triumphant, as Zion slumped to the stallion's neck, he shouted: "We've got him, Luke!"

But not if Black Wing could help it, for, strain as Mate and Goblin did, as they never had, they couldn't gain on him. They could only keep even. That was something, something they couldn't have done, if things hadn't been going wrong with Zion. Fatally wrong, it looked, for he was hanging on the side of his horse. Falling? Not yet, for he managed to pull himself back in the saddle. But every instant they thought he must drop. Yet still he clung, and Black Wing ran.

They were in the foothills now. The rest of the posse was far behind, too far to be of any service in this crisis. It was up to the sheriff and Chartres. And Black Wing was running straight for the rock-ribbed, brush-choked cañon before him.

"If he makes it," shouted Chartres, his eyes on the reeling figure, "he'll take terrible toll, as long as he's able to pull a trigger! Don't be foolhardy, Pat! A Jore with his back to the wall. . . ."

"He won't make it!" Dolan predicted hoarsely.

And he did not! Within a few yards of the cañon's mouth they saw him again hanging on the side of his horse, making a desperate attempt to regain his balance, but slowly, surely slipping. Then, losing his hold altogether, he fell to the trail. Black Wing raced on a few yards and stopped, whirling to look back.

With an effort that wrung a groan from Chartres and aroused pity in Pat Dolan's breast, Zion got to hands and knees and dragged himself toward the cañon. But when safety was all but won, he collapsed and lay still.

"Rode his last trail." Dolan was sure. "Waal, alive or dead, I said. I'd rather it had been the other, but it would have been all the same to him in the long run."

Needing both hands to bring his strung horse under control, he put up his gun, convinced he had no more use for it.

With Chartres he yanked to a stop not more than ten feet from the motionless form that lay, face up in a patch of sun, long lashes peacefully locked on restless eyes, nerveless fingers resting just on the butt of the gun at his waist.

"Tried to draw with his dyin' breath," the sheriff commented grimly, leaping down beside Chartres. "Deadly to the last. Well, he's harmless enough." The rest died stillborn, and a mighty tremor shot through him.

For, so suddenly they never knew how it came about, they were looking into a gun in a Jore's hands. And a Jore was ordering them in a cold, steely drawl: "Hold up your hands!"

Stunned, they obeyed him. They wouldn't have dared to do otherwise. For there was a flash in the blue eyes, on that wild face a madness of purpose that told them death hovered close, so close they felt its chill above their heads, while Zion, never taking his eyes from them, the black gun unwavering, sprang up unhurt and approached Pat Dolan.

So maneuvering that at all times his weapon covered both men, he jerked the sheriff's gun from his holster and thrust it in his belt. Then he explored his person for other weapons, extracting a .45 from a shoulder holster under his vest. As cautiously, then, he disarmed Chartres. Each movement as swift and deft as though often rehearsed. If he gave a thought to the rest of the posse coming at a gallop, he showed no sign of it, coolly surveying his captives.

His weird eyes flicked from Dolan's star to his face. He said simply: "You're the sheriff."

"I am," said Dolan, certain that death lay in the admission. The Jores had it in for him — with reason. Now a Jore had him — the most dangerous Jore in the clan. He expected no mercy.

He was even surprised at the few seconds of life that were

his, as Zion pointed to Chartres, so strangely regarding him: "Who's he?"

With some far-flung hope that the name might overawe him, instill in the mad brain a glimmer of reason, Dolan said: "That's Luke Chartres."

"Is he helpin' you hunt Jores?"

"No!" denied Dolan emphatically. "He's nothin' to do with me. He is. . . ."

"I know! He's after Black Wing." And Zion laughed, a sound to freeze the blood in their veins. "You thought you had got him. You thought he couldn't run. That's what I wanted you to think. I let you catch up a-purpose. So I could play 'possum on you. So I could catch you, see?"

Dolan's heart gave a mighty bound as he caught the faint ring of hoofs far below them, and to keep Zion from hearing, fighting for time, he suggested: "And now that you caught us?"

A cunning light broke upon Zion's face. He pointed to Chartres again: "That's up to him." Addressing the man directly — "If I give you a chance to save the sheriff," demanded Zion, "will you do what I ask?"

"Anything," swore Luke Chartres.

"Then," Zion ordered swiftly, connectedly, as though this was something he'd learned by heart, "go down and stop them men! Tell 'em if they come afoot after you stop 'em, I'll kill the sheriff! Tell 'em if they come back to hunt for you . . . after they do what I want 'em to . . . I'll kill the sheriff! Tell 'em to go back to Big Sandy and turn my uncles out of jail! But not till sunup tomorrow. Remember that! Tomorrow . . . just as the sun comes up. And tell 'em to tell my uncles I said to go straight to the Picture Rocks, or I'll kill the sheriff!"

Wrenching his eyes from that wild face, Chartres looked at

Pat Dolan, ashen with understanding. Hoofbeats rang loud on the hush.

"Go!" Dangerously the blue eyes flashed. "I'll do what I say I will! I'm Zion Jore!"

Hesitating no longer, Chartres caught up his horse, over the sheriff's agonized protest. "Don't, Luke! Better let him kill me than free them outlaws!"

Never had Chartres admired a man so much. However high Pat Dolan's ambition, he was worthy of it. He said huskily: "I've got to, Pat. Can't you see? He will do it! I can't be a party to it." He sprang on Goblin and swung away.

Zion stopped him. "You'll come right back," he warned, "when you tell 'em that."

Looking straight in that upturned face, so heart-rendingly weary and young, Chartres said in a strangled voice: "I, too, do what I say I will, Zion."

Chapter Twenty-One

AT A JORE'S MERCY

In the quaint vernacular of old Dad Peppin, Zion Jore might not have all his buttons, but he had more of what he did have than most men — more imagination to conceive a plot, more daring to carry it out, no fear to hamper him, no restraining doubts. His was the genius of madness.

This genius had enabled him to accomplish the all but impossible feat of capturing the sheriff, that he might hold him as hostage and force the release of his uncles. It had been easier than he expected. He had anticipated trouble in separating the sheriff from his men and had planned to lead them on and on, trusting to some fortunate chance of place and circumstance to accomplish that night what the two fast horses of Chartres had done the first hour.

Now, in that wild, wild cañon, with lilac dusk falling, he was holding the sheriff and Chartres. Cross-legged in the grass, Winchester across his knees, a few yards from where they sat, bound hand and foot, in uncomfortable postures against a boulder, he watched them, as tirelessly as a wild thing watched its intended prey. There was no doubt in his mind of ultimate success. He had done his part, and, being what he was, the posse, now thundering back to Big Sandy to electrify the whole country with news of the capture, would do the rest.

But there was grave doubt in the harassed brain of Sheriff Dolan, trussed up like a Thanksgiving turkey ready for the oven, helplessly writhing, as if already suffering the roasting that would be his, if he survived this. He'd get the horselaugh from the Jore sympathizers, from everyone, for letting a crazy kid put a trick like this over on him. Better never to leave this spot — nobody laughed at a man that died for a cause. No. His fighting blood spoke — better to live, to do it all over again. He prayed the posse would do as Chartres had told them, feared they would not, feared they would bring a force back to rescue him, and forfeit his life. For he wanted to live — to rid the world of this young menace, if nothing else.

He looked over at Luke Chartres. What was he thinking, there, in the dusk, which brought that haunted look to his face? Not fear — that, he would swear. Luke had proven his courage in coming back here, after his talk with the posse, submitting himself to other whims of this mad young fellow, when he could have gone with them and saved his own skin. In more ways than one, Luke Chartres was a mighty big man.

Now in the dusk, strainedly, Dolan burst out: "Kid, can't you ease these ropes on my legs . . . give me some freedom? You needn't be afraid I'll run . . . you, with that gun."

Zion's eyes blazed with a gleam so fierce that Dolan was forced to lower his. "How much freedom do you give Jores?"

Death hovered close then.

"How free is my dad?" Zion fiercely demanded. "You got to take your own medicine. It won't be very long. Not your whole life . . . like my father."

"See here, young man," Dolan cried earnestly, "you can't compare us thataway! It's my duty to put people in jail, if they break laws. They needn't break laws."

"You're holdin' Jores," Zion summed it up, "and I'm holdin' you."

Groaning with the same helplessness René had felt in

argument with Zion, Dolan fell silent, rather then risk further antagonizing.

Still as the grave, that deep, dark, narrow vault, where the young fellow sat with his captives. The Thoroughbreds grazed, but the stallion, golden skin glimmering in the dusk, never strayed far from where Zion was. Now the men saw him come up and, thrusting his nose beneath Zion's arm, nudge him, nickering.

And naturally, as he'd answer a human, they heard Zion say: "Not yet, Black Wing. I told you three things."

Out of the hush that fell again, Chartres asked softly: "Son, what did you mean . . . three things?"

"Why," Zion answered readily, "I got to do three things before I go home. This is the first one."

"And the second?" quietly prompted Chartres.

"Get Dad out of prison!"

Pat Dolan, leaning to listen, saw the face of Chartres flash with that look of hate Race had wondered at. That, he now remembered, the man had shown at any mention of the clan, particularly of Joel Jore. What could he have against Zion's father? This intrigued Dolan more even than Zion's calm intention to release his father from state prison. He would lose quick enough if he tried that, unless — a superstitious shiver ran through the sheriff — he was in league with the powers of darkness.

"And the third thing?" quizzed the Val Verde rancher.

"Kill Shang Haman!" hissed Zion. At their gasp of horror at this frank declaration of murder, the more awful for being spoken in this wild spot, at this dark hour, by one who had them absolutely in his power, Zion said tensely: "Shang squealed on us. But that ain't why. He killed Dave!"

"Dave?" Dolan's professional instincts were roused. A Jore he hadn't heard of? An unreported killing. "Tell us about it."

As though hungry to talk, but not relaxing his vigilance one jot, Zion told them about his cousin, Dave Jore, Abel's son, who had "growed up" in the basin with him and Eden, told it with so much feeling and circumstance, that they followed Dave's brief, blameless life, and brought up with shock at his grave with the cross. For Shang had killed him.

"They don't believe me." Deep that rankled in Zion's heart. "They believe Shang. He told 'em that you done it, Dolan. But . . . you didn't."

"No" stated the sheriff with some emotion, "I didn't, Zion."

"I know that. It was Shang. Dave was goin' out of the basin. I went with him to Sentry Crags. I said good bye, and was goin' back. Shang was on watch. I heard the shot, and I found Dave . . . dead." The rifle gleamed under the fierce clutch of his hands. "Anyhow," he went on, "I'd have to kill him. He pesters Eden. If it wasn't for the men. . . . Since they got caught, I ain't slept good for thinkin' what might happen if Shang went back."

"Zion" — Luke Chartres strained at his bonds, his face singularly white in the gloom — "Shang's gone back. He went this morning. He's been wanting to go ever since your uncles were jailed. But I kept him here till. . . . Wait!" — frantically as Zion sprang up, half whirling toward Black Wing. "Don't leave us tied up like this . . . helpless!

But already Zion had changed his mind and was actually smiling as he sat down again. "I forgot," he confided, pushing his black hair back, "my pard's up there. René can handle Shang all right. He won't let him in."

But Zion didn't know that René had left the basin to hunt him. Nor did Chartres and the sheriff know it. And they felt a curious relief at the thought that René Rand was on watch at Sentry Crags, even found a curious comfort in remembering his vigilance that had discouraged the sheriff about getting in. For they hated to think of a girl — and such a girl as rumor depicted Eden Jore — at the mercy of Shang. They despised him, using him only as men must use rotten tools if no better can be obtained. Dolan had planned to get him off, if he turned state's evidence. But this talk of a killing gave a new aspect to the situation.

"And if he's there when my uncles get home," Zion said, "they will sure handle him!"

Yes. If the Jores were freed, they would handle Shang. Seizing this opening, Dolan put the question that had kept him in dire suspense ever since Chartres had sent the posse racing for town: "How will you know if they are freed, Zion?"

Zion's laugh was crafty. "My eyes will tell me. I won't believe nothin' but my own eyes. When it gets good and dark, we're goin' to ride down to Sentry Crags where we can watch. We'll be there in the mornin' and watch 'em ride in."

Suppose they didn't come? Suppose the posse didn't release them? Suppose the Jores, once released, did not go to the Picture Rocks? Zion had sent them word that, if they didn't, he'd kill the sheriff. Well, the sheriff thought, the Jores weren't likely to be concerned about that — a solemn thought for Pat Dolan, then, that his life depended on the very men he had prosecuted so relentlessly.

Night descended on the Montezumas with silver trappings. The wind, accompanying it, played taps on the cañon's ribs of rock. A prowling coyote filled it with mad, mocking song. Chartres sat with his nameless thoughts. And Zion watched.

"Zion," suddenly the Val Verde rancher spoke, "when the sheriff told you my name, I had the impression you'd heard it before."

"Sure," Zion owned.

"Where?"

"At home."

"You mean in the basin?"

"What other home do you think I got? It's the only place I ever was, till I come out to see things. It's the only place I ever want to see again." His voice throbbed with longing.

The man sat silent for a long time. Then: "Tell me when you heard my name."

Moved by the kindness of his tone, something he hadn't known since he left home, Zion said: "I heard it twice. Once, when Dad run Sahra and Black Wing in. Long ago, that was. He said Luke Chartres would raise a howl to heaven about those two horses. And Mother said. . . ." His voice broke on her name.

"Your mother said . . . ?" The man's voice broke, too, doubtless in sympathy.

"She said Sahra was hers. She said a lot more was. But Sahra and the colt was the only things she'd ever ask of Luke Chartres. She said she wouldn't ask that for herself . . . but for her children. Meanin' me and Eden. So Dad and her could take us out of the basin and give us things. That's what she was always sayin'. I ain't sure what she wanted to give us. Things we could not get in there, I guess. We couldn't get much . . . after we lived honest."

"Honest!" cried Chartres.

"Yes. So Dad could take us away where folks wouldn't know we was Jores. But" — his eyes flashed the old hostility — "they took him away!"

"And then?" pressed the man, in a low, trembling tone.

"Then Mother didn't care what come. She used to learn us things. To be tellin' us just to have patience and God would answer her prayers. Now she don't pray. And she don't laugh or sing. That's why I'm bringin' Dad home, so she'll be happy again."

"She loves him yet?" Luke Chartres murmured, as one repeats an astounding fact to one's self.

Amazed at the question — "Bars don't make no difference with love!" — Zion shouted. "Or bein' apart or dyin', she says. She says . . . ," he couldn't go on, his thin shoulders were shaking.

After a long time, Chartres asked: "When did you hear my name again?"

Wearily Zion looked up. "When my pard come. He told us somebody was helpin' the sheriff clean up Jores. We asked who it was. He said Luke Chartres. And Mother, she . . . I found her on the couch, cryin' and sayin' to nobody . . . 'My God, why hast thou forsaken me?' "

In the dead of that fateful night under a high-riding moon and moving stars, three riders crossed the wild Montezuma to Sentry Crags to watch for the return of the Jores.

"When they go in," Zion said, all Jore again, "I'll turn you loose." — no need to state the alternative.

Chapter Twenty-Two

THE RIDER'S NAME WAS DEATH

Far up in the headwaters of Placer Creek, René Rand paced his lonely camp and kept the trail hot to the ledge above it that he might strain his eyes on the gap between two buttes to the east, where Race would first show up, when he came back. *If he came back,* René would think, all but frantic. Race had been gone five days now, each one an eternity, each one making it harder for them to find Zion. For the law was hunting Zion, too. And every day the hunt would broaden.

Why didn't Race come? Had something happened to him? Not likely; Race looked out for number one. Had Race walked out on him? No chance; Race was twice as crazy about that horse since Revel had given it to him, crazy to get possession. Race depended on his being able to persuade Zion to turn Black Wing over to him. Then what was keeping Race?

He said he'd be back the next night when he left. He'd just gone to Big Sandy to hear the latest, so they'd have some idea where to begin the search. He, René, couldn't go. He was a fugitive — something new, not to be able to go where he wanted to; to know folks considered him too dangerous to run loose; that he'd be arrested on sight and locked up, so he couldn't keep his promise to Eden. He'd do anything to do that — even the rabbit act. He'd steer clear of towns and let Race find out things, as Revel must have foreseen he'd have to, when she'd bribed Race to come with him. But if it was going to take Race this long . . . ?

175

For the seventh time that morning, and the morning was young, he climbed the ridge, scouring the glaring sage flats, with no better results. Then he dropped down on the ground to watch, although he told himself that this was the last way to bring Race, for a watched pot never boils. As if to hasten his coming, he turned his gaze to the haze-swathed Montezumas, his thoughts — where most of his thoughts had been these frantic ages of watching — with Eden in the Picture Rocks. He thought of her watching for him, as he watched for Race, in ten times the suspense. He envisaged her up in the crags, her blue eyes haunting the Picture Rocks' trail in longing and hope and fear that seemed to reach him, to reproach him for doing nothing, to urge him to do something.

Frantically pacing the wind-swept knoll, he thought of her and Revel up there alone. It worried him. He shouldn't have left them. But he couldn't stand to see them worrying so about Zion. Now, he couldn't see anything else for them. Yance and Abel would go to prison, for life, as Joel had. And they'd always be alone in that wild basin. If he did take Zion home, they'd be worse than alone. For the state wouldn't give up trying to bring Zion to justice. In time, it would win. For there wouldn't be force enough now to guard the pass indefinitely. And to see Zion taken away to face the consequences of acts he wasn't accountable for would kill his mother and sister. Better, for them, if Zion never went back to the basin, better if Dolan. . . .

A horrible fear shot suddenly through René's heart. Was that why Race hadn't come back — because there was no rush, because Dolan had got Zion?

Then his eyes, swinging back to the gap, saw that for which he had watched so long. At least he saw a mounted man. But with the caution he must now observe, he watched

until positive the rider was Race. Then, tearing down to camp, he leaped on the bay — kept up, saddled, ready to take the trail the instant Race returned — and galloped to meet him.

Riding close eagerly, he sought Race's eyes for the news he was frantic for, but feared to ask. But Race's eyes, shifty always, were on the jump now. René couldn't catch them. Nor could he get in a question.

"Kid," Race was babbling, as he yanked up, "I got something! I swear to heaven, I don't know what. It scares me . . . what I got. You've heard of Luke Chartres's runners, Goblin and Mate?"

"Sure," René affirmed wonderingly. "You can't be around race tracks, and not."

The man sputtered: "He beat 'em. Not just a plain win. He walked plumb away from 'em!" — talking of races, when. . . .

"Race, what are you talking about?"

"That horse of mine." Race blew up, his swarthy face ignited by the flame that always spelled Black Wing. "Kid, you've seen coyotes play with ranch dogs? You've seen how they lope off a safe ways, and set down and set down and laugh at 'em, till the dogs get close, then they do it all over again? Plumb tantalizin' 'em! Well, that's what Black Wing. . . ."

"But Zion," René cut in anxiously. "What did you hear about him?"

"Naturally" — Race frowned — "Zion was on him. Zion robbed the Big Sandy bank Monday, and a posse took after him. The sheriff and Chartres on Mate and . . . I tell you, kid, that horse. . . ."

"Race," the young fellow begged him, "get your mind of Black Wing! I know he's the whole show to you. But not t

me. Me . . . I've gone 'most crazy for thinkin'. Tell me what happened."

Angrily Race threw up his hands. "Holy smoke, ain't I tellin' you as fast as I can? Zion robbed the bank. A posse took after him. He decoyed Pat Dolan and Luke Chartres away from the rest, got the drop on 'em, and swore he'd kill 'em, unless the posse went back and let the Jores out of jail and sent 'em back to the basin!"

Let Yance and Abel out? "Race, did they do it?"

"So quick it made their heads ache. Think they'd risk the sheriff's life? Risk Luke Chartres's precious hide? Zion Jore" — Race's eyes had a nervous glitter — "ain't to be monkeyed with. They done what he asked. Now every loose man in the county's joined the big hunt for him."

"You mean" — René was suddenly faint — "Zion killed Dolan and Chartres?"

"No! He turned 'em loose, when he saw his uncles ride into the basin. Now he's goin' his old gait again. He told Dolan he was goin' to get his father out of the pen and kill Shang Haman before he went back to the Picture Rocks. But," added Race with a grim laugh, "there ain't much danger of his doin' that last. For Shang was in the basin when Yance and Abel got home."

Shang in the basin. But René didn't dare to think about that. Whatever had happened was over. Yance and Abel would have settled with Shang. But nobody on this earth but himself could possibly stop Zion Jore from this mad endeavor to free his father.

"He'll do it, too!" he told Race wildly, spurring back to break up camp and get to doing something, trying to get some idea what to do out of this man. "He'll do it or die tryin'. That's what'll happen. Unless we stop him. We've got to stop him, Race. Where is he? Where was he seen last? You must

know something. You've been gone. . . ."

"See here, kid!" Irritably Race swung on him. "I can find out as much as the next man. But I can't perform miracles. If anybody knows where Zion Jore is, he's keepin' it to himself. There's a big reward on him, savvy? And it piles up every day. That's what's been keepin' me . . . tryin' to pick up some clue. But all I got was the story of a cowpuncher who told Dad Peppin he'd sighted a man on a cream horse in the Montezumas, headin' south. That was yesterday. Tomorrow, you may hear he's a hundred miles off, headin' north!"

"No, you won't," René said excitedly, leaping down to get ready. "He said he was goin' to free his father, didn't he? Well, that's where he's headin' . . . south, to the state prison. Yesterday, you said? Race, we've got to head him off."

But Race was strangely unresponsive. Making no move to help René, who was hurriedly throwing their few camp belongings into the saddlebags, he sat apart, lost in guilty thought, until René was buckling the flaps.

"Kid," he said then, and he looked like a sheep-killing hound, "I ain't goin'. I hired *you* to get that horse."

It was out, at last. His eyes shifted to René to see how he was taking it. What he saw was so surprising that it might have been the first time he had seen him since that far-gone day on the tracks. He saw — not the sick, hopeless lad he had driven such a hard bargain with, bullied so mercilessly that day he got off the train in Big Sandy, but — a cool-eyed, firm-jawed young Westerner, hard as nails, fired by a desperate purpose, and adhering to a sense of obligation far greater than he owed Race Coulter.

"No, Race," — René's smile was cold — "you don't worm out of this. I agreed to get Black Wing, and I'll do it. But you've got to be there to take him. You've got to help. I can't go this alone. You know I can't show up places."

Race reverted to bluster. "You'll have to. I can't risk gettin' caught with you . . . mixed up with the Jores, like you are. A outlaw! I'd be aidin' and abettin'."

"Yeah?" René drawled. "I'm outlawed because I aided and abetted you. But suit yourself, Race. If we don't find Zion, Dolan will. And where will Black Wing be then?"

In the Val Verde stables of Luke Chartres — the mere thought gave Race fever and chills. Torn by this fear and the fear that had tortured him ever since he left the basin, he was reduced to begging. "But, think of the fix this puts me in. Zion Jore's got it in for me. Years ago, just a kid, he almost killed me over that horse. What'll he do to me . . . now, man-grown, with who knows how many notches on his gun . . . when I ask him to turn over Black Wing? No, kid, I ain't goin'!"

Sure that a stiff bluff would bring him to time, René sat down on his saddlebags. "That's right. Well, we'd better forget it. I'll go back to the basin. And we'll let Chartres take the risk."

Race stared at him, beaten. Then, sullen of face, he got up, growling: "Come on, then! Let's get it over with quick!"

But the hunt for Zion Jore wasn't to be quickly gotten over with. Mapping the probable route he would take, they rode south. Extending their horses recklessly, considering the long search that might be ahead, they hoped that Zion's pursuers would drive him into hiding for a while, so they might head him off. Riding furtively, they kept to the foothills and unpeopled places, for René's description had been broadcast the length of the state, and they ran a grave risk of his being recognized as an ally of the Jores. But three hard, hot days, and a hundred and fifty wearisome miles, gave them no clue to Zion.

Then, one evening, while René waited in camp, in the bare, desert hills near Malo Tanks, Race went into the little settlement for supplies, and brought back the discouraging news. "Just like I told you," he broke it gently, "next time we'd hear of that kid he'd be a hundred miles off, headin' north. While us and everyone else has been combin' this southern country, he's been goin' the other way. Just yesterday, he held up the Yava stage north of Big Sandy."

Bitterly René blamed himself. He might have known Zion would do the unexpected. He was too cunning to tell them where to set a trap and then walk right into it.

"And now what?" asked Race.

"Get north as quick as we can," said René.

Race didn't demur. In the days passed and in the days and days of riding back to the country where Zion had been last seen, Race conceived a vast respect for René Rand. He recognized that the young fellow's range training made him the natural leader in a mission of this kind. Out here, where he was like a fish out of water, he deferred to René in all things.

Though suspicious by nature, he came to trust René as he never had another man. Nor could he ever get it out of his mind that Black Wing was not the primary object of this hunt, that René was hunting Zion only because Zion had the stallion.

"Kid," one day, jogging along, Race said out of the thin air, "you're sure a square-shooter."

"How, Race?" René was astonished at this praise.

"The way you're stickin' to your promise to get me that horse. Most men, in the fix you was in, would agree to. But when they got well, they'd forgit all about it."

René smiled wearily. "That's why I can't forget it. The better I am, the more I remember the shape I was in."

"And that," declared Race, with a glance at René's young

face, so tired and worried beneath his sombrero, "is why you're a square-shooter. Any other man would consider the debt paid, when she gave me the horse. But you're stickin' to the spirit of the deal as well as the letter. Standin' by till I git delivery."

René put him straight. "I can't take credit for that. It jist happened we'll both get what we're after at the end of this trail. I'm out for Zion."

Yes — that was his goal, the one aim and purpose of his existence, to take Zion back to Eden. He didn't look beyond it. Strangely, there seemed to be nothing beyond it. There seemed to be no today, no tomorrow, just this riding, hiding, fighting down his horror lest Zion elude them, reach the prison, and do whatever mad thing he had in mind — just this, and allaying Race's terror of what might happen when they found him, and watching a changing landscape, by the changing shine of sun and stars, for a yellow horse.

But there was a yesterday. René lived it a thousand times — a yesterday that seemed to contain all the happiness he had ever known. Home-hungry, he had found home. Lonely, he had found kin. In that yesterday, he had found love in blue eyes, by the blue lake, in the heaven of the Picture Rocks.

Ten days on the trail, and they were covering the wild, broken mesas of the Yava without another hint as to Zion's whereabouts. Frequently, when they were near some town, René waited while Race went in for information. But Race's rare talents in his line availed him nothing. Oh, he heard about Zion, and little else, wild, fantastic rumors, that did not help.

Then, utterly without warning, bright and early one late-August morning, they came on Zion's trail, so hot it smoked.

It was up in the gaunt, sandy, forsaken Black Spout

region, the rendezvous of two-bit rustlers, horse thieves, and the like, where a man who had committed a petty offense, and made himself scarce, was said to have "gone up the Spout."

Up it, René and Race went in their quest. Suddenly, rounding a sharp bend, they came upon a camp so unexpectedly that René had no chance to slip out of sight and let Race sound out things. They had been seen. There was nothing to do but face it out, and trust to luck he wouldn't be recognized.

So they rode boldly up to the group of men gathered before the rude shelter, built in a mesquite thicket, a score of the hardest-looking men they had seen in all their journeying, and who were, they noticed with misgivings, strangely disturbed about something. The sudden arrival of strange riders here might well cause a commotion. But René was sure they hadn't caused it. Their attitude suggested an ordeal passed, as men stand, awed, stunned, amid the wreckage of a cyclone. So these men stood, too stunned to extend even the common courtesies of the range.

Uninvited, René got down. Then he saw what they were grouped about; saw the wreckage, covered by an old bit of canvas, that failed to hide its still, dark outlines from the eyes. René's eyes, as creeping horror filled him, turned, with horrible intuition, to search the remuda of horses below the camp, fully expecting to see among them a horse whose skin of gold was marked only with a jet-black wing. When he failed to see it, relief giddied him.

"Had an accident?" he asked the men, with a nod at the tarpaulin.

There was a long wait. Each fellow looked at his neighbor. Nobody wanted to speak first.

Finally one whiskery, weasel-faced individual took the responsibility on himself, laconically venturing: "You might call it that." Seeming to feel this didn't suffice, he added: "He tried to ride a hoss."

"And it throwed him?" queried René, strangely tense.

"Throwed a dead man when it did," said weasel-face.

"He told us" — shrilly this burst from a hard-faced young man — "he told us the rider's name was Death."

There was a strangled cry from Race. His face was pasty with fear.

René cried wildly: "Zion Jore told you! He's been here! When? Where's he gone?"

The first speaker gave him a long, hard look: "Nobody said it was Zion Jore. But you guessed right. Young Jore stopped here last night. And Fresno . . . that's him" — hoisting his boot toward the tarpaulin — "got infatuated with that yellow horse and 'lowed to elope with him. He figured all he had to do was git on and vamoose while the kid was asleep. But there's them as says Zion Jore don't sleep, and I believe it! Fresno no sooner hit that stallion's back than the kid was settin' up in his blankets. He whistled. The horse whirled. And Zion yells . . . 'The name of the man that sits on him is Death.' And it was."

"You mean," faltered René, "Black Wing killed him?"

"No, no," was the slow response. "I don't mean that. But he's just as dead as if he had. He was fool enough to go for his gun, and . . . he was dead, when he hit the ground."

Chapter Twenty-Three

CAUGHT

No more, now, to follow the trail of Zion Jore. No more doubt that, at last, he was definitely on his way to free his father. His reported depredations marked his course straight south, toward the little desert town where the state prison was. Residents, for a hundred miles about it, were plunged in panic. Bars were inflicted on doors to which they were strangers. Loaded guns were laid on convenient shelves or window ledges. But what use were bars and guns in this case? The wildest rumors were rife. The least credulous gave them some credence. And why not? Half the sheriffs of Arizona, hundreds of citizens, were doing their frantic best to stop Zion Jore. Yet through them he passed, invisible, save to the unfortunate few to whom he chose to reveal himself.

Among these, there was a poor Mexican wagon tramp, encamped with his wife and numerous offspring at Gila Run. Into their camp rode the young fellow in buckskin on the buckskin horse, demanding food. But they had none to give him, none for themselves even. By all their saints, they swore it. If they had, would their little ones be crying for food? Would not the *señor* believe? The *señor* had.

He had gone, but, in departing, had taken one of their horses, the best and strongest. While yet their souls bemoaned their loss, he had returned the animal, groaning under its weight of corn meal, flour, fat slabs of pork, beans, coffee. At their insistence, that they had nothing with which to pay, he had laughed. "Livin's free!" And such a feast as they had then. *Bandido,* that one? A thousand times no. Zion Jore was *muy caballero!* — but not to the Gila Run trader who had been forced to supply the feast.

By Halifax, things had come to a fine pass — held up in his own store by that young killer and, at the point of a gun, forced to take goods from his own shelves and load them on the horse with his own hands, every ounce it would carry. No, he hadn't tried to reclaim it. Look what happened to Jake Wheeler in Big Sandy, when he tried to take his money away from them Mex' kids.

"He's a fool for luck, and he knows it," Race told René, when he brought this story back to their camp on the Moqui. "He had a run-in with Zion Jore and lived to tell of it."

Since the day they had left that camp in the Black Spout, Race had proved a gloomy companion. That still, stark, tarpaulin form haunted him. He couldn't shake it from his mind. Highly superstitious, like all his kind, Revel's prophecy had sunk deep. Desire for Black Wing had kept it in the background, although he had observed that the last half had come to pass — hell had followed the horse. Now, it seemed true to him in its entirety.

"Suppose he's jinxed?" — thus, he voiced his morbid thoughts, as they trailed south through the heat and dust. "They'd have to be a hitch some place. He's too perfect. You can't get away from it, kid . . . hoodoos does follow some things. There's houses that bring bad luck to everyone that lives in 'em. Calamity trails some men. Suppose there's a jinx on Black Wing? Suppose it is death for anyone to. . . ."

"Zion rides him," René tried to reassure him.

"Yeah!" Race laughed, without mirth. "And he's what an insurance company would call a mighty good risk." And, a morbid half mile farther on, Race added gloomily: "I ain't such a good risk myself. You seen what happened to Fresno, when he tried to take Black Wing."

Fear was getting the best of Race. But he stuck. René was forced to admire his singleness of purpose. No matter what hardships they met, he never grumbled. He never murmured about the expense. Nothing mattered to him but Black Wing. But there was a limit to what his nerve would stand. Tonight, it seemed, the last straw was laid on.

He came tearing back from Dine's Post about midnight, his eyes wild, his face ghostly, as he yanked up in the firelight. "They're after you, kid!" he cried, and his rein hand shook. "That gang in the Spout figgered you out! They're huntin' for you, as hard as for Zion! They say you come out to help him bust in that prison. They've heard, somehow, you're the Reno Kid. And they've hung a bad rep on you. Say you're a gun-toter from Nevada. Kid, you can't expect me to take the risk! You go on and git the horse! I'm goin' back to Big Sandy!"

Silently René stared into the fire. It wasn't right to make Race run this risk. Race had had nothing to do with helping Zion escape that day in Big Sandy, nothing to do with the fight at the pass. These were the things the law had on him, serious charges, which would reflect on Race, if. . . .

"They're on the watch for me, too," Race confessed nervously. "That gang said there was a pair of us. They've got me mixed up with the Jores. Why, they described me so good up there at the Post, I recognized myself. Kid, I'd have to keep under cover, too. I couldn't be any help to you."

"All right." René looked up. "You go back."

But, through the night, visions of Black Wing in the Val Verde stables bolstered Race's nerve, and he carried on.

A month had passed since they had left the Picture Rocks. September was nearly gone. In the mountains, the nights were touched with frost. But down on the desert, where they were now riding, the sun was still merciless. Days, they traveled monotonous wastes of greasewood and cactus, many a day, waterless. Feed was scarce. Even Stonewall, good horse, if there ever was one, was leg-weary and worn, while Race's roan was near the end of its string. Ceaselessly Race fretted now about what this run was doing to Black Wing.

Deeper the desert closed around them, a white, glaring land, a dead land, slain by the scourging heat and drought, but holding its lovers against the charms of green lands, by the promise of its brief and glamorous resurrection, when spring rains brought it to glorious blossoming and the dainty palo verde was blazoned with gold, the giant cactus in white, waxen bloom, and others tipped with flame.

And the hunt was narrowing down. On several occasions when Race or René — for it was as safe now for one as the other — ventured to some remote habitation, they found he was only an hour, a day ahead of him. Once, Race, speechless with rapture and terror, pointed to a cream horse, just disappearing over the skyline, that had all the appearance of Black Wing.

But they never came up with him. And ever the way grew more perilous, more infested by searchers, more frequently marked by narrow escapes. Race was nearing a nervous break, and René lost heart. Only by great, good fortune could they hope to overtake Zion before he reached the prison town.

Then, one sweltering afternoon, entirely out of provisions in the foothills of the Estrellas, a barren, thinly populated region, where a stranger would be remembered for months, they came upon a prospector's camp and decided to stop. They even risked riding together up to the hut of logs and mud in the shade of a wide-spreading cottonwood, where their hail brought an old desert rat to the door.

"How's chances to buy some grub?" Race asked him.

"Bad," the old-timer replied, grinning. "And there's a mighty good reason."

"How's that?"

"Zion Jore paid me a call last night!" Although childishly pleasuring in the sensation he had created, he affected to make nothing of it. "Yeah . . . he cleaned me out. Oh, he paid me for what he took . . . twice ag'in what it was worth. But that don't help the ol' grub box! My pard's gone over to Mesquite to lay in a supply. He'll be back before dark. If you care to wait, I'll fix you up."

Race turned to René: "How about it?"

"We'll be time ahead," the young fellow thought. "And our horses need rest."

So they stripped their saddles off, nervously aware of the interest with which their host was sizing them up; alarmed, as the old fellow's curiosity got the best of his manners.

"Come fur?" he quizzed.

René dodged. "Quite a spell."

"Goin' fur?"

"That depends."

The old man chuckled. "Reckon it does. Reckon I know on what. I'll bet a stack of blue chips, I know who you be."

"Yeah?" drawled René, his heart at a standstill.

"I'll bet my hat that you're some of them fellers on the hunt fur Zion Jore."

"You win!" René's tired smile was nothing if not genuine.

But the old man didn't warm to it. On the contrary he froze up to them. "Waal," he said coldly, "I wish you luck, though I'm pro-Jore myself. You see, I knowed Jerico. So I'm bound to be prejudiced. But that young fellow's unbalanced . . . no two ways about it. And he ain't safe at large."

Whereat he retired to the hut, and they relaxed in the shade of the cottonwood. Race slept. But René's brain wouldn't let him. It kept whirling, as they say a drowning man's does, whirling back to every kind, thoughtful thing Zion had ever done for him; every golden moment with Eden; every dark hour Revel had watched over him. And by all Zion's countless kindnesses, by all his love for the loyal, blue-eyed girl, by every moment of Revel's faithful watch, her every motherly touch, he longed to halt Zion in this mad expedition but suddenly knew he could not; suddenly knew that Zion would free his father, for he had utter faith in Revel. She had said Joel would come home. How could that happen unless someone freed him?

Then, when sunset was painting the ridges below them exquisite shades of purple and gold and crimson, the partner showed up, boosting his burro up the trail to the hut, stunning Race and René, already saddling, with the bellowed announcement: "Joel Jore's broke prison!"

"By Jingo!" cried the desert rat in the door of the hut with curious satisfaction and pride. "The kid done it."

"By Jingo!" mocked the one pulling up by the steps, "you're as gullible as the rest! You must think he's got wings or somethin' . . . to do that! He was here last night. Nope" — turning to include Race and René — "the kid hadn't anything to do with it. Joel broke out on his own hook. They say he had inside help . . . some guard in sympathy with him. Of course, he's been hearin' by the prison grapevine all Zion's been doin'. And, naturally, made the break to save his son from committin' some awful crime. They're turnin' this country upside down for him!"

The relief was almost more than René could bear. For weeks he had lived in terror of what Zion might do to free his father. Now, in the reaction, a thousand thoughts raced through his brain, kept him from hearing the soft scuff of horses' hoofs in the sand behind the hut, the cautious steps of the seven armed men creeping up.

For this changed everything. Zion would hear of Joel's escape and, his mad project no longer necessary, would head back to the Picture Rocks. René felt sure of this. So sure, he resolved to turn back at once. This very night, he and Race would line out for the basin. He was turning to draw Race aside and tell him, when he froze in his tracks at the familiar command: "Hands up!"

Chapter Twenty-Four

STRICKEN

At last something had been done. The sheriff and six deputies congratulated themselves, as they disarmed and bound their prisoners. This catch, of course, wouldn't stop the howl of criticism going up. Nothing but the capture of Zion Jore would do that. But it would show that the law was still functioning.

It was more than they had expected to do, when they rushed into the Estrellas, following the old prospector's report that Zion Jore had stopped at his hut the night before. Certainly, they hadn't expected Zion would be anywhere around there, nor had they hoped much to pick up his trail. For the day-old trail of Zion Jore was about as non-existent as a sidewinder's after a sand storm.

They had been as dumbfounded as their captives, when — approaching the hut, and seeing there the bay and roan described by the Black Spout gang as the animals the Jore confederates were riding — they slipped quietly up and threw their guns on the pair, the Reno Kid, right-hand man of the Jore gang and Zion Jore's partner, and his associate, Race Coulter, whose connection with the Jores was a mystery, but who must be a bad one to be in such company.

Unceremoniously they boosted their prisoners into their saddles, roped their feet under their horses and, in sunset's red afterglow, began their triumphal procession to the nearest jail, ten miles away.

"Talk up, kid!" The sheriff was questioning the young fellow they jostled among them. "Come on! Where's Zion Jore? Where was you to meet him? What was your lay for breaking prison? Talk up! Don't pull any more of that don't-know stuff."

"I don't know," insisted René.

"Who's this *hombre?*" The sheriff hooked his thumb at Race, who was riding with head bowed down like a man on his way to be hanged. "Where does he fit into this picture?"

"No place," declared René earnestly. "I told you he just fell in with me. He was goin' my way."

"All the way, huh?" an official suggested coldly. "He's come quite a spell. From 'way back East, I hear. Figger on usin' him in that break? Come on . . . talk!" When René wouldn't, he said shortly: "Waal, don't then! We'll find someone more expert in the art of stimulatin' conversation."

Giving René a rest, he went after Race. But Race couldn't talk. He was scared too badly.

Riding along, painfully bound, racked by the jostling, while sunset's red faded to dusk, René felt mighty sorry for Race. He had been a faithful trail mate through hazardous, heartbreaking weeks. He was a pretty good scout, for all his shortcomings. He just wasn't accountable where Black Wing was concerned. His longing to possess the horse had grown on him, until it had got to be a craze, one that would never be realized now.

Oh, they'd let Race go eventually. They'd have to. Race had committed no crime. But he would lose Black Wing. For no one but himself could ever induce Zion to give up the horse. He couldn't do that — behind bars. That's where he'd be, for no jury would free him, after the things he'd done for the Jores. He'd be locked away in the same prison where Joel Jore had spent five years, in the same cell, maybe. Buried alive, as Joel had been, to eat out his heart with thoughts of the same dear folks in the Picture Rocks.

In steady progress toward that cell, his captors left the ridges and dropped into a narrow arroyo, riding between sheer rock walls that seemed to merge in the gloom, weighing and pressing on him, till he wished they'd spur up and get out of them. For, somehow, they symbolized his whole future — these grim, dark, imprisoning walls that seemed to come together at the bend in the trail just beyond and lock tight, leaving no way out. But he knew there would be a way out. Beyond that shoulder of rock, the arroyo would open up and continue to the smooth country south.

Might it not be so in his case? Might not some sudden turn of events open up a way for him? He despaired of anything like that and, despairing, was hustled around that bend at a fast trot, and there his way confronted him.

With a muffled curse, the leaders yanked up, staring. The rest, riding against them, also halted and stared. Race Coulter's head rose and froze that way, although his trembling body inclined to his captors as to safety. Wild hope filled René's heart.

For, there in the trail, coolly sitting the golden horse of the Picture Rocks, was Zion Jore — there in the trail, an impregnable barrier, the big rifle at careless ease across his saddle, but so turned that the black muzzle seemed to point to the heart of each man. And seven pairs of hands went up, as if manipulated by one and the same string. And seven pairs of eyes looked to Zion Jore for life, while they watched — afraid to speak, afraid to stir, afraid it wouldn't make any difference what they did.

Even René's blood was chilled. For the Zion here in the trail, so dangerously cool, was a sinister being, not the Zion he had known in the basin. Even in the dusk that hid so much

— yet did not hide his deadly weariness — René saw the change. There was a hard line to the jaw and, in the restless blue eyes, a cold blaze. René did not wonder that these men — brave men, they were — awaited his will in mortal fear. Zion had the look of a killer.

But there was, he saw, in that awful pause, no change in Black Wing. The horse was in perfect condition. Months he had been in constant flight, through ordeals that would have killed an ordinary horse. But he showed no sign of them. That this was due to the care Zion took of him, the way he put Black Wing's comfort before his own, René was to learn.

But at that moment he marveled and thrilled to the stallion's perfections, as he had the day he first saw him in the little green valley in the basin. Bright, in the dusk, gleamed his satiny skin as then. His head was held with the same high pride as when he'd kinged it over the mustang band. Proudly he stamped now, and René heard an iron ring. And wondered how in the world Zion had managed to get him shod?

As for Race, at this, his second close look at the stallion, all his first longing, with interest accrued in five years, swept him. But, equally keen, was his terror of the moment when Zion Jore would recognize him. He wanted to scream that he was René's friend, so Zion would spare him. But that would identify him with the Jores to these officers. He was between the devil and the deep blue sea.

Zion took no notice of Race. Fastening his gaze on the sheriff, he asked, with a nod at René: "What are you doin' with him? He ain't done nothin'. It's me you're after . . . Zion Jore."

At that cold, metallic tone, Race a thousand times preferred to take his chances with the law.

"You think you can take him to jail?" Zion's wild laugh intensified that preference. "He's my pardner!"

They stared, incapable of an answer. After a moment's cool survey, Zion reined the stallion to one side of the trail, and motioned outward: *"Drift!"*

The deputy, leading René's bay, dropped the rope as if it were a live rattlesnake and spurred out. The rest followed, all but the one leading Race's roan, and he asked, with commendable courage: "How about this one? Does he stay?"

René was about to say yes, but Race got there first, screaming, as Zion's eyes flicked to him: "No! I go! I go, I tell you! You can't leave me here! I demand the protection of the law!"

But the deputy was taking his orders from Zion Jore.

Inquiringly, Zion looked at René, but, getting no sign, said shortly: "Take him along."

René realized this was best. If Race left with Zion and him, he'd be classed with them, would be a fugitive, too, and if they were caught, pay the same penalty. This would convince them he wasn't mixed up with the Jores, and they'd turn him loose. Race could hunt them, if he chose. Race knew he'd get Black Wing for him, if that could be done.

So René thought, as the riders vanished in the gloom. But Zion still sat the saddle, motionless as a sculpted figure, until their retreat had beat itself out on the night.

Satisfied, then, that they couldn't get back in time to be dangerous, he rode back to René, changing as he came. No change he had undergone had ever been half so welcome. Suddenly he was the old Zion; his face youthful, glowing with eagerness, his eyes reflecting the old worship, as, seizing René's arms in their galling fetters, lovingly shaking him back and forth, he cried brokenly: "Gee, pard, you look good to me! You'd look good to me any time. But now . . . now I'm most wild to see someone from home."

But Zion didn't look good to René. Seen close, like this,

there was a grayness and strain that didn't come of natural fatigue, a look of physical suffering. His eyes were sunken. His cheeks were sunken. He looked the very ghost of Zion. He looked, René thought, with an awful tension about his heart, as *he* had looked when Zion carried him into the Picture Rocks.

Now, as the young fellow got down, it wasn't with his old, free, easy spring, but like an old man, carefully easing himself to the ground and doubling up, his face plucked with pain.

"Zion," René cried anxiously, "you're hurt!"

Gamely Zion grinned. "Just so you could notice it." He laid his hand on his right side. "Just nicked . . . here."

But René knew it was more, and he said hoarsely: "Cut these ropes off me, so I can see."

"It ain't nothin'," insisted the boy.

But when René was down and had pulled open Zion's buckskin shirt, baring the wound, he was appalled by what he saw.

"Zion," he tried to keep the fear out of his tone, "when did this happen?"

"When?" Zion stared at him, making an obvious effort to think. "Oh, I don't know. About a week ago . . . up around Lasco. They were takin' pot shots at me. I felt a sting. Didn't hurt much then. But" — reeling up to rest against Black Wing — "it does now . . . some."

It must hurt a lot. It would have to — a wound like that. It hadn't been much at the start. The bullet had entered his side and had been deflected by a rib, René found upon examination. It would have given little trouble with proper care. But it was badly infected now, red and ugly, getting in its poisonous work already. For, now that his need for action was over, Zion was so weak he could hardly stand and his mind was hazy.

"Zion," — René bent over him — "we've got to get out of here. We've got to get to some safe place . . . so you can rest . . . give it a chance to heal. You can't go on like this."

But Zion wouldn't hear to anything else. "No place is safe," he said wistfully, "but the Picture Rocks. An' I . . . can't rest till I get back."

His head sank to rest on the arm thrown over Black Wing's neck. With sinking heart, René watched. Presently Zion looked up. "Dad's out," he whispered. "Did you know that, pard? I'm done . . . out here. I was lookin' for you, when they nabbed you up there. I knowed you was huntin' me all along. But I was afraid you'd try to stop me from what I was doin'. Now. . . ."

Too weak to hide the homesick longing it had once shamed him to show Black Wing, he sobbed. "Now . . . I want to go home. I want to see the folks and the ol' paint rocks."

That night, encamped in a safe place, miles from the arroyo — a place as safe as any place could be for a Jore, which wasn't safe at all — the boy slept fitfully, and René sat beside him; sat, with leaden heart, under the brooding desert stars, his black eyes turned toward the Picture Rocks, hundreds of hostile miles to the north. Over Zion's heavy breathing, he seemed to hear a distracted mother sobbing that the Book had said to *let the dead bury the dead.* And, sharp on night's jet screen, he saw a sister's face, imploring.

To that face, quiet, reverent, as a votary at the shrine of his saint, René vowed: "I'll bring him home."

Chapter Twenty-Five

A RACE WITH DEATH

How did he keep that vow? Only the recording angel and René will ever know. The great saguaros — those grim sentinels that stand, century upon century with gaunt, upflung arms, witness of all the desert's savagery and tragedy — might have told something of the heroism of René Rand, as he passed beneath them, taking his wounded partner home. Or, beyond the belt of spiny growth, the gray sage might have told, or the pine and juniper that, on the higher levels, gave friendly shelter. But shrub and tree have no tongue.

And old Piney Torm — stirrup brother of Jerico Jore in the old days, and the one human being who saw them — is scarcely less silent. So the story will never be told. For René never spoke of it — never, if he could help, thought of it.

Each time they must have water, they must risk capture, and the necessity increased in degree and frequency, as Zion's fever mounted. Before food could pass their lips, it must be obtained at awful risk. No longer dared they approach human habitation, but must live off the land — that lifeless land. A jack rabbit, brought down by a shot, at all but as much risk to their own lives, was a feast. A sage hen, killed by a stone, when a shot would have been suicide, was a banquet to be remembered for days. There were days when they did not eat, days, when they ate strange, repellent things. What passed for food on that trip, René never dared to think.

All those endless, October days they lay in hiding. All

those brief, black, chilly nights they were riding, piercing a land up in arms against them. It was, to René, no longer a mystery how Zion had eluded the cleverest traps set for him, no mystery that they were doing it now.

For the wild's every sound and stir had a meaning for Zion Jore. He could tell by the flight of a desert bird if all was well, or whether its sharper vision saw something inimical to them, but not visible from their earth-bound horizon. A fleeing road runner or coyote, the distant whir of a disturbed snake, were to Zion warnings as positively as the gong that had aroused Big Sandy. And then they had Black Wing, a guard more alert, with keener sense of hearing and sight than any watchdog. His perceptions seemed to quicken, as Zion's failed.

René, who had thought he had few tricks of range-craft yet to learn, learned a thousand and one from this young fellow who had lived as wild as any mustang. In those first few days, when the infection from Zion's wound, although spreading alarmingly, did not hinder their progress, he depended on him to direct their flight, relying on Zion's uncanny instinct — sharpened by pain and his wild longing to get home — to find hiding places where there were none; to dodge posses and chance travelers; to slip them through dangerous territory, with no more disturbance than the shadow cast by the wings of a bird of passage. Even in those last few days, when delirium made it necessary to tie Zion to the saddle, René listened to his mutterings and was guided by them.

So, steadily, incredibly, by God's mercy, they passed, invisible to human eyes, through that hostile land, passed, with many a close, close call, many a terrible ordeal that left scars on René's soul that never healed.

Like this — at the desert water hole, south of Mustang Basin, Zion's fever was raging. His parched, burned body cried for water, driving them, finally, in broad day to the lonely spring. Here it was, that Zion, helped from the saddle by René, first fell and could not rise alone. Here, the first delirium came — in a swift, treacherous onslaught that tore René's heart.

He had helped Zion to the shallow pool and, supporting him with one arm, filled a cup and held it out to him. But to his dismay, Zion struck it from his hands, staggering back, horror in his fevered eyes, shrilling: "It's poison! Don't drink it! Look! Can't you see them skulls and bones . . . dead things? Things that died . . . drinkin' it!"

"Where?" cried René in amazement.

"Here! All around! You're steppin' on some. You must be blind."

Blind to this — yes, for the white, flat, sun-caked ground about was as bare as a table top. Sick with understanding, René said quietly: "You're dreamin', Zion."

That seemed to anger him. "Think I can't see? Do you want to poison me?" Suddenly, leaning close, his eyes blazing with hot ferocity: "You ain't René!" he screamed, his thin form tensing. "You're Shang! You're Shang! And I've got to kill you!"

He sprang. And René, with tears streaming down his face, struggled with him, until he fell back exhausted.

Fever's flame subsiding, Zion took the brimming cup and drank it at a gulp, and another, and another. Then, when René advised against more, he lay weakly back, his white face to the north.

Helplessly René watched him, not knowing which way to turn. Knowing Zion must have medical attention. Yet death, in more horrible guise, might be the penalty for getting it — death, on the gallows. The responsibility seemed too much. If only he could talk to Abel or Yance, so far away in the Picture

Rocks. Or with Zion's father, out here somewhere, fighting through the same dangers, to the same refuge of the Jores. But he couldn't talk to them. He must decide on this alone.

"Zion," — René knelt over the young fellow — "we can't let this run. I've got to get things . . . medicine, bandages . . . I'm goin' to hide you some place and risk ridin' into the nearest town."

Zion went wild at the thought. "They'd catch us! I'd never get back to the Picture Rocks!"

"I've got to get you well, Zion."

"Just . . . get . . . me . . . home."

"I've got to fix you up," René said steadily, "so you can get home."

Zion's eyes held René's face the longest time they had ever held to anything, turning from it, at last, to stare into sunlit space. After a time he said: "Take me to ol' Piney's, then. You remember, I told you about Piney. On the Moqui, his place is where the river forks. He's a friend of the Jores. Dad used to talk a heap about Piney. I hunted him up and rested there, when I come down. He'll fix us up. But we'll just get things . . . and go on. We can't stop. We ain't . . . got time."

No, there was no time to lose in getting Zion home.

In feverish haste to be going, Zion raised on one arm, whistling Black Wing to him. Taking that velvety muzzle in his hands, looking deeply into those all but human eyes: "Home, boy." — René heard him say. — "Home . . . to the Picture Rocks."

As eagerly the small ears shot up. "You've got to take me," Zion charged Black Wing, "you and René. I can't look out for you, no more. You got to look out for me."

The stallion nickered softly.

A hand twined in the golden mane, Zion tried to rise, but sank down with a groan. Setting his teeth on pain, he put the other hand out to René. "Help me."

"But we can't go yet, Zion. You ain't able. You couldn't stick to the saddle."

"Then, tie me on."

It was useless to argue with him. René was helping him on Black Wing, when Zion fell back against him. "Pard," he faltered, in trembling shame, "I just thought. . . . Something in my head ain't right. I get notions . . . like a while ago. I . . . ain't safe for you." Before René could grasp what was in his mind, Zion unfastened his gun belt and handed it to him. Then, steadying himself against Black Wing, he drew the big rifle from its scabbard, and placed it in René's hands. "Reckon," he said, his lips quivering, "I won't ever be usin' it again."

On the gray dawn of the second day following, they approached the sequestered cabin of Piney Torm at the forks of the Moqui. The old frontiersman saw them coming, recognized the golden buckskin on whose back was roped the inert figure of Zion Jore, and reached inside the door for his rifle, before stepping out to meet them. But, seeing that the rider with him wasn't a deputy with Zion captive, guessing who he was, this friend of the Jores, he threw down his gun and wrung René's hands.

"I've heard of you, young man," he cried huskily. "I've heard everything you've done, since that day you helped Zion git away in Big Sandy. And I'm almighty proud to shake your hand." Fearfully, his eyes went back to Zion. "Is he . . . ?"

"No," said René.

But Zion seemed so near it, when they got him in the cabin and laid him on Piney's bed, and Piney's old face assumed such seriousness as he examined Zion's wound, that René had to strain his voice to ask, "Will he . . . make it?"

"If he was anybody but a Jore," Piney made slow reply, "I'd say no."

"But Jores die."

Piney nodded. "Hard . . . though." And, a busy moment later: "You can't scarcely kill a Jore. They're well nigh indestructible. It's the spirit in 'em. It holds 'em up when the flesh is gone. If this shack was to burn," — he overcame the habit of silence to illustrate the Jore spirit, as he set a pan of hot water by the bed, and ripped up a clean flour sack for bandages. "If this shack was to burn, what would be left? Just a pile of ashes, with that stove stickin' out, warped some, but there . . . recognizable. All ash, but the iron. Waal, Zion's all burned up now but the iron in him. It may break down in time. Inside a week, I'd say, if he was anybody but a Jore. But he's Jerico's grandson, so . . . let's hope."

Then, talked-out, he silently did all he could for Zion's comfort, cooked René a hot breakfast, and abruptly announced his intention of riding to Moqui for medicine for Zion. But René halted him, as he was riding off, to ask if he'd heard anything of Joel.

Piney shook his head. "And no news in this case is best. I hear they're holdin' an investigation at the prison. Think some guard helped him."

"He'll be apt to stop here, won't he?"

"I'm hopin' not," said Piney gravely. "Possemen's as thick as fleas. I wouldn't want you boys to stop a minit, warn't that you had to."

Then he was gone, and René sat by Zion, trying to hope. But, looking at that wasted face, now overcast with an unnatural, bluish flush, the most he dared to hope was that Zion would live to reach the Picture Rocks. All day he had babbled of the basin, was babbling now.

"It's dead here, Eden," René caught. "I'm goin' out. I

can't stand it . . . shut up."

His burning eyes fell upon René beside him, seeming to note for the first time the clothes he was wearing. For joy and wonder illumined his face. "Dave," he whispered. "Dave," — laying a trembling hand on René's buckskin — "where did you go, when you left yourself behind? I called and called . . . but you was gone. Dave, don't leave me again. We'll have . . . big times."

Happy in the big times he and Dave would have, he lay so quietly René thought he slept. Weariness closed his own eyes. The next he knew, Zion was struggling up, panting: "Black Wing . . . hears something."

René leaped to the window. Stonewall was grazing peacefully in the yard. But Black Wing's head and ears were up, and he was making that peculiar whistling noise that was his warning.

Running outside, René looked in all directions, but saw nothing. Yes. A half mile to the west, a hawk had started from its nest in the top of a dead pine, screaming — enough for one who had studied wild lore under Zion Jore.

Scrambling to the roof of the cabin, he scanned the country in that direction. Almost instantly there flashed into his view a band of mounted men, coming at a fast trot through the pines.

"Riders comin'!" he called to Zion, as he leaped down and burst within.

"Then," said Zion shrilly, "let's get goin'."

There was nothing else for it. They couldn't risk the faint chance that the men — a posse, beyond a doubt — would pass this cabin up or, finding them here, fail to recognize them. They would have to hide out until it was safe for them to come back.

Somehow, René got Zion on Black Wing's back and roped

205

him there. His own foot was in the stirrup, when it occurred to him they might not come back. Knowing everything Piney had was at their disposal, he raced back and ransacked the cupboard, rolling the food in blankets stripped from Piney's bed and, emerging with the bundle, he tied it behind his saddle.

As he swung on Stonewall's back, the posse lifted over a rise, saw them, and gave chase. It was the closest call yet. But they shook them off in the rough hills north. In the terrible days that followed they eluded others. And always, grave as this menace was, René realized that the most dangerous contestant in this race for the Picture Rocks was not the law, but Death.

Chapter Twenty-Six

THE SACRIFICE

Still victor in that grim race, although often he had to look to make sure of this, René rode out in a gap between two buttes, that bitter dawn that ushered November in. Reining up, hauling on the rope to stop Black Wing, who, instead of being led, was forging eagerly ahead, René cried, in breaking tones: "Look, Zion!"

There was no movement in the still form on Black Wing's back and, terrified lest the race was lost, René cried again: "Zion, look . . . the Picture Rocks!"

Ah, that power to force Zion's eyes apart, giving him strength to turn his head, while silent, happy tears flowed down his wasted cheeks. Zion looked and looked — at the great, fluted cup, towering over the black range against the lightening sky, but a few miles away. Black Wing stamped impatiently. All night he had sensed the nearness of his home range and towed Stonewall along.

"Home!" René cried though tears of great joy. "We'll make it, Zion."

But they couldn't go farther then. It was getting too light. They would have to find a place and hide till night. The country swarmed with searchers now. He had sighted three posses from their hide-out yesterday.

"Tonight," René promised Zion, praying that he would be in time, "we'll be home."

But Zion's sunken eyes, fixed on the split in the great cup, mirrored such agony as could never have been inflicted by death's victory. "We can't . . . get home," he moaned.

"Sure we can. When dark comes."

"We'll never . . . get home. There's men there. I see fire."

In sudden terror René's eyes swept the entrance to the pass, where once had blazed the campfires of Dolan's men. He saw nothing.

"Below," moaned Zion, "that . . . little cañon."

Then, from a small notch south of the pass, René saw a wisp of blue smoke curling up. A man was there, climbing through the jack-pines to the pass, and René knew that guards were camped at Sentry Crags, posted there to keep in Yance and Abel — to keep out Joel and Zion and him. His heart seemed to die in his breast then. So far, so desperately, they had fought to this haven. Now it was barred to them.

He was almost glad to see that Zion had relapsed into that coma he had been in most of the time since leaving Piney's cabin. He lay limp upon the stallion, his black hair mingling with the golden mane. He wasn't suffering. He was more dead than living, only the iron in him still enduring. René knew he must get him home tonight — or never. Iron couldn't last forever.

High on one of those broken buttes, behind which Zion had raced the posse to Sentry Crags, René found an overhanging shelf of rock, wide enough too conceal their horses, and with a niche far back under the sloping roof, where Zion would be protected from the wind that blew with a cutting edge and the smell of snow.

Snow freighted the clouds now heavily, obscuring all hint of the rising sun. Big, wide-spaced flakes were falling, the beginning of a real snowstorm, the first of winter, early — even up here.

Fumbling, with cold-stiffened hands, he untied Zion and

carried him into this shelter. He dared not build a fire. But he covered Zion with Piney's blankets, and, fearing this wasn't enough, although bitterly cold himself, he spread his own coat over Zion, who, heated by a fatal flame, did not feel the cold.

Then, too worried to rest, to think of eating, although some of the bread and venison he'd brought from Piney's still remained, René went out to the edge of the shelf and stared off at the Picture Rocks, crouching there, shivering, studying the ground for some way to get past the guards. It seemed hopeless. From their camp in that protected cañon, the guards could view all approaches to the pass. They would watch against anyone making a break at night. Abel and Yance played that trick on them. They couldn't be fooled the same way twice. Yet he had to get Zion home tonight.

"Pard. . . ." Zion's faint cry reached him.

Crawling back, René found him fighting at his blankets, feverishly insisting: "Someone's . . . comin'."

René listened. He could hear nothing. He thought Zion was growing delirious again. "It's the wind," he told him. "It makes queer noises . . . howlin' through these rocks. It's snowin', Zion. Comin' down fast. Snow makes things sound different. See Black Wing out there . . . restin'? He'd let us know if someone was around."

"Someone is!" insisted Zion wildly. "Go see."

To quiet him, René went out and looked. He even climbed to the top of the ledge. But in all that vast scope of broken cañon and mountain, already taking on a tinge of white, he saw nothing he shouldn't see but, going down to tell Zion, he saw that Black Wing was uneasy. His head was up, and he was looking all about, his nostrils working, as though he weren't sure in what direction lay the danger he warned of, but drawing that peculiar whistling breath.

Racing back to the ledge, René scanned the landscape again. There was no sign of anything hostile to them. No tracks marred the thin, white covering that lay over everything. But he was nervous, too. Black Wing never gave a false alarm. Was he warning of the nearness of that dangerous contestant in this race, as dogs are said to howl at its dread approach?

In mad haste to refute this, he plunged down the slope, bringing up short at sight of a man, who was standing there beneath the wall, silently watching him. Instinctively René reached for his gun. But he never drew. Nor was this because the man had the drop on him, or had made any threatening movement. But because his dark-ringed, hollow eyes were blue, a rare and piercing blue; because his face, so grimly set in seams of anguish, with all the bronze worn off, was the face of a Jore; because, unkempt, as this man was, dressed in mismatched odds and ends of clothes — there was about him a dash and daring that might have won any woman to renounce it all.

His lips moved, almost without sound. "Am I in time?"

At René's nod — "Thank God!" — said Joel Jore. He leaned weakly against the wall. "Piney told me. I stopped there. I've come night and day since. I saw you come in here. Where is he?"

René showed him where Zion lay. But he didn't follow him in. He couldn't bear to witness that reunion. He could hardly bear the echoes that came to him, a man's crying, great, racking sobs that broke him up, the delirious joy of a homesick, dying young fellow that man had parted from five years ago and had never expected to see again, now seeing him — like that.

After a bit, when all was quiet, René went back. Joel knelt on the cold stones, holding Zion in his arms. Zion's eyes were shut. He seemed in final sleep. But René heard his whisper: "Gee, Dad . . . gee." And, with a confidence that made René's eyes smart, he added: "I'd a-got you out . . . I bet."

"Sure," Joel said, as confident.

"But you . . . beat me . . . to it."

The man's arms tightened. "Thank God, I could, son. Why did you do it?"

Zion seemed to be rallying his thoughts. They must have been scattered far. His voice seemed to come from afar. "For mother. She missed you." His smile was piteous. "It hurts . . . missin' folks." He sighed, and slept.

Gently Joel laid him down and, covering him, groped his way out. Silently René followed him. For a long time the man stood staring at the great dome. What must it have meant to him? Everything he loved in life lay within those whitening rims.

He turned abruptly. "Tell me about them. I've heard everything that outsiders is mixed in. Lots of news goes to prison. I've heard all you've done. I've thanked you a thousand times . . . in my cage. I never hoped to do it face to face. But I'm doin' it, son, from my heart."

René said: "Don't."

"But" — Joel flung a hand up at the big cup — "of what goes on in there, I never hear. Not a whisper. How's my wife? And my little girl?" A sad smile crossed his weary face. "I keep forgettin', Eden will be a woman. Tell me about them."

As hungrily as René, that May day on the far off track, had listened to Race tell of the Jores, for the pleasure of hearing someone speak of his homeland, did this Jore, crouched there beneath that ledge, the snow beating about them, listen to René — now inextricably a part of the Jores' red history — tell of home. If the young fellow, in his love and longing, showed his heart in this talk of Eden, it must have had her father's full approval, for he begged for more.

When René reminded him — "You'll be seein' them soon." — pain that he was at a loss to understand twisted Joel's face out of its seams.

"When I hear what Zion was doin'," said the man, when he had stored in his heart every scrap of this talk of home, "what he hoped to do, I about went mad, and made the break. I'd found friends . . . even in prison. They helped. All along the line, friends helped. I just aimed to get Zion back. And" — his eyes, fixed on the great cup, flashed naked hate — "settle a score of long standin'. But I hear Shang Haman never come back from the basin. So my brothers must have settled for me."

After a time, he said: "Just one thing, and I'd be at peace with the world. Luke Chartres. . . ." His eyes now blazed with a light of personal outrage. "How could he help the sheriff for that horse? What kind of stuff is he made of? And I . . . I was fool enough to think that with me out of the way. . . ." His laugh was a brittle thing that broke in his throat.

They sat in silence, while the snow went swiftly on, hanging wreaths on dead boughs, shaking out the white folds of its enveloping shroud, drawing a veil between them and the great dome, casting over the wild scene a light that made all seem unreal, spectral.

Joel asked suddenly: "You know there's a watch up there?"

"Yeah. Zion spotted their fire."

"Have you made any plan for gettin' in?"

"Not yet. I just know I am gettin' him in . . . tonight."

The man's eyes kindled at this spirit. But he shook his head. "Tonight" — his voice broke — "will be too late. We've got to beat that. Revel will be wantin' to see Zion before he . . . goes. Zion must see his mother. Son," he said tensely, "we must get him home today."

Tears stood in René's eyes. "How?"

"The guards up there don't know we're together. I can draw them off, while you and Zion slip in the basin. I'll ride out near enough so they can see who I am. They'll come for me, and I'll run. It's not likely they'll follow far, for they'll have orders to watch that pass. So I'll drop from my horse and make a stand in that draw you can see from here . . . just down the trail. I'll have to, for my horse is too fagged to run. But I can keep 'em occupied, and, if some have stuck to camp, they won't lose any time comin' to help their partners, knowin' they've got Joel Jore, the lifer, cornered. There's nothin' to it, René."

René cried earnestly: "You'd never get out of there."

"I don't expect to."

René's voice trembled. "You mean, you'd die, or go back to prison for the rest of your life, so Zion can spend his last moment at home?"

Joel Jore answered: "I'd die every day of every year left to me for Revel. I've died every day of every year I've been down there, thinkin' of the wrong I done her . . . in ever lovin' her, lettin' her love me . . . a Jore. I don't expect to get away from that . . . ever. I don't deserve the happiness I feel now . . . doin' this for her."

"Then," pleaded René, loving him as he never had another man, "make her happy, too, by goin' home. You take Zion in! I'll draw the guards off. It won't matter much if I'm caught. I ain't wanted for anything serious."

"You've done enough for the Jores." Joel's heart was in that smile of thanks to René. "Too much . . . if I didn't feel a Jore would reward you. And it's doubtful if they'd follow you. This is my job. The snow will be a big help . . . it will hinder their aim, and be as a screen for you and Zion. And now, promise one thing, whatever happens to me, you'll go on with Zion. You won't turn back, no matter what."

"It's hard to promise."

"Hard, yes. But that's your job."

René promised.

"Then" — tightly Joel clasped his hand — "we'll carry this through all right."

"When?"

Joel got up. There was a radiance on his face, as if the sun had suddenly emerged to shine on it and nothing else. But this glory was not of the sun, buried above gray cloud drifts, more thickly spilling their cargo of snow.

He said quietly: "Now."

Chapter Twenty-Seven

THE HOME STRETCH

High in the spires, through driving snowstorm, as through rain and shine, blue eyes haunted the Picture Rocks trail. Long, long weeks they had watched in awful longing and fear, for sweetheart and brother, for father, as well, since news had reached the basin that he had broken prison. Of late, with such wild hope as heart never dared before, did this daughter of a Jore watch for the coming of yet another. Now, as her gaze left the trail, straying fleetingly over that wild, grand, wintry panorama, her expression crystallized into wonder.

Excitedly she whirled on the sentinel. "Uncle Abel, riders just dropped in behind that flag-shaped butte."

"That's queer," said Abel, frowning and striving to pierce the snow between. "Nothin' to come from there but wolves. Who'd be prowlin' up in that wilderness? None of the guards. They're in camp . . . all six of them."

Her upturned face glowed with eagerness. "Do you suppose that it's. . . ."

"Chartres? No, lass. He'd be alone. And he'd come from Big Sandy."

"But it could be," she insisted pleadingly. "Something could take him out of the way. Somebody could be with him. Somebody, who had to come. There's bound to be a lot of red tape. It could be, couldn't it?"

"It could," he was forced to admit, "but it ain't. You're buildin' false hopes, Eden. That's too much for even Luke

Chartres to swing. It's just a pipe-dream."

But she said, with a faith that touched him: "No, it's not. It's one dream that's coming, true. I know it. He'll come. And when he does" — never did hope star eyes to such brilliance — "we'll be through with all this." Her gesture seemed to sweep into nothingness the law's grim guardians, the contested pass, the eternal rims she stood upon, even the Winchester, propped against a rock, within easy reach of Abel's hand.

But Abel Jore knew better than to dream. Always, dreams turned into nightmares — for Jores.

Yet, as intent as the girl, he watched that butte, as excited, too, when one of the riders she had seen emerged from behind it — too far off, too snow-obscured for recognition. But as he came on, more in the open, they knew by his horse — a black, they had never seen — that it wasn't the Val Verde rancher. Before they could study him further, he dropped into a ravine, and was lost to sight.

Glancing back, Abel was surprised to see no sign of the other riders. "Funny they don't show up. Sure you seen more?"

"Yes. It was just a glimpse. But I counted three."

Definitely uneasy, Abel Jore picked up his rifle, wiped the snow from it carefully, made sure it was ready for any emergency, and then crouched, waiting. Beside him, a slim, little, snow-powdered figure, crouched Eden. The eyes of both, straining on the end of that ravine where the black would emerge, saw his black head bob out, and, a moment later, he struggled up the steep bank to level ground.

Then they saw him through that white, slow, drifting veil of snow, across too wide a space to make possible the distinguishing of any feature. But something in his riding, some dearly remembered swing, shrieked his identity to them.

"He will come," Joel Jore's wife had said, "through snow and ice and storm."

Now he was coming — coming, although he knew the pass was watched, or he wouldn't have taken that rough route. Coming, in reckless defiance of it, they thought, in his desire to get home, right into the open, where, in a moment more, the guards would see him.

"Quick, lass" — the nightmare had commenced — "bring Yance! I can't fire the signal without drawin' the attention of the camp."

But the small, taut, snowy figure did not stir. The blue eyes — hopeless, wide, and fearful — never left her father.

"Go! Get Yance!" said Abel huskily.

But she whispered, with fear-frozen lips: "There isn't time."

Nor was there. Before she could reach the cabins, whatever was to take place here would be all over. There was time for nothing, except to watch that loved form coming through the storm, but — not to them; to die a thousand deaths; to pray that Dolan's men be stricken with blindness; that God make it snow so fast — anything, so the guards didn't see him.

But, mocking their prayers, there was an actual lessening in the fall. Even before they feared, the guards saw Joel. For all was wild commotion in the camp down there. Men were running from their tents, pitched in the jack-pines, others already springing to their saddles. And Joel, as if just aware that he had been seen, was spurring his jaded horse madly toward the pass.

"He'll never make it!" Crazed with his sense of helplessness, Abel paced the crags. "They'll cut him off before he gets halfway in. He must see that as well as us. Why don't he turn and run? This ain't like him. Reckless, he was, but cool in a crisis. Prison can't have worked this change. Girl, there's something funny going on."

She saw nothing but her father riding to death or capture and those six, hard-riding forms bearing down on him. And she moaned. "Oh, stop them! *Do* something!"

"There's not a thing I can do," Abel groaned. "They're out of range. They'll get him before they ever come in reach of my gun."

But he lifted the gun and fired six fast shots.

"When that happens," he said grimly, "I'll need Yance."

They had a faint hope, then, that it might not happen. For Joel seemed to realize that he couldn't get in. They saw his head turn toward the oncoming men, saw him yank his plunging horse to a stop and, for one awful instant, in which a howl of recognition went up, look about him in apparent confusion, then, wheeling straight away from the pass, strike off down the Big Sandy trail.

"Lass," cried Abel Jore, "them other riders. . . . Joel's up to something. Do you reckon . . . ?"

No! She knew. Her gaze, flashing to that butte, had been stopped short by sight of a bay horse, dark against the snow, and, bright as a patch of sunlight on it, a buckskin. And she screamed: "It's them! I see Black Wing! It's René and Zion! Dad's luring the guards off, so they can get in!"

Now Abel saw them, waiting, unseen by the officers, who were in hot pursuit of Joel, and almost far enough down the trail to permit René and Zion to beat them to the pass. They were, too, almost in shooting range of Joel — in range. For they heard snow-muffled shots. Saw Joel leap from his horse to the shelter of the trailside undergrowth, and run for the draw beyond.

"He'll make it!" Abel cried, with a mighty throb of thanksgiving. "He can hold 'em back there, till me and

Yance. . . ." — then broke off to curse a fate that had ever been the implacable enemy of the Jores.

For suddenly, out of the storm, a rider had loomed, directly in Joel's path. An enemy, whoever he was, unless — wildly they prayed he was that other rider for whom Eden had so hopefully watched.

But Joel, finding himself between two fires, cut off from the draw, where he had hoped to hold the guards while René and Zion slipped in the pass, was forced to take refuge among the boulders beside the trail — meager shelter, but enough to daunt six of the most dauntless men, when held by a Jore with his back to the wall. The guards pulled up in sharp respect. And the fateful rider pulled up, uncertain what course to take, then, circling those rocks, rode like the very wind to join the guards.

In this respite, Eden's eyes flew back to the ravine, and she cried, her tortured soul in her words: "They're coming!"

Yes! They were coming down the home stretch at last at a headlong gallop, the long mile from the ravine's end to the portals of the pass; coming, with that grim contestant, in this race for home, fighting to hold second place in the whirlwind finish.

For the deputies, stationed here by Sheriff Dolan, who had deserted their post in their endeavor to capture Joel Jore, now saw the other fugitives breaking in. And, leaving two of their number to guard the trapped convict, lashed madly for the pass.

"It's a stand-off for distance." Abel's hand quivered on his gun, in eagerness to do what he could when the time came. "But Dolan's men's got the best footin'. Zion can make it on Black Wing! But René. . . ."

Out of the snow behind them lunged a horse, and Yance flung off.

"They're back . . . all three," Abel explained the situation. "René and Zion's breakin' in. Joel's tolled the guards off. They've got him cornered in them rocks."

Rushing to Abel's side, Yance looked. Up from the left, through the deceptive snow haze, he saw the guards pounding and, down from the right, neck to neck, a bay horse and a buckskin racing. His eyes fixed on the buckskin, his clenched fists beating the rocks before him, as if that would hasten their coming, he was yelling: "Black Wing can beat that! What's holdin' him back?"

Suddenly, they saw the pale horse pull away from the bay, saw a fast-widening stretch of snow between. For the first time, saw Black Wing run. Run, with neck outstretched, body hugging the ground, mane and tail astream. Run, with that low, smooth, space-consuming stride, inherited from a long line of racing kings. They saw Crusader's son, drawing heroically on every trick, trait, and attribute of his glorious heritage to bring the helpless grandson of old Jerico to sanctuary.

For, now, it appeared, Zion was lashed to Black Wing's back. They glimpsed his white, senseless face in the golden swirl on Black Wing's neck, as the guards, seeing the most wanted of the three in danger of reaching safety, goaded furiously.

"Get set!" Abel's drawl had a steely ring. "They're about in range! They've forgot there's guards up here! Don't kill unless we have to. But stop 'em!"

Shoulder to shoulder, the Jores, known as two of the most dangerous men in the West, crouched behind those rags of rocks, coolly biding their time — two brothers, rejected by the world of men and hence grown nearer, dearer to each other than all the world beside — except for that third brother, out there, at the world's mercy. And Joel's willingness to forego a man's life and a man's death, that his son might have both, inspired them with a determination to insure this and to sacrifice as much for him, made them dangerous.

"Now!" Abel's gun blazed.

Between the guards and the entrance to the pass, there dropped a curtain of hot lead, harmless, if they didn't try to pierce it; deadly, then — death for anyone but a Jore, or a friend of Jores, to go behind that screen. It fell and stayed there, the levers of those rifles working almost with the speed and precision of machine guns, while Zion Jore — all unconscious of their roar, dead to the fact that over him was falling the shadow of the home rims — passed within the protection of that leaden hail.

Then, the guards, cheated of this victory, swerved their horses from the hot face of that screen but, seeing still a chance to cut off the Reno Kid, spurred straight toward him.

Seeing them coming, René thanked fate he had released the stallion, trusting him to take Zion in alone. All but forgetting his own danger, in wonder at Black Wing's running, even slowing to turn back to Joel, then remembering that Zion wasn't home yet and his promise not to turn back, he settled down to gain the safety of that leaden screen himself.

Steadily the Jores' guns blazed, while Joel, hearing them, placed his faith in them and watched in awful suspense from his shelter in the rocks, while the rider, who had driven him there — a fine-looking man, in a white Stetson — thundered after the guards, cursing, as a sensate thing, the snow that had made him an hour late with the message that would have prevented all this.

Eden Jore, who had risked life in her race down that steep, slick, icy cliff, long before the shooting began, tore with all the frenzy of despair at that rock barrier on the floor of the pass. Getting an opening in it just as Black Wing plunged up and seeing her brother, all frenzy left her. The long suspense was over.

There, with the black walls soaring a thousand feet above her — piled as high as grief for the Jores this day — she loosed Zion's bonds and drew him down into her arms. And there, surrounded by the cold snow and the cold rocks, she gently rocked him back and forth.

"Eden," — his opening eyes focused on that sweet, sorrowful face with joy hardly of this earth — "Eden, you was right."

She didn't seem to know what he was talking about.

"About out there," he murmured. "It's better here. I'm home . . . to stay."

To stay. Two pine crosses now.

He stirred. "Where's René?" For he hadn't known when they had roped him on for this mad dash home.

Over the shooting that was one prolonged roar, she heard the pounding hoofs of Stonewall, and, in an instant more, René dropped down beside them. One look at his thin, strained face told Eden more of the story than pine and cactus could, had they tongue, or even old Piney Torm. And all the love and gratitude of her loyal heart were forever his.

"You brought him home." This was her simple greeting.

"He's not home . . . yet." René's smile — for Zion's benefit — struck her to the heart. "We must get him home . . . quick."

She understood.

Lifting Zion — with tragic ease, for he had no weight — René put him on Black Wing's back. He was reaching for the rope to tie him there, when Zion weakly waved him back. Insisting, with the spirit that would be the last thing to die in him: "Not . . . like that. I'm goin' back with my tail up. Like I always seen myself . . . goin' back to the Picture Rocks. Pard, give me my gun."

Slowly, with Eden and René on either side of him and the big rifle in his hands, Zion Jore rode down the home trail, the iron left, when all else was ash, holding him erect in the saddle.

Erect, he rode in sight of the cabins by the lake, across from the painted bluff. The dogs ran out with a welcoming clamor. A woman came running, a black-clad woman, with face of marble. His heart aching with pity of the shock awaiting her, René looked away and saw — with shock to himself, in his own old cabin door, eyes glued on Black Wing — Race Coulter.

Chapter Twenty-Eight

GOOD BYE

Up the steps to the big house, René carried Zion. But when he would have borne him in, Zion resisted with all his failing strength.

"Not in there!" he protested. "Don't shut me up. I want to be out . . . where I can see the lake and the ol' paint rocks."

Since the cold could no longer hurt him, they dragged the couch from before the fireplace out to the west porch, and there they laid him, under the protecting pelt of the big grizzly he himself had brought down.

There he lay, head pillowed high, the big rifle, to which he still clung as a faithful friend, across his lap, his restless eyes eagerly feasting on the dear, familiar scenes that had haunted him through all his wanderings — with joy unspeakable, on mother and sister, who masked their own heartbreak to smile bravely back; on the painted bluff, whose grotesque, savage host seemed, through swirling flakes, to come to life, to caper and dance, in high carnival over his return; on the lake, dimpling for him, as soft snow petals touch its ruffled surface and, dissolving, became a part of it; on the white hills he never more would roam; on the white walls that, once more, shut him in — shut out every troubling thing and seemed to fold him in their mighty arms.

He closed his eyes, tears of happiness welling from beneath his lashes, sighing, happily: "Here everything likes me."

Seemingly, he had no memory of that meeting with his father. Or, if he had, he thought of it only as a dream, one of his many, many dreams of home. René was thankful this knowledge was spared Revel. Looking at her, bending over Zion, smoothing his tangle of long, black hair he believed God had spared her any divination of this. She could not be so brave, must surely have lost her reason, utterly, had she known Joel was fighting for his life at the very gate of home.

Quietly rising, he slipped off the porch and led the horses to the corral. But he didn't turn them in. He just stood, listening, his eyes on the snowy crags, not knowing what course to pursue. He wanted to go to Joel. But a solemn stillness now hung over everything. Whatever the outcome, temporarily, at least, the fighting was over out there. And he might be needed here.

"Kid, what was that shootin'?"

He turned to see Race beside him. Race had stuck like a burr to him since he came. But this was René's first word with him.

"It was Yance and Abel, Race. Joel was with us. He's cut off."

Soberly Race said: "That's tough." He studied René for a moment's space. "You're all in, kid. Go rest. I'll put the horses up."

"I ain't puttin' 'em up. They may be needed. No tellin' what may happen out there. Yance and Abel won't stand by while they take Joel. If there's any more shootin', I'm goin'. I'm just waitin'."

Waiting with him, his eyes on the crags. "It's tough," said Race and, with a back nod at the porch: "Things like that . . . tough."

There was a new note in Race's voice. Now, as he looked at Black Wing, there was a difference in his expression. The

225

greedy light his eyes had always reflected, when the stallion was in his sight or thoughts, was conspicuous for its absence. He was, René observed, changed in every way, subdued, chastened.

"A lot of water's run under the bridge, since we parted in that arroyo, kid." Thoughtfully Race pushed up a pile of glistening snow with his boot toe. "They let me go that same night. Had to talk hard, though. And I come here, fast as I could travel. The Jores let me in to wait. Give me your ol' cabin. There I've been. Oh, they treated me all right . . . fed me and let me alone. First time in my life I really was alone. Sort of got acquainted with myself. Didn't like myself much." With sudden, startling passion, something almost of dislike in the look he flashed at Black Wing. "I wisht to heaven I'd never seen that horse."

Stunned by this speech, René could only ask: "Why, Race?"

"He's give me nothin' but grief. That's all he's give you, too . . . and everyone who's had anything to do with him. You forget all that . . . lookin' at him. But" — a shudder swept the man — "Fresno ain't lookin' at him. Nor Zion won't be long! Nor Joel. Kid," he somberly declared, "this is the blackest day the Jores has known. And just when I thought things was breakin' for them. Do you know Luke Chartres has been here?"

"What?" cried René dazed.

"No tellin' how many times. But twice since I came. You'd think he was one of the clan. Oh, I ain't stringin' you! That's how I got in. Sheriff Dolan wrote Chartres a passport in here, and I got him to pass me by the guards. Kid, sure as you're livin', there's something in the wind. I throwed out some hints to Yance. But you know how he is . . . close-mouthed. Abel's worse, while the women. . . ."

226

Just then René saw Eden beckoning to him and rushed up to the porch. Race, nervous, decidedly out of his element here, followed closely.

But what René feared had not yet come to pass, although it couldn't be far off. Zion had asked for him. His partner's face was one of the things on which his eyes must rest as their glow swiftly dimmed.

On it, now, they lovingly dwelt, as René sat down by him and took his hand. Happily Zion said: "We made it, pard!"

René's smile was crooked. "We sure did, Zion."

Again Zion's eyes must make the rounds to assure himself of this. René, whose own gaze never left his face, saw them suddenly halt near the corrals and fix with intensity on something, the old lightning flaring in them.

"Shang!" he gasped, making a desperate effort to rise. "I . . . saw . . . Shang!"

René whirled. But there was nothing. He said sadly: "Zion, you're dreamin' again."

"It's no dream!" he cried wildly. "I saw him. Not slick . . . like he used to be, but . . . rough . . . hungry . . . like a wolf!"

Could it be that Shang Haman's shadow was over this farewell, his malevolence strong enough to reach them from — where? Next thing, René told himself, *he'd* be seeing things.

"You seen him that day at the springs," he reminded Zion. "Remember? You thought I was Shang."

Zion's memory of that was painful enough to make him doubt himself. He lay back, fighting for breath. But he couldn't rest. His eyes continued to search around the corral for Dave's murderer.

Quietly Eden drew René aside. "It's possible," she choked back her grief to tell him, "that he did see Shang. Shang's still in the basin. He came back soon after you left. Mother ordered him to go, but he wouldn't. When my uncles came, he took to the hills. They couldn't find him. They haven't tried lately. But he couldn't get out. They've kept a close watch at the pass. The storm may have driven him down."

René resolved to investigate. Stopping by the couch to take a look around, he saw Zion's eyes again rivet on something, his thin fingers twine about the big gun and heard his faint, fierce gasp: "There . . . he is."

Nor was it any fever-conjured creation, although as horrid as one, that wild, disheveled figure, they all saw spring from behind the corral, dodge behind Stonewall and, grasping the trailing reins of Black Wing's hackamore, leap to his back and bolt.

It was Shang, far from dapper but more devilish than ever. His silverware, if he still had it, had lost its luster. What had been a pale silk shirt was blackened tatters, his sleek, blue jowls hidden beneath a beard of two months' growth.

Shang had lived like the wolf he looked, in constant terror of his life, in this basin where the very rocks scowled at him; where the painted host, even in his securest days, had made him nervous, came down from their rocks at dark to hem him in, to gibber taunts, gloat over him, freezing, starving, hunted, as he thought. So had they maddened him that, when he heard the shooting — believing Dolan was at the crags, and all he needed to escape this living tomb was a horse — he had risked coming out, to leap on the first horse in sight, one he had long coveted, the only one on earth fleet enough to outrun the wrath of the Jores.

But eyes that missed no unnatural thing, while the faintest glow remained, had marked him. As he struck the saddle, a laugh rang out, that wild, weird laugh that had transfixed the gang in the Black Spout, that transfixed those about the couch, so they could only watch Zion Jore, miraculously sitting up, his rifle aimed and cocked, but its fire checked, while he called in a voice to which vengeance gave power to reach that figure spurring off: "The name of the man that sits on him is Death!"

He whistled in the same breath — the shrill, sweet whistle that Black Wing loved as no other sound. It stopped the running horse like a rock, held him, anchored there, while in a very ecstasy of fear Shang lashed and cursed and belabored him with brutal fists; held him, until Shang, seeing that rifle aimed at him — for René dared not touch it, lest to do so give impetus to the bullet long overdue — and feeling beneath his leg the heavy, leather rifle scabbard, jerked it free, and brought it down in a savage swing upon the head of the stallion. And this, Black Wing's spirit could no more brook, than would Zion Jore suffer the indignities Hank Farley had heaped on him in Trail's End.

Black Wing moved — but not on. With a maddened scream, he hurled himself upright. For a flash of time, poised there, forefeet flailing the air, his golden, outraged form arched. Then, so suddenly that it scarcely registered in the horrified watchers, he crashed backward. When he rolled to his feet, the devilish figure of his tormentor did not move.

Dave Jore was avenged. Shang had paid in full for all his crimes. They all knew it — even Zion. His mother and sister knew it, with horror and thankfulness that fate had relented to settle the score and spare Zion this last violence. Race Coulter knew, in terror that started cold sweat from every pore, that, again, the prophecy was true. René — with some awed reflection of that other prediction, that when Joel came in snow and storm one who heard it would be gone — was leaping down the steps to verify this, when he saw a band of riders storm up the trail — Joel Jore, his brothers, Yance and Abel, and between them, rode a man in white Stetson, Luke

Chartres. Behind them there were six others, with stars, who yanked up beside the crumpled form. René realized that the law had come to the Picture Rocks and knew, somehow, that it did not constitute a menace. But he had no time to wonder at this. Zion was making his last request.

"Pard," — as René sprang up the steps — "Black Wing! My whistle won't work."

Like lightning René ran for him, as the Jores and Chartres threw down at the porch. The stallion had moved back to the corral and stood there, his great eyes rolling hate and fear at the snowy thing the deputies were examining. But he let René catch him and lead him to the couch, for everyone was there. Joel knelt at the head of it, his arm about Revel. René gave the lead rope to her, and the stallion stepped up, thrusting his velvety nose under Zion's hand, caressing the hand that could no longer caress him, soothed by the voice he would never hear again, voicing last love and praise.

"Good boy. Now . . . our work's done. Now . . . we can . . . rest. Good bye, Black Wing."

He lay back then — at rest. Unmanned by the sight of Eden's grief that need no longer be repressed, by his own loss, René looked away from the scene. His dark eyes were brimming, his lean jaw quivering, he was reaching for the rope to take Black Wing away. But Revel didn't relinquish it to him. Instead, she held it out to Race Coulter.

Race stared at it and stared at her, stared at the couch and out at that blotch in the snow. His face went gray and his eyes shot sparks of terror, as he struck the rope from him, screaming: "Not me! I won't have him! Don't make me take him!"

And he ran from temptation, ran, as if Death were after him, ran to his cabin to gather his few effects and get back to the nearest race track, to recoup the losses he had sustained in this mad venture, and forget, if that were possible, this golden, accursed horse of the Picture Rocks.

Hearing, as he ran, the mournful howl of the big hound, Capitán, in wild, fitting requiem to his young master Zion.

Chapter Twenty-Nine

DREAMS COME TRUE

Winter's snow was gone. Spring's warm sun had made green the range lands, on which the blossoming sage made brilliant purple patches. Again, one could sit comfortably on the shaded gallery of Trail's End and look across at that great, fluted cup, towering a thousand feet above the jagged summits of the Montezumas. One wondered, if one was curious, as was this latest guest, enjoying the sunset with his picturesque old host, just what had happened to the Jores in the months since they had dropped out of the news.

Old Dad Peppin, pleased about it all, answered: "Pardoned . . . every mother's son of 'em!"

Of course. That had been in headlines. "But how did it come about? Politics? I hear Pat Dolan's hat's in the ring. Goin' to be your next Congressman. For he's a mighty popular man. Always had a hunch he engineered it. Pretty slick, if he did . . . considerin' public sentiment."

"Dolan," Dad Peppin sniffed, "didn't have a thing to do with it! He's popular because he's well advertised, thanks to the Jores. And, to give the devil his dues, he's honest enough to stick to his principles. Folks can afford to be generous and elect him. It'ud be a shame, if he lost out all around. But the Jore pardon came about, because Luke Chartres went out for it.

"But," he admitted, as if it still made him nervous to think about this, "Luke didn't git it any too quick. Got back to

232

Sentry Crags jist in time to save the Jores from bein' wiped off the earth. For Yance and Abel was bustin' out of that pass shootin', to take Joel away from Dolan's men who had the handcuffs on him, when Luke tears up with a pardon for everyone . . . but Zion. No need to pardon Zion. He'd never have been held to account . . . even if he'd lived. But he'd've been restrained some place, and he couldn't 'a' stood restraint. So it's a God's mercy he passed on."

"But why," quizzed his curious guest, "did Luke Chartres take up cudgels for the Jores? Strikes me as strange."

"It wasn't strange," Dad assured him. "It was natural. Luke Chartres is Revel Jore's brother."

"Holy Smoke!"

"That's what I thought. And then I thought Holy Smoke to myself for not havin' guessed it! You see, the Chartres family is a stiff-necked outfit. Regular blue-bloods, like their hosses. And when the daughter of the house eloped with Joel Jore, they give out she'd gone to Louisiana to live with kin, and washed their hands of her. Wouldn't let her name be spoke, and all that tommyrot. Somehow the rumor spread that Joel's wife was from some high and mighty family. But nobody guessed she was Revel Chartres, and wouldn't have, but for that horse."

"Black Wing?"

"Waal, I was goin' back a generation further. To Black Wing's mother. Revel Chartres, as she was then, owned the racer, Sahra. Oh, there wa'n't no papers to that effect. Dads don't usually make out papers when they give presents to their kids. And when he died, Luke inherited everything. Revel made no claim. Sahra was the only thing she wanted from home. So Joel shanghais the mare and colt away from Val Verde one night . . . only way a Jore knew to git it. When Luke saw they went in the Picture Rocks, he give up.

233

"But some years later, runnin' into a snag in his racin' career, he thought of Black Wing. The colt would be grown, and might pull him out of the hole. So he decides, there bein' no legal reason why he couldn't, to git the Jores out of the way and claim the stallion. Kill two birds with one stone! For he hated the Jores like pizen, for the disgrace they'd cast on his name.

"But when he saw Zion, his own sister's son," — Dad's old face lightened, as if this were more to his liking — "it come to him what an unnatural thing he was doin'. And when Zion caught him and Dolan and held 'em as hostage, and Luke talked to the young fellow . . . waal, Luke told me the tortures comin' to him in the hereafter holds no terrors, after what he endured, hearin' Zion tell about Revel, and readin' between the lines. And he tumbled some Joel wasn't the devil he'd pictured him.

"So," Dad went on, with particular satisfaction, "soon as he can, Luke goes up to the basin. He makes it up with his sister. Finds out Yance and Abel don't wear horns neither. And when he sees his niece, Eden . . . 'A Chartres!' he brags to me. Poppycock! Eden's a red-blooded Jore, from the ground up. Anyhow, their sufferin' plumb undone Luke. And he went out to git a pardon for the lot."

Slowly his guest digested this. "And Black Wing?" he asked, still curious.

"Waal, now" — old Dad hitched around — "that's a funny thing. Seems Revel give the stallion to that other *hombre* who was out for him, the joker in this deck, Race Coulter. Nobody exactly knows the straight of it . . . to square some obligation the Reno Kid owed Race. But Race is superstitious. And after seein' the horse kill Shang Haman . . . a good riddance, if ever there was one . . . Race wouldn't have him. And Chartres vowed he wouldn't touch him with a ten-foot pole. So they turned him loose to run in the basin. And there he'll run till he comes to a natural end. For nobody'll ever bother him.

"They say" — suddenly serious, solemn, with a faraway light in them, Dad's old eyes went up to the blue-misted dome — "they say he don't run alone. They say his hoofs is heard of nights poundin' them rims, like an avengin' demon! They say. . . ."

"But," the other interrupted, a skeptic and, hence, not curious in this respect, "you know better than to believe that!"

"No," said Dad slowly, "I don't. And neither do you. I like to think so. I like to think Zion's never left the basin, but runs up there, wild and free, without any responsibility. I said as much to René Rand one day. And he says it might be. He says the spirit of Zion Jore will never die."

A long pause, in which Dad sat alone with his thoughts, not so solemn, for he chuckled outright. "Things don't die much in the Picture Rocks. Take this René lad . . . he's the best proof of that. You've heard about the Reno Kid? A Western fellow that got stranded in a foreign land, took sick there, and come out here, with the Grim Reaper hot after him and ready to swing. Got all shot up, went through the mischief bringin' Zion home, and come out of it all sound as a dollar. This country's sure been good medicine for him. I know, for I seen him before and after."

"Wasn't he in love with the Jore girl, Eden?"

"And is!" Dad beamed. "And to that extent it's a caution. Or would be, if she wasn't as head over heels in love with him. Marriage don't seem to cure 'em."

"Married, huh?"

"Right in this house!" Pride fired the old man's face. "Yes, sirree! Right here in Trail's End. Private weddin' . . . jist the few hundred Jore friends who could squeeze in. Big Sandy hung buntin'. Give 'em a send-off such as we reserve for our own nobility. A sweeter bride, you never see! A flower, she was, with her blue eyes . . . purple-blue, like's on the rims now . . . and all swaddled up in that white lace stuff the Chartres women's been married in since Genesis. Afraid to kiss her, I was. But she up and done it herself. Up and kissed ol' Dad Peppin on her own initiative."

Too masculine to relish second-hand kisses, the guest supposed: "They're making their home at Val Verde, then?"

"Another good hunch gone wrong," Dad said, grinning. "You couldn't pry them kids from the Picture Rocks. Say it's the purtiest place on earth. I'll be able to give you my impression of it next week. For I'm goin' up with them, when they come back. They've gone over to the Navajo country for a few days' visit with Joel and Revel, who's spendin' their second honeymoon at Revel's old home. And goin' to stay, if Luke has his way. He wants Joel to take charge of Val Verde. But René's goin' into the cattle business in the basin with Abel and Yance. Abel says it's allus been his dream, and he's beginnin' to believe a Jore can tie to a dream."

Dreaming himself, forgetting he had any guest, this old friend of Jerico stared off at the great cup, fancying that the golden blaze in the sky above it, and on its rims, and on that one split — a pass forever open — was not the glow of the setting sun, but the reflection of the happiness that had come to the Picture Rocks.

About the Author

Cherry Wilson enjoyed a successful career as a writer of Western stories for pulp magazines for twenty years, beginning in the mid 1920s. She was born in Pennsylvania, and moved with her family to the Pacific Northwest when she was sixteen. Having had some experience writing for newspapers, when, in 1924, her husband became ill, she decided to try her hand at Western fiction. Over the course of her career she published over two hundred short stories, short novels, and serials. Five serials were published as hard cover novels, and six of her stories were brought to the screen. The majority of her work appeared in the highest paying of the Street & Smith publications, *Western Story Magazine*. Her stories were highly regarded by both readers and editors, and quite often her work was singled out in letters to the editor, along with Max Brand's, as being some of the best to appear in *Western Story Magazine*. Her novels include STORMY (Chelsea House, 1929) filmed as STORMY (Universal, 1935) with Noah Beery, Jr., and Jean Rogers and EMPTY SADDLES (1929) filmed as EMPTY SADDLES (Universal, 1936) with Buck Jones and Louise Brooks. THUNDER BRAKES, also published in 1929 by Chelsea House, the book publishing division of Street & Smith, was reprinted in 1997 in a hard cover edition in the Gunsmoke series by Chivers Press. However, much of her work has not been read in many years, having appeared originally only in magazines. A good example is

Cherry Wilson

"Ghost Town Trail" from *Western Story Magazine* (10/25/30) which has been collected in THE MORROW ANTHOLOGY OF GREAT WESTERN STORIES (Morrow, 1997) edited by Jon Tuska and Vicki Piekarski. THE THROWBACK will be her next **Five Star Western**.